THE
GOLDEN
BELL

THE

GOLDEN

BELL

ROBERT L. STONE

First published in 2022 by Stony Mere Limited

Paperback ISBN 978-1-915036-53-7
ebook ISBN 978-1-915036-54-4

Typeset by seagulls.net
Cover design by Emma Ewbank
Project management by whitefox

STONY MERE

Stony Mere Limited, 8 Little Common,
Stanmore HA7 3BZ, Middlesex

For Helen

'Yehuda Halevi'
by Yehuda Amichai

The soft hairs on the back of his neck
are the roots of his eyes.
His curly hair is
the sequel to his dreams.
His forehead: a sail; his arms: oars
to carry the soul inside his body to Jerusalem.
But in the white fist of his brain
he holds the black seeds of his happy childhood.
When he reaches the belovèd, bone-dry land—
he will sow.

(Translated by Stephen Mitchell)

CONTENTS

AUTHOR'S NOTE

This is a work of fiction. Everything in this book could have happened; much of it certainly did happen; some of it probably did not.

Where possible I have drawn on real people in telling the story: the list of who's who in the story on page 275 indicates which major characters were real and which were not.

You can find suggestions about further reading on page 285 if you want to know more about the extraordinary characters who inhabit our story.

The first language of Yehuda and his family and friends was Arabic, but they also knew Hebrew (and wrote their poetry mostly in Hebrew). There is a glossary of the Arabic and Hebrew terms occasionally used in the book on page 281.

PART I

ANDALUCÍA AND TOLEDO

1

AWAKENING
CÓRDOBA, SPRING 1088

> Rav said: A person will have to give account on the Day of
> Judgement for every good thing which they might legit-
> imately have enjoyed and did not.
>
> *Palestinian Talmud, Tractate Kiddushin, 4:12*

As the serving boys came out of the house carrying jugs of wine,
Moses ibn Ezra took a moment to admire the garden, which had
almost reached perfection on this fine May evening. Roses bloomed
between lilies and flowering grasses. The hornbeam hedges shimmered. Green catkins danced against darker leaves. Moses breathed
deeply, savouring the honeyed scent of the mock orange bushes,
and running his palm over the cool grass beside his divan.

A dozen poets lounged on divans and cushions around the
lawn, dressed in the fine linen robes and turbans of courtiers and
scholars, sober browns and maroons brightened by flashes of
colour at the broad cuffs. The men were talking quietly, waiting for
the poetry contest to begin. Court poets and philosophers, Jewish,
Muslim and Christian, were always welcome at Isaac ibn Ezra's

wine parties. Moses was visiting his brother Isaac from Granada and this evening's party was being held in his honour.

As Moses turned to speak to his brother, he noticed a boy entering the garden – he was not a servant: he was dressed in a rich linen robe like the other guests. Moses thought that he must be about thirteen, though he carried himself with a quiet grace beyond his years. His skin was fair, lighter than most in the garden, as arresting as his auburn hair and the deep brown of his eyes. Moses watched the boy bow slightly in response to Isaac's nod of greeting, then walk around the lawn to a vacant divan by the elegant stone fountain.

'Who's the boy?' Moses asked Isaac.

'That's Yehuda Halevi. His father is a business associate of mine in Tudela. Yehuda has come to Córdoba to learn medicine, and his father asked me to look after him and find a suitable teacher. So he's lodging with us.'

A young poet, Shalom ben Japhrut, sitting on the other side of Isaac, leaned across and winked at Moses. 'And such looks, such grace, eh, Moses? Maybe he should be the subject for the first round of the contest!'

'Don't count on it, Shalom,' said Isaac. 'I think you'll find he has a few poetic surprises of his own, if we can get him to speak at all. Wait and see.' Isaac held out his cup to be filled by a serving boy and raised it high. 'Let the contest begin,' he declared. He drank from the cup and smiled at Moses. 'So, brother, are you recovered from your journey? Perhaps you would prefer to sit out the first round? Yes? Then you shall set the subject for the rest of us.'

Moses ibn Ezra was a little younger than his brother, in his early thirties, lithe where his brother was plump, his dark, wavy hair longer and less well-groomed than Isaac's, his beard fuller. The family resemblance was in the eyes. Both men had the habit of fixing you with their startling blue gaze until you began to feel uncomfortable; only then would they smile.

Now, Moses's eyes were abstracted. It was true that he was tired. The journey from Granada had taken only three days, but in these troubled times all journeys involved anxiety and circumspection. Tensions were increasing between the various Muslim rulers of Andalucía, and between them and the Christian kingdom of León-Castile; among the bands of warriors encountered by travellers, some were undisciplined and dangerous.

Moses realised that he had to shake off his exhaustion. He mustn't spoil the party. Isaac had gathered together the best Hebrew poets of Córdoba in his honour, and it would be churlish to cast a gloom on the proceedings. So Moses decided to give them an enlivening challenge. No scholarly or liturgical themes, then. Let them begin with sensuality.

He raised his cup and drank a deep draught. 'Very well,' he said with a broad smile, 'I'm ready. Let's start with something easy. A warming-up exercise. No prizes awarded for this round. Isaac's garden is famous for his collection of biblical flowers, so let's have a biblical theme to start with.'

Moses walked across the lawn to the fountain beside Yehuda's divan and picked one of the white lilies growing under the rose bushes that framed the fountain. He stood still for a moment, listening to the rhythmic splash of the water and revelling in the scent of the lily. Winking at Yehuda, he turned, held up the flower like a sacred offering, walked slowly to the centre of the lawn and placed the flower on the grass. 'There she is,' he announced. 'Shoshana, a lily among the thorns. She is beautiful, sensuous, fragrant. Serenade her!' He returned to his seat.

Everyone smiled, but behind the smiles their minds were working furiously. After a while, Shalom ben Japhrut, the youngest and brashest of those present, spoke up. 'I have it! Shoshana, the lily, speaks to me. Let it be in the form of a *muwashshah* from her to me! I'll start the opening quatrains, and you can all follow.' Switching easily from Arabic to Hebrew, Shalom began:

> *Shalom, I swear by you,*
> *by your lively imagination,*
> *because it is you I desire, I say*
> > *come to my house, Shalom.*
> *Drink from the wine in my cup,*
> *eat a little bread at my table,*
> *breathe the scent of my spice,*
> > *spend the night in joy, Shalom.*

Another poet, Manasseh ibn Tarphon, took up the improvisation:

> *You will sleep upon my bed,*
> *which I have perfumed with oil of myrrh.*
> *I have wafted spices*
> *where my beloved Shalom will lie.*

Manasseh was followed, one by one, by everyone else in the garden, apart from the boy. The poets wove a light and delicate structure around Shalom's opening quatrains – applauding a particularly evocative or witty passage, laughing and tutting at the same time when the erotic imagery became a little too explicit. After the last poet had finished, there was a pause while more wine was poured and food was brought out. The group relaxed into quiet conversation around the garden, some discussing the *muwashshah*, some exchanging gossip from the Court and the city.

As the sun set, torches were lit around the garden, carefully placed to cast a cheerful light without obscuring the brilliance of the stars. The poetry contest continued, an elaborate series of improvisations in elegant Hebrew. Isaac awarded prizes for the best verses – small jewels, or baskets of rare candied fruit from the East. The boy remained silent throughout, watching and listening, but offering no poetry. He did not join in the conversation between the rounds.

Around midnight, Moses ibn Ezra held up his hand for silence and said, 'Well, I think it's time for me to throw out another challenge. I'll begin a *ghazal* of six couplets in praise of this garden, and let's see who can finish it.' He stood and recited:

The garden wore a coat of many colours,
    its grass a brocaded cloth.
Every tree donned a braided robe,
    its wonders displayed to every eye.

In the silence that followed, Isaac noticed that the boy was gazing at the rose bush by the fountain, his lips moving. 'Yehuda,' he called, 'are you inspired? Has the muse seduced you at last, my young friend? Come on, let's hear it!'

Yehuda was clearly embarrassed by the sudden attention. 'No, I wouldn't… I don't have the…'

Moses caught his brother's eye and Isaac stood and walked over to his ward, raising him to his feet. 'Don't be ashamed, young man. We all have to start somewhere. Among all the golden verse tonight, we've heard some dreadful lines of leaden doggerel, and no one has sought to shame the authors by pointing out the travesties – I'll name no names, though I could!' The guests hissed and murmured in good-humoured protest. 'Come,' Isaac said to Yehuda, 'let's hear it. Can you complete Moses's *ghazal?*'

Yehuda hesitated, then nodded. He walked over to the bush and picked a large yellow rose. Holding it up and looking straight at Moses, he said, 'Let Shushan, the rose, succeed Shoshana, the lily:

Each new blossom, renewed by Spring,
  emerges smiling to greet its coming,
and at their head comes Shushan, the Rose, the king,
  for his throne is now set on high.
He emerges from his guard of leaves
  and casts off his prison clothes.
Whoever does not toast him with wine,
  that man shall suffer for his sin.'

There was a stunned silence. Anxiously, Yehuda took a step back – had he done something wrong? Had he gone too far in building upon Moses's poem? Then Shalom ben Japhrut shouted, 'Astonishing!' and the group applauded enthusiastically. As the applause died down, Moses ibn Ezra said, 'Well, that was something, young man, a perfect mix of wine and divinity with a hint of menace. Gentlemen, a Jewish Sufi has appeared among us! Isaac, give him the prize.' Isaac grinned and presented Yehuda with the prize: a ring set with a ruby. Moses put his hand on Yehuda's shoulder. 'Can you improvise an encore for us, Yehuda?' Looking up, he said, 'Let's not neglect the stars. They'll think we've forgotten them in our obsession with Isaac's plants! Let's have something for the stars.'

Yehuda gazed at the brilliant display of stars for a long time, then looked at Moses and said, 'The stars seem tonight as if they are trying to huddle together. How about this?

The stars of the world have joined today.
Among the host of angels none are found like these.

The Pleiades long for such unity,
For no breath can come between them.
The star of the East has come to the West;
He has found the sun among the daughters of the West.
He has set up a bower of branches,
And made of them a tent for the sun.'

The applause was enthusiastic once again, and Isaac laughed, proud of his protégé. 'Well, brother, you are called the greatest living poet in Hebrew, but watch out! Here's a rival for your throne!'

'Yes, brother!' said Moses. 'A star of the East has indeed come to the West, it seems.' He turned to look at Yehuda. He was smiling, but there was an intensity in his eyes that the boy found disconcerting.

*

The next morning, Yehuda woke to the smell of yeast from the courtyard – which meant that the servants were already preparing the day's bread. The murmur of the girls' voices and the quiet rhythm of their kneading were the only sounds in the house. His hosts must have allowed him to sleep late, knowing that he was not used to wine parties.

Still drowsy, Yehuda watched the pattern of sunlight reflected on the ceiling from the water butt outside the window. He closed his eyes, recalling the warm glow of the previous evening's sunset, the scent of the flowers around the lawn, the reflection in the lily pond of tables laden with dates and figs. Above all he remembered the elegance of the poets reclining on their divans, their faces illuminated by the flickering torches as they smiled and congratulated him.

After a while, he opened his eyes. The servants had finished kneading the bread and the house was silent. He decided that he ought to get up or his hosts would think him a laggard or unable to hold his wine. Washing quickly, he threw on a white linen tunic and went to the *majlis*, the main reception room of the house.

Isaac ibn Ezra's daughter, Deborah, was sitting alone on the cushions against the wall, poring over a sheaf of manuscripts. Absorbed in her reading, she didn't notice Yehuda standing in the doorway. Her olive skin glowed against the drab green of her cotton housecoat, and he longed to touch it. He gazed at her delicate nose and full lips, memorising her face. She was the same age as him, but she looked so sophisticated, leaning among the brocaded cushions, her sandals discarded on the Armenian carpet.

Deborah fingered a loose strand of hair and tucked it behind her ear. She was frowning, troubled by what she was reading. Closing her eyes, she lowered the manuscript and pinched the bridge of her nose. As she opened her eyes and looked up, she noticed him. She pushed the manuscript under a cushion and stared at Yehuda defiantly, as if he had caught her doing something wrong. Her eyes were the same penetrating blue as her father's and Yehuda looked down, disconcerted by her reaction. Deborah squared her shoulders and took on the formal tone of the gracious hostess.

'Good morning, Yehuda ben Shmuel Halevi. I trust you slept well?'

Taking his tone from hers, he responded, 'Very well, thank you, but too long, I think.'

'Would you like something to eat? I can go and fetch some food for you if you wish.'

'That's very kind, thank you, but I'm not hungry.'

Yehuda wondered how long Deborah would wish to continue this exchange of courtesies – he was struggling to understand the urbane ways of Córdoba, a very different world from the remote provincial outpost of Tudela where he had been brought up. After a moment, Deborah scrambled to her feet – she appeared to have had enough of the formalities. She ran barefoot to the courtyard door and looked outside, checking that the servants were still by the kitchen, out of earshot. Returning to the cushions, she gestured to him. 'Come over here. My father and mother have gone to visit a sick relative, and Uncle Moses is leading a study session at the synagogue. Sit by me and listen, before they get back.'

He did as he was told, and Deborah whispered, 'When I was serving breakfast this morning, my father and Uncle Moses were talking about you. Uncle Moses said that you have an extraordinary talent as a poet. You must really have impressed him at the reading last night!'

He wanted to break into a wide grin but was afraid of looking like a fool. At the same time, he knew that he couldn't carry off the arch insouciance affected by grown-up poets. He took a deep breath to calm himself, but that only made him conscious of the alluring smell of Deborah's hair. When she leaned across and put her hand on his, he forced himself to keep still, to enjoy the touch without breaking into a sweat of joy and confusion. 'So,' she said, 'did you realise what an impression you had made?'

Not being sure what kind of answer she expected, Yehuda decided on the simple truth. 'Yes, I think I did, but I don't understand why. The lines I spoke seemed to come naturally to me, with a little adjustment to get the rhythms right. It wasn't difficult.'

'That's exactly the point! That's what natural talent means.' Deborah rolled her eyes, but then looked at him again, her face solemn. 'The important thing I want to tell you, though, is that Uncle Moses said that your gift must be cultivated. He wants you to go to Granada and study with him, and he asked my father to write to yours and get his agreement. What do you think?'

Yehuda looked down at the ruby ring that Isaac had given him and rolled it round his finger, watching the light on the facets of the ruby. He was confused, and a little resentful that his success meant that things might have to change. 'I don't know what to think, Deborah. I like it here. I like Córdoba. I like this house, your parents – being with you.'

She smiled, blushing slightly – O God, the blush on her cheek, so lovely, so delicate! He made himself go on: 'But Granada is also a great city, and Moses ibn Ezra is a great poet. It would be really something to study with him, wouldn't it?'

'Yes, of course it would. It would be wonderful, Yehuda,' she said. 'At least, I think so, but… there's something you need to know about Uncle Moses.' She hesitated. 'It's just that… well, he's…' Deborah looked at him anxiously.

'Is there something wrong? Why shouldn't I go?'

After a moment's hesitation, Deborah said, 'Listen, I'm going to show you something. You must not talk about it to anybody. I don't know what it means, Yehuda, but it's very… well… there is something amiss here.'

She felt under the cushion and took out the manuscripts that she'd hidden there. Shuffling the sheets, she found the one she was looking for and handed it to him. 'Look at this. I found it in the guest room – it's by Uncle Moses.'

Wondering why she was suddenly so serious, he took the paper from her. It was the draft of a Hebrew poem, heavily worked on, with many corrections and scored-out passages. A clean version of two stanzas of the poem was written at the bottom of the page:

Many denounce me, but I do not hear them.
 Come, lovely fawn, and I shall subdue them,
And time will shame them, and death will confound them.
 Come, lovely fawn, let me feast
 On the honeycomb of your lips, let me be satisfied.

He was seduced, and we went to his mother's house.
    There he bent his back to bear me.
Night and day I was alone with him.
    I stripped off his clothes and he stripped me.
    I sucked at his lips and he sucked me.

The colour drained from Yehuda's face, but to cover his embarrassment he muttered, 'Yes, that's his style. It's very allusive – "death will confound them" is good. It's a reference to Ezekiel, "Their kings are aghast, their faces confounded." But it's also in the First Book of Samuel—'

'Yehuda!'

Startled, he looked up. Deborah was staring at him. 'I'm sorry,' he said, 'I suppose I was getting a bit carried away.'

'Yes, you were. I don't think it really matters how "allusive" it is. Are you just showing off, or do you really not get the point?'

He squirmed. People didn't talk to each other like that back in Tudela, especially not girls, especially not girls who looked like Deborah.

'I'm sorry. You're right. Yes, I do get the point. Or rather, I don't. It is indeed very strange. What do you make of it?'

She frowned. 'I'm not sure, Yehuda. I'm not even sure I should be sharing this with you. I hardly know you, but… but I do care for you and if you are going with Uncle Moses to Granada, then I felt I must tell you. I can't imagine him writing something like that. He's always been nice to me and pays me a lot of attention, and listens to me, more than most grown-ups do. I thought he just liked me, but sometimes he seems to be staring at me, and it's embarrassing. He doesn't stare only at me, but at other girls too. And not just girls, boys as well. Sometimes it really disturbs me. When I found this poem today, it felt like that.'

Looking down at the poem his hand, Yehuda ran his finger along the text, as if to feel its meaning. 'Yes, I liked him when I met him last night. He made me feel included in the party. But this, I agree with you, there's something wrong here. Look at that last stanza. I've never seen anything like that before.' He handed the poem back to her.

Reaching for the sheet in Yehuda's hand she froze, her eyes widening as she stared over his shoulder towards the door behind him. Yehuda turned and saw Moses coming in from the sunlit courtyard.

'What are you two studying so intently?' Moses asked, squinting as he adjusted to the less intense light of the room. He walked towards them but stopped short, recognising the manuscript. His blue eyes widened a little, but his expression was inscrutable. 'Is that what I think it is? How did you get it?' He reached out and took the paper from Yehuda's hand.

Deborah rose and stood in front of Moses, her eyes downcast. 'I'm sorry, Uncle. I was helping the servants to clear up after the party, and I was cleaning your room. These papers were on the floor. I picked them up. I'm really sorry.'

She waited, head bowed, for the rebuke. Yehuda could see that she was very frightened. But nothing happened. Nobody spoke. Moses stood, stroking his beard and looking down at her. Yehuda still couldn't read his expression, but he didn't seem angry.

Moses turned to Yehuda, who looked straight back at him, nervous but defiant. He was not going to allow Moses to do any harm to Deborah. He thought he saw a twitch of amusement on Moses's face. Was Moses really enjoying this? Moses didn't speak but turned and walked back to the courtyard door.

The servant girls were wrapping the bread dough in damp muslin, ready to take it to the baker's shop. Moses called out,

'Rebekah, would you be so kind as to bring some of your delicious rose sherbet, if it's not too much trouble. Can Chaya take the bread to the bakery?'

An awkward girl, a little older than Deborah, Rebekah bowed while wiping her floury hands on her coarse woollen smock. Chaya, much younger, just stood and stared wide-eyed at the famous courtier-poet. 'Yes, sir, she can,' said Rebekah. 'There's only a few loaves. There's not as much needed as yesterday, what with last night's party and all.'

'Not as much needed, so not as much kneaded,' said Moses.

'Beg pardon, sir?' Rebekah was worried that she may have said something wrong.

'Nothing, just a bad joke, Rebekah.' He leaned back into the *majlis*. 'Deborah, Yehuda, would you like some rose sherbet? It's excellent on a dusty day like today, and very good for your health.'

They nodded. Still afraid that Moses's apparent lightness of touch might be a pretence, neither of them was willing to speak.

'Very well, then, Rebekah,' Moses said, 'rose sherbet for three, please.'

Rebekah bobbed again, gathered up the loaves and shooed Chaya ahead of her into the kitchen.

Moses walked up to the *martaba* and arranged the silk cushions on the carpeted platform. He turned to Deborah and Yehuda. 'Come and join me here. I think a little explanation is in order.' Still nervous, they stepped on to the *martaba* and sat opposite Moses. He looked down at his poem, stroking his dark beard and rocking back and forth a little, as if in time to some tune in his head. Without looking up, he said, 'So, Yehuda, what did you make of this?'

Yehuda glanced across at Deborah, as if for a prompt, but she shrugged, evidently as perplexed as he was. He stalled. 'Do you mean the poem, Rabbi?'

'Yes, Yehuda, the poem.'

'Well, sir, I was just saying to Deborah that it is full of allusion, like the phrase "death will confound them". It—'

'And no doubt,' interrupted Moses, 'Deborah told you that you were missing the point. Told you quite forcefully, I imagine, knowing her. Yes?' He turned to her with a smile that she did not return – she just lowered her eyes and muttered, 'Yes, Uncle.'

'And as usual,' Moses continued, 'Deborah would have been right. She would have been more concerned about the implications of the second stanza. And if you weren't concerned about it, Yehuda, then you are less discerning than I give you credit for.' Yehuda was now both frightened and intrigued, wondering where this was heading. 'So, I'll explain why you should be concerned about it, but not in the way Deborah might think. Listen and learn.'

With a clatter of brass, Rebekah entered the *majlis*, carrying a jug and three beakers on a tray. Kneeling, she put the tray on the *martaba* and asked, 'Do you want me to pour, sir?' Her eyes flicked to Deborah and Yehuda, who could see how much she disapproved of children being allowed to sit on the *martaba*, which in a well-run household was reserved for distinguished visitors.

'Thank you, Rebekah,' Moses replied, 'but that will not be necessary. It will be a privilege for me to pour your wondrous infusion.' Rebekah blushed, tried to rise gracefully and bow at the same time, and retreated to the courtyard.

Moses poured the rose sherbet and handed the beakers to them. He held his own beaker to his nose before taking a sip, rolling the sweet cordial around his tongue as if it were fine wine. 'Desire,' he said. 'Let's begin with desire. What Aristotle defined as "a conation for the pleasant". But the Sufis have many more elegant ways of describing it, recognising it as the beginning of everything. Yehuda, you'll be familiar with the Arabic poets, like Abu Nuwas or Ibn Zaidun?'

Yehuda nodded, but Deborah drew herself up, her nostrils flaring. 'So am I, Uncle, and also with the work of Ibn Zaidun's beloved, Wallada bint al Mustakfi, and she's a far better poet than he was!'

Yehuda thought Deborah looked magnificent in her anger.

Moses raised a hand as if to defend himself. 'Ah, I'm sorry, Deborah. I wasn't meaning to ignore you, nor indeed women poets. It's just that I know what you know, but I don't know what Yehuda knows: I only met him last night, remember?'

Looking mollified, Deborah said, 'Yes, Uncle, I'm sorry.'

Moses nodded and went on, 'So, desire, as I was saying, is what awakes us. It's what makes us human. It is essential to acknowledge it. Ibn Zaidun wrote:

> ... *Delicious those*
> *Days we spent while fate*
> *Slept. There was peace, I mean,*
> *And us, thieves of pleasure.*

'Yes, "thieves of pleasure".' He returned his beaker to the tray and leaned forward, his hands on his knees. 'I could tell you things about Ibn Zaidun and Wallada that would burn your ears. Such passion, such love, and, ah, such bright desire!' He looked at Yehuda, his blue eyes twinkling sardonically. Had he guessed how Yehuda felt about Deborah? 'That's the point, Yehuda. They celebrated their desire, with great verve and in great poetry. And then... oh, and then, such loathing! As Deborah has reminded us, Wallada was even more eloquent when her passion turned sour. But here's another point, the key point. The Sufis teach us that there is nothing good or evil in desire. Good and evil do not reside in the desire itself but in what we do with it.'

Moses started to rock back and forth. His voice took on something of a singsong quality. 'For us Jews it's the same. The Talmud tells us that we have two drives, the good inclination and the evil inclination – in Hebrew the *yetzer hatov* and the *yetzer hara*. No emotion is good or bad in itself; what matters is whether that emotion is placed at the service of the good or the evil inclination. Thus, desire in the service of the evil inclination is lust and dissolution, but in the service of the good inclination it is love and mutual satisfaction and companionship. It is written in the Talmud that without desire and the fear of the evil inclination, humans would never marry, have children or earn a living.'

Stroking his beard, he continued to rock, his eyes downcast. Deborah and Yehuda exchanged glances. Yehuda was used to rabbis launching into homilies at the slightest provocation, but he was beginning to suspect that Moses was evading the issue. Deborah also looked uncomfortable, but Yehuda couldn't fathom her expression – she seemed sad, bereft, rather than worried. He got the impression that she was searching for something in his face. He thought she might speak, but Moses continued, apparently lost in his own thoughts.

'Now, some rabbis, and of course some Sufi teachers, say that the only way to ensure the victory of the good inclination is to overcome desire, to suppress it, to wipe it out. Others say that to do that is to deny what we are as humans; it leads us to serve God as half-human. We cannot and should not deny what we feel – we can and should acknowledge it, and then master it. I say, with the great Rabbi Akiva as well as Ibn Zaidun, that we should be aware of our desires, feel them, confront them, harness them.'

Unable to restrain himself any longer, Yehuda pointed at the poem in Moses's hand. 'But that's not "confronting" the desire, it's revelling in it!'

Deborah gasped and put a restraining hand on Yehuda's arm. Far from being offended, however, Moses responded warmly to his outburst. 'Yes, you're absolutely right,' he said, 'that's the problem we all face. When the desire is for something we are told we should not have, must never have, what do we do with it then? What?' He looked intently at Yehuda, as if trying to draw an answer out of him, but Yehuda remained silent, and Moses paused and looked down at the poem, running his finger across the text as Yehuda had done before. He said quietly, as if to the text, 'We offer it up, that's what we do, we offer it up. We acknowledge its source.' After a long silence he looked again at Yehuda. 'You've read the wine songs of the great Arabic poets?'

'Yes, Master, some of them.'

'And do you think that those men were drunkards? Of course not! They were pious Muslims. Their lives and all their poetry were dedicated to their God. They would no more have lived a life of drunken debauchery than you, or they, would live on pork.'

'So why did they...?'

'Why did they write wine songs? Because they knew the true nature of intoxication, they knew the true nature of desire, as I do, as any poet must. Any desire, Yehuda, any desire is sacred. It is from exactly the same root as the desire of husband for wife and of wife for husband. It's the desire celebrated in the greatest biblical poem, *The Song of Songs*. And that desire, in turn, is from the same root as Man's desire for God. All poems of desire are metaphors for the longing for the divine spark! And when the desire is one that cannot be fulfilled? Then it must nevertheless be acknowledged, must still be explored. We never, never follow the desire into action, but we must celebrate its divine origin.'

He clenched his hands together and looked intently at Yehuda, who nodded, beginning to see how complex was the world of poetry that he was seeking to enter, but also how seductive it was. 'It's a hard road, Yehuda,' Moses said, 'a dangerous road. But if you're going to be a poet, it's the road you have to take.'

*

This was the beginning of a series of *shiurim*, of lessons that Moses held almost daily for Yehuda, in which Deborah was also included when she could be spared from her household duties. Moses proved to be a great teacher as well as a great poet. He started to teach Yehuda not only language and prosody but also how to access that spirit, that *ruach*, that was the source of poetry, opening his senses to see, hear, smell and touch the world that God had made, to draw in its spirit and to breathe it out into words.

Isaac persuaded Yehuda's father to allow Yehuda to move to Granada to study poetry with Moses, on the understanding that he would also continue his medical studies. They arranged for Yehuda to serve as an apprentice to Abraham ibn Daud, the physician to Abd Allah ibn Buluggin, the Amir of Granada, while also studying poetry and philosophy with Moses. Abraham ibn Daud was a pious, learned man, who knew all the Greek as well as the Arabic medical sources and was experienced in their practical application. He loved to pass on his knowledge, and Yehuda absorbed it enthusiastically, but Abraham dwelt always in the mind, no more interested in true friendship with Yehuda than with his patients.

The work with Abraham, however, brought Yehuda into frequent contact with Amir Abd Allah, who took him under his wing. Abd Allah was quite different from Moses or Abraham. He was curious about people, loved to hear their stories, and was skilful at drawing them out. He took a liking to Yehuda and became the closest Yehuda had to a father in Granada. Yehuda sometimes found it a little unnerving to be familiar with an amir, yet he was the only person to whom Yehuda could open his heart, despite the amir's preoccupation with the dangers that Granada was facing.

In the two years that Yehuda spent in Granada, those dangers gradually overwhelmed the city, as well as its neighbours. The Almoravids, fierce Sanhaja Berber warriors devoted to the reform of Islam, had been invited to come over from the Maghreb by the rulers of Andalucía, to help them to fight Christian invaders from the north. They were led by Yusuf ibn Tashfin, who had taken the title 'Commander of the Muslims'. After the allies had defeated King Alfonso VI of León-Castile at the battle of al-Zallaqa in October 1086, Yusuf returned to Marrakesh. He grew weary of the chaotic behaviour of his Andalucían allies, however, and in 1088, encouraged by a number of fiercely uncompromising clerics and Sharia judges from Andalucía, he decided to return there to extend his empire and overthrow rulers whom he, and the clerics, regarded as decadent and irreligious. This was just after Yehuda had joined Moses ibn Ezra and Abraham ibn Daud in Granada – which by 1090 was threatened with invasion by Yusuf and his Almoravids.

2

DISRUPTION
GRANADA, 1090

For two and a half years the Schools of Shammai and Hillel debated; the former said: It would have been better if human beings had not been created; the School of Hillel said: It is better for human beings to have been created than not to have been created. They took a vote and came to this decision: It would have been better had human beings not been created; yet, since they have been created, let them pay attention to their actions, those past and those before them.

Babylonian Talmud, Tractate Erubin 13b

The major-domo stepped past Yehuda into the amir's private chamber and Yehuda heard him say, 'Rab Abraham's apprentice is here, my lord.'

'About time,' the amir replied, rather abruptly. 'Well, show him in, show him in. Don't keep us waiting.'

Returning to the corridor, the major-domo shook his head and whispered to Yehuda, 'He's still in a bad way, my boy, but you usually cheer him up. Go on, then, in you go. And good luck!'

Abd Allah was at his usual place by the window overlooking the courtyard of the palace, but he was slumped on his cushions with his back to the window, staring at the floor. Yehuda had never seen him like this, his clothes dishevelled, his turban partly unravelled, his face grey and drawn. As he looked up at Yehuda, his expression softened for a moment, but the frown soon returned. 'So, here you are at last, young man.'

'Yes, my lord.' Yehuda bowed, then held up his medical bag. 'As soon as my master came back from examining you, he sent me here with a tincture of *hypereikon* and poppies in honey.' He opened the bag and pulled out a glass flask, the golden medicine glinting in the sunlight from the window. 'You are to take a spoonful three times a day, before meals.'

Yehuda offered the flask to the amir, who leaned forward to take it and opened the stopper, sniffing at the contents suspiciously. 'Is this for my stomach problems or for my melancholy, my boy?'

'For both, my lord – the spirit and the body are connected, and *hypereikon* has a beneficial effect on both.'

'And can it cure the advance of a hostile army?'

Yehuda smiled. 'No, my lord, but it can certainly help you to feel less depressed about that, as well as easing your stomach cramps.'

To Yehuda's astonishment, Abd Allah laughed and patted the cushions by his side. 'Oh, Yehuda, you're miraculous. Come and sit by me – you have a unique ability to say exactly what's needed, and you're not afraid to joke with me if that is indeed what's required. You're going to make an outstanding physician. No, you already are one!'

Yehuda lowered his eyes and bowed, before moving to sit by the amir. 'Thank you, my lord, but if I have learned anything in that area of life, I've learned it from you.'

'Now, now, my young friend, the art of flattery is not such an admirable thing for you to learn.' He sighed and slumped again on the cushions. 'I suppose, however, that it's a necessary skill nowadays – to flatter one ruler while slandering another.'

Seeing the puzzled look on Yehuda's face, he went on, 'Oh yes, I don't suppose you would know about the intrigues in Córdoba or why Yusuf finally decided to move against me. When Yusuf was welcomed by Amir Al-Mutamid of Córdoba and summoned me to join them there, I decided not to go. I sent my envoys, Ibn Hajjaj and Sha'ah Allah to placate him, but instead of supporting me they spoke against me. They told Yusuf that the people of Granada would welcome the Almoravids here, which is certainly not true. Already Al-Mutamid of Córdoba had spoken against me, wrongly believing that I'm seeking an alliance with Alfonso and the Christians. This has been going on since last year, when I sacked my chief judge, the Quadi Al-Khulayi, for plotting against me. He fled to Yusuf, along with others, and they all spoke against me. It's Muslim against Muslim, yet again.'

He stopped, closed his eyes and shook his head. Yehuda decided that it was best to remain silent. After a while, Abd Allah opened his eyes and looked at Yehuda with a wan smile. 'I am starting to think, Yehuda, that if my clothes could speak, they would also slander me, for this is the destiny decreed by God. Never have I witnessed days and nights more distressing to my heart and more calamitous to my soul than in the last few months.' He straightened up again and took a deep breath. 'Enough of this, my friend, I must stop complaining and decide what to do.'

'What to do, my lord?'

'Yes. The Almoravid army is now encamped only a few miles away…' The amir sat up and looked sharply at Yehuda. 'What are you muttering, boy?'

Yehuda looked startled. 'I'm very sorry, my lord, I didn't realise that I was speaking aloud.' When Abd Allah gestured for him to continue, Yehuda said, 'I couldn't help thinking of what another king said when he was in the same position. You'll recall, my lord, that in one of his psalms, King David wrote:

> *Though a host is encamped against me,*
> *my heart shall not fear.*
> *Though war should arise against me,*
> *even then I am confident.*
> *One thing I ask of God,*
> *one thing I seek,*
> *to dwell in the house of God*
> *all the days of my life.'*

'Yes, Yehuda, that's comforting, I suppose, but I think King David must have written it after he'd won the war! I haven't won or lost yet, or even fought, but I'm in an impossible position. All my fortresses are surrendering to the Almoravids, starting with Lucena.' He sighed, then looked sternly at Yehuda. 'A city of Jews, I might add, Yehuda. When Lucena rebelled against me earlier this year, I put their rebellion down peacefully and showed them mercy. Yet still the Jews were the first to surrender.'

'I…' Yehuda looked down at his hands, uncertain whether to respond or not, but Abd Allah said, 'Go on, my lad, what do you have to say to that?'

'My lord, surely the rebellion was not about faith but about taxes? It ended when you exempted them from the new taxes you'd imposed on them. And there were Jews fighting in your army at the battle of al-Zallaqa as well as in King Alfonso's army.'

'True, true,' Abd Allah said quietly. 'Anyway, the taxes were to help pay a tribute to keep the Christians at bay. We all paid tribute to Alfonso before the Almoravids returned, and some of us even fought alongside the Christians. Only last year Alfonso sent Rodrigo Diaz, El Cid no less, to fight alongside the amirs of Zaragoza and Valencia against Ibn Rashiq of Mercia. Everyone's fighting everyone else. It's impossible to know who to trust.'

Abd Allah groaned. 'But why am I giving you a history lesson, boy? I need to think. I must decide what to do.' He rose from his cushions and started to pace around the chamber. 'Yusuf, the "Commander of the Muslims", has summoned me once again, this time to his camp. My mother and my advisers tell me that I should go out and meet him and ask for his forgiveness. They remind me that the Almoravids are not barbarians who massacre the conquered, though they do put the occasional sinner to death. But...' He winced and sat on the cushions again, clutching his stomach.

'The pain again, my lord?' Yehuda asked quietly.

'Yes, the pain again.'

'May I?'

When Abd Allah nodded, Yehuda gently moved the amir's hand from his stomach and placed his own hand there. The spasms he felt were relatively mild. 'As Rab Abraham told me, my lord, the stomach pains and your anxiety are linked. Let me give you a first dose of the tincture, which will certainly relieve the cramps and may also help the anxiety.'

Abd Allah nodded, and Yehuda reached into the bag for his amber spoon. When Yehuda had administered the dose, Abd Allah said, 'Thank you, Yehuda, you don't need to wait. I'll rest a little until it takes effect. Please convey my thanks also to your master.'

Later that day, Abd Allah decided that he would go and make his peace with Yusuf ibn Tashfin. He wrote much later, in his memoirs, 'So I went out to meet the man feeling as though I was being driven to the jaws of death, not knowing my fate. I was like someone risking his life but I put my trust in Fate.' At first, he and the queen mother were well-received, and Yusuf treated them with respect and kindness. Soon after their arrival, however, Abd Allah was placed under close surveillance and later put in fetters, while Yusuf's officials sought to extract money from him. In due course, he was told that most of his treasures would be distributed by Yusuf among his troops, while he himself would be sent into exile in Meknes, in the Maghreb. The Almoravid army entered Granada and Abd Allah and his mother were sent to the Royal Palace to gather the goods that they would be allowed to take into exile.

*

The following morning Rab Abraham did not appear in his consulting room as usual, so Yehuda decided to go and look for him. As soon as he left the courtyard the confusion and the noise overwhelmed him. People were hurrying everywhere, some with travelling bags, others still in their indoor *jalabiyyas*. Terrified children were running to keep up with their parents. A well-dressed merchant brushed past Yehuda, followed by three servants carrying boxes on their heads. He shouted, 'They're coming from the North Gate – we have to go through Amilia.' Someone else called, 'No, Abbas, they're all over the city. There's nowhere safe now, best to just go home.'

Gripping his bag to his chest, Yehuda hurried along a narrow street through acrid smoke. As he passed the house of Fuad ibn Said, the innkeeper, a commotion of thumps and shouts culminated in an angry roar. Startled, Yehuda backed into the doorway opposite. On the upper floor of the house the *mashrabiyya* balcony screen shattered, its fine tracery smashed to pieces. Hurled through the screen from the inside, a cedar wood chest crashed to the ground and broke open, tumbling bolts of cloth, silk ribbons and jewelled slippers into the dust.

A warrior leaned out of the broken screen, panting from the effort of lifting the chest. He straightened his black turban and adjusted his tunic. The man's face was veiled in the Almoravid fashion, only his eyes showing – but Yehuda was close enough to clearly see the anger and the power in those green eyes. He drew back into the doorway in which he was hiding.

The warrior shouted in a heavy Berber accent, 'Thus perish all luxury and vanity, the snares of Satan! We are commanded to live simply, a life of *zuhd*, an ascetic life. You people have been seduced by the effeminacy of Andalucía. You've been corrupted.' He drew his sword and pointed it at the frightened crowd. 'And we Almoravids have come to restore the purity of the faith. *Allahu Akbar!*'

'*Allahu Akbar*,' a few of the crowd responded hesitantly, though most of them stood silent, their faces blank.

The warrior repeated the call, louder than before. Half a dozen Almoravid soldiers marched out of the house, kicking aside the pieces of the chest as they stood on either side of the door. Two more soldiers followed, dragging between them a short, fat man. It took Yehuda a moment to recognise Fuad ibn Said, the innkeeper, his brocaded robe torn and soiled, his face bloodied from a wound at his temple. Fuad stared around him, his mouth opening and closing without a sound. As the Almoravids tightened their grip on his arms, Fuad fainted, hanging between the soldiers like a ragged puppet.

'Stop! Stay where you are!' shouted the warrior on the balcony. The crowd had been turning to slink away, but at his shout, they froze. 'You seem unsure about God's message. So now we will teach you how evil is rewarded.' He pointed to the group below him. 'This is Fuad ibn Said, curses be upon his name. Many of you know him – I am told that he is Fuad the brothel keeper, Fuad the adulterer, Fuad the usurer. Mahmud, show these people how the wicked perish. Your sword!'

The tallest of the Almoravids stepped forward and stood, hands on hips, looking up at the balcony. 'My lord, you want this man to die by the sword like an honourable soldier? Should he not perish like the diseased cur that he is!'

When his leader nodded, Mahmud slapped the prisoner across the face to rouse him from his faint. Fuad opened his eyes and looked around, as if uncertain where he was. Mahmud slapped him again. Fuad shook his head and focused on Mahmud, still dazed. Drawing a dagger from the red sash at his waist, Mahmud raised it so that Fuad could see it clearly. Fuad pulled back against the soldiers who were holding him.

'No, no, my lord, I beg you. Have mercy!' Seeing the leader looking down from the ruins of *mashrabiyya*, Fuad attempted to sink to his knees, but the Berbers held him up. 'Please, please, my lord, don't let him kill me. Save me. I have done no harm!'

'No harm? You have done great harm, you miserable dog. You have lived a life of debauchery, you have rejected Allah the All Knowing and you have corrupted the young. Mahmud, I say again, show these people the reward for doing evil.'

Yehuda trembled as he watched Mahmud knock the bedraggled turban from Fuad's head. Holding his dagger high, he spat in Fuad's face and shouted, '*Allah al-Adl* – God the Most Just.' Yehuda was astonished to see Fuad relax, his face no longer contorted with fear. Looking steadily into Mahmud's eyes, Fuad took a deep breath and said, just loudly enough for Yehuda to hear, '*Allah al-Rahman, al-Rahim* – God the Most Compassionate, the Most Merciful.'

There was a moment of silence as Mahmud hesitated and looked up at the warrior on the balcony, who gestured for him to continue. Stepping forward, Mahmud grabbed Fuad by the hair, yanked back his head and pulled the dagger slowly across his throat. Blood spurted from the wound, a little of it even reaching Yehuda and spattering his face. He heard the gurgle of breath leaving the merchant's throat as the two soldiers let the twitching body slump to the ground, blood gushing onto the ribbons and jewelled slippers in the dust.

Glaring at the crowd, Mahmud raised his bloody dagger and shouted, '*Allahu Akbar.*'

This time, the people replied with more force: '*Allahu Akbar.*'

The warrior on the balcony shouted, 'I am Yusuf ibn Tashfin, Commander of the Muslims. We are not here to harm you and you have nothing to fear from us if you abandon your infidel ways and return to God. In the words of Sheikh Al-Sarraj, renunciation is the first step for those who set their faces towards God. To those who renounce evil, we shall be merciful. But as for those of you who are stubborn, you who set your faces against God, you have just seen, and you will soon learn for yourselves, how we Almoravids deal with backsliders.'

Ibn Tashfin raised his sword arm. A skein of yellow silk that had somehow attached itself to his chain mail unravelled and dangled at his armpit. Snatching at the silk, he tried to rip it away, but the threads were tangled in the links of the mail. Furiously, he tore at the skein, which eventually gave way, leaving just a few strands caught in his armour. Ibn Tashfin glowered down at the crowd and noticed Yehuda in the doorway across the street.

'Hey you! Jew! What are you staring at? This is a matter of Sharia law and doesn't concern you. Unless of course you want to embrace the true faith. Is that what you want? Is it? Speak. What is your name?'

'My lord, your humble servant's name is Yehuda ben Shmuel Halevi.' Yehuda stepped forward, his head bowed, eyes downcast, wiping the blood from his cheek with his sleeve.

'A boy, a stripling!' Ibn Tashfin said, in a lighter tone. 'So, tell me, Yehuda al-Lawi, is that a physician's bag you are carrying? Are you a physician?'

'I am apprenticed to a physician, my lord, to Abraham ibn Daud, physician to the amir.' Immediately, he realised his mistake. Stepping back, he looked up at Ibn Tashfin and stuttered, 'I mean, physician to… to Abd Allah ibn Buluggin, my lord, the… the…'

'The former amir,' Ibn Tashfin prompted, 'the amir until yesterday. Don't worry, Jew, I'm not going to punish you for calling him the amir. Ibn Buluggin was a weak ruler. He allowed Granada to sink into sin and lassitude. But he himself is an honourable man. You have served him, you know he's an honourable man, yes?'

Yehuda straightened his shoulders and met Ibn Tashfin's gaze. 'Yes, my lord, he is one of the most honourable men I have ever met.'

'Aha! I admire that, young man. You are not afraid to speak the truth even to your master's enemy, are you?'

'No, my lord.'

'Good man. But Abd Allah is no longer my enemy since he surrendered. What's more, he's a Berber like me, in fact my blood relative, and he fought alongside me when we defeated Alfonso of León-Castile at the great battle of al-Zallaqa. Do you think we Almoravids are barbarians, to kill those whom we depose?'

Yehuda shook his head. 'No, not barbarians, my lord.'

'No, my young friend, we are not. We are merciful, as God is All-Merciful. So, Abd Allah will be sent into peaceful exile. Before which,' he said, pointing to the bag in Yehuda's hand, 'he has need of your services. He was injured, unfortunately, when my excessively zealous officials put him in chains. Your master, Rab

Abraham, seems to have fled, like most of your cowardly race, so you'll have to do.' Leaning further over the balcony he called, 'Mahmud, Hassan, take this young man to the palace – and don't manhandle him. He's to be taken straight to Abd Allah to see to his wounds.' He turned again to Yehuda. 'Tend your former amir skilfully, Jew. No harm will be done to you, and if you do your work well, you will be rewarded.'

Addressing the crowd in the street, Ibn Tashfin concluded, 'As for the rest of you, go back to your homes and now live your life in peace. As I said before, you will not be harmed by us as long as you follow the law.' The crowd dispersed in silence, their heads bowed, as four of the Almoravids carried Fuad's body away.

*

Mahmud and his companion, Hassan, didn't say a word as they marched Yehuda through the busy streets, now a little calmer than before, and out of the town. The road up the hill to the palace was almost deserted, and Yehuda could hear the rustle of the warriors' mail behind him and smell the sweat on their blue woollen robes. They didn't meet his eye even when he could see them at a turn in the road or as the three of them filed through one of the gates in the outer fortifications. It was impossible to tell whether they resented being taken from the fray to act as escorts to a boy-doctor or whether they welcomed the break and the chance to see the famous Palace of Granada. The silence of the Almoravid guards unsettled Yehuda and he felt an unaccustomed nervousness. He had never before encountered anything like these fierce ascetics who had erupted from the deserts of the Maghreb. They seemed out of place in the fecund gardens of Andalucía.

Some of Abd Allah's own troops were still stationed around the palace, allowed by Ibn Tashfin to remain as a royal bodyguard after the rest of the amir's army had dispersed. There was an awkward moment as the party approached the Great Gate of the inner wall. No one seemed quite sure of the etiquette, since the Almoravids were the victors, but Abd Allah and his bodyguard had not yet vacated the palace. Mahmud and Hassan stopped dead ten yards in front of the guards, each of them taking hold of one of Yehuda's arms. The palace guards stood in silence, glaring at Mahmud and Hassan, clearly waiting for them to speak – they weren't going to let anyone in without an explanation. The Almoravids also said nothing – equally clearly, there was no way they, Sanhaja Berbers, were going to explain themselves to a bunch of Zanata Berbers.

The guards tightened their grip on Yehuda's arms and he saw Hassan's hand move towards the handle of his scimitar. As the stand-off continued, Yehuda's heart beat faster. Terrified as he was, however, he was astonished to find some cool and detached part of himself, thinking, 'Is this how I die, the victim of a procedural deadlock? Is this how God disposes of His creatures?'

A loud voice broke the silence. 'Yehuda al-Lawi! What are you doing here, my boy? Are you on another mission to bring poetry to the wounded?' Jamal bin Qasum, the captain of the guard, had come out of the guardhouse to investigate the unwonted quiet at the Great Gate. A short, stocky man, he stood now with his hands on his hips and a broad grin on his handsome face. He seemed unperturbed by the turbulence of the city and addressed the two Almoravids as if they were old acquaintances. 'This young Jew's a remarkable young man, you know. After the skirmish near Lorca last year, his master, Abraham ibn Daud, treated me for a rather nasty wound on my leg, and young Yehuda recited some of the filthier poems of Wallada to distract me while Abraham stitched up the wounds!' Mahmud and Hassan's grip on Yehuda's arms relaxed a little, and Hassan even smiled, until Mahmud scowled at him. 'So, Doctor of Words,' continued Jamal, 'are you on another poetic mission today?'

'No, Captain, no poetry today. I've been sent by Amir Yusuf ibn Tashfin to dress the wounds of my Lord Abd Allah ibn Buluggin.'

'Why you and not your master?' replied Jamal, glancing at the two Almoravids.

'Because he cannot be found, Captain.'

'Well, then, gentlemen, you are all very welcome! It's my privilege to admit you to the Palace of Granada.' He waved them through in a gracious gesture that included Mahmud and Hassan as well as Yehuda. The Almoravids took their hands off their sword hilts. Honour had somehow been satisfied. They nodded curtly to the smiling captain and nudged their charge towards the gateway. The Zanata guards pulled open the postern gate to let the three of them through.

Inside the Royal Courtyard, coffers, trunks and canvas packs were scattered all around, while servants and guards hurried in and out bearing more packs and cases. The dusty air was filled with a constant babble. Supervisors snapped instructions to the servants. Clerks read out inventories and porters thumped each item in turn, responding with a rhythmic, 'It's here; it's here; it's here.'

Yehuda had walked through the Royal Courtyard hundreds of times. Always, it had been virtually deserted, except at the fixed hours when the horse guards gathered to ride out at the beginning of the evening and morning watch. On those occasions, the water carriers scattered water to settle the dust raised by the horses. Now, there were no horses and no water carriers, only a storm of noise and red dust.

Surveying the chaos, Mahmud spoke to Yehuda for the first time since he had been assigned this escort duty. 'So, Jew, where do we go now?' His voice was gruff, but not unfriendly.

'I don't know, but I can see Lady Ameira over there in the corner – we should go and ask her where Abd Allah is.'

'Very well,' said Mahmud. 'Lead on.'

The queen mother stood at the edge of the frantic activity, quietly giving instructions to the major-domo. As she turned towards them, her green brocaded robe shimmered and glowed, seemingly immune to the surrounding dirt. She held a chiffon veil in front of her face, perhaps in modesty or perhaps against the dust, and Yehuda's attention was drawn, as always, to her eyes, their expression cool and detached in the midst of all this turbulence. Yehuda knelt in front of the lady and bowed his head. The Almoravids remained standing, staring straight ahead; they refused to be awed by a mere woman.

'Well, Yehuda, it's good to see you,' Lady Ameira said. 'Although the circumstances are hardly auspicious, you and your companions are welcome.'

'My lady, I have been sent by...' He hesitated, reluctant to utter the name of the victor in the queen mother's presence. 'That is to say, I have been sent to attend to Lord Abd Allah, who I understand is wounded. Would Your Majesty be so kind as to tell me where I might have the honour to find him?'

'Why, Yehuda,' Ameira replied, 'where else but in the garden? The world has collapsed, he's lost a kingdom, we don't yet know if we are to be allowed to escape with our lives, let alone our goods, and my most admirable son is in the garden, dictating his memoirs. I am sure that he'll be delighted to see you. You can discuss the finer points of autobiography with him while dressing his wounds. Gentlemen,' she added, turning to Mahmud and Hassan, 'when you've conducted Master Yehuda to the amir, please do take some refreshment before you resume your... ah... your duties in Granada.' The Almoravids, to Yehuda's amazement, bowed to the lady, who instructed a footman to take the visitors to the amir – she persisted in calling him amir until the end – and then to take 'these two gentlemen' to the kitchens.

Abd Allah ibn Buluggin was indeed sitting in the myrtle bower, his favourite spot, dictating to old Faruddin the Scribe. It appeared at first that the ravages of the city hadn't reached this green haven, yet his attire was dishevelled and dusty and his right hand, holding his left forearm, was stained with blood. As the footman led the Almoravids away Yehuda approached the amir and opened his bag.

'Welcome, Yehuda, you are very welcome, but please wait a while; I don't want to lose my thread. Just sit here by the fountain – you look as if you need a rest anyway.'

Old Faruddin had been Abd Allah's amanuensis for many years. The amir always talked so quickly that the scribe could barely keep up. The dictation sessions resembled a contest – Faruddin would tut and mutter and wave his quill. Eventually he'd say, 'Again, my lord, I'm sorry but you'll have to say that sentence again.' The amir would snort and shake his head and complain that he couldn't remember what he had just dictated, and then repeat the sentence as fast as before.

But that day, it was less of a struggle. Abd Allah was more patient, keeping up a slow and steady flow that was fine, eloquent and wise. He sat cross-legged with his eyes closed, as if in meditation. The first phrase Yehuda heard him dictate was, 'Words that emanate from the heart make an impression on the heart.' After a pause, he said, 'A person cannot appreciate the value of good unless he has experienced evil. It should be realised that reason stands in need of learning, that no learning can be complete without the acquisition of experience, and that no experience can be complete without some hardship and tribulation.'

After a while Yehuda stopped listening to the amir. He was thinking of the letter that he had received from Deborah the night before, a letter that had frightened and confused him, bringing equal joy and grief. The joy was to see her handwriting and read her words, and to imagine her writing the letter at her usual place by the *mashrabiyya* screen, the sunlight through the lattice dappling her arm. The grief was to read of the disruption of life by the Almoravid warriors in Córdoba and the fear that Yusuf ibn Tashfin would eventually turn against Amir Al-Mutamid as he had turned against Abd Allah. Even if he and Deborah had been together to share it, the hardship and tribulation of those times would have been terrible to bear.

Deborah also hinted at a dispute between her father and her Uncle Moses, Yehuda's mentor. There had already been some talk of this among the poets in Granada – Deborah's name was whispered in the rumours, but nobody would talk to Yehuda openly. He longed to be with her, to know at first-hand what remained unsaid in the letter. He didn't dare to ask Moses, for Moses was withdrawn and morose; it was always impossible to ask him questions when he was in that humour.

Despite the anguish of reading the letter, Yehuda had felt again a frisson of joy when he looked up from it to see the brightness of the stars and the ripple of the moonlight on a hornbeam tree swaying in the breeze. The stars were the same ones that she was watching, and the wind was blowing from the southeast towards Córdoba, where she lay. Yet Córdoba felt as distant from him as the Little Bear glittering in the northern sky.

The voice of the amir startled him out of his reverie. 'So, young Yehuda, are you dreaming of a lost love? You look so melancholy – yet you're so young. Come here and tell me of your sadness while you tend to my wrists.'

The amir's wrists were badly injured. The fetters had not cut very deeply, but the lesions had been carelessly cleaned and dressed and were in danger of infection. Yehuda cleaned the wound again and brushed in albumen and seaweed ash with a feather, binding the treated wound with linen. While he was working, the amir plied him with gentle questions.

'So, young man, why so forlorn?'

'My lord,' he replied, concentrating on dressing the wound to avoid looking into his eyes, 'you know better than I what is happening in Granada. Terror has gripped the whole city. People are dying, you are to leave us, and the Almoravids will take control.'

'Yes, my son, all this we know. We struggle to accept it as God's will, as accept it we must. But your grief isn't only for Granada, is it? Nor for me, nor even for yourself. I know that look. I remember it from my youth. This is about Deborah, is it not?'

Yehuda was embarrassed to feel tears running down his cheek. The peace of the myrtle bower, the kindness of the amir and the familiar routines of the work had seduced him into letting go of that self-control that both Rab Moses and Rab Abraham had drilled into him. All the horror of the day came to the surface – the fear among the crowds, the burning houses, the killing of Fuad – and when he remembered the grief of Deborah's letter, he could hardly speak.

'Come, Yehuda,' said the amir. 'Leave the dressing now, it's secure enough.' He caught the eye of Faruddin, who silently nodded, took up his parchment and quills and returned to the palace. 'Now,' the amir continued when they were alone, 'what is it that weighs so heavily on you?'

He patted the bench beside him, and Yehuda sat, wiping his cheek with the back of his hand. The breeze grew a little stronger, carrying the scent of jacaranda from the neighbouring bower. 'My lord, I received a letter yesterday from Córdoba. It was indeed from Deborah. Fear has gripped the city, as here in Granada. It's as if the foundations of their lives have been undermined.'

'Yes, indeed. As the psalmist wrote, "When the foundations are destroyed, what can a righteous man do?" It's the will of God… but this we know already. What else?'

Yehuda hesitated, looking down and dabbing at a trace of blood on his sleeve.

'What else?' the amir repeated.

'Deborah… Deborah tells me that her father's affairs have been badly affected by these troubles, and he's decided that they must leave the city. They'll probably go west to Seville or northwards, towards Toledo.' The amir's eyes widened at the mention of Toledo – he himself had been a commander at the tragic battle in which it fell to the Christians fifteen years before – but he said nothing, nodding at Yehuda to continue. 'Her father has had some quarrel with his brother, my master Moses.'

'Yes, my son,' the amir said, 'rumours have reached us in Granada. Have you not heard them already?'

'People stop talking when they see that I'm listening, or they say that I'm too young to hear of such things. But that's not the reason they won't tell me, is it?'

'No, Yehuda, it isn't. And in any case, you are older in wisdom than many of those gossips. Perhaps I should tell you what they say, but today has already been distressing enough for you. Are you sure you want to know?'

Yehuda took a deep breath, aware again of the sweet scent of jacaranda mingling with that of the myrtle. 'Yes, my lord, I am ready.'

After looking at Yehuda for a long while in silence, the amir said, 'Well, Yehuda, what the gossips are saying is that the great rabbi and poet Moses ibn Ezra has… compromised himself with his niece Deborah, daughter of Isaac ibn Ezra, and that is why Moses returned so suddenly from Córdoba.'

Yehuda blushed. 'I don't believe that, my lord, there can't be any truth in it. Moses would never... He could never do such a thing.'

'My own informants tell me that they have found no evidence of any transgression. They say, however, that Deborah has been kept closed up in Isaac's house for these past three weeks.'

'No, she can't have done anything wrong! Even if he had tried, Deborah would not have allowed him to touch her!'

Abd Allah put his hand on Yehuda's shoulder. 'Calm down, my son. You don't have to convince me. It doesn't matter what I think, or what the gossips are saying. You know what you must do. First talk to Moses; you need to hear what he has to say. And then go to Deborah. Above all, you must go to Deborah.'

Yehuda shook his head – he dreaded the thought of confronting Moses. For two years Moses had been his master, and though the rigour of his instruction was leavened with much kindness and more wit, he still held him in awe and feared his anger.

But he could not admit this to the amir, so he said, 'How can I leave you, how can I leave Moses at this time?'

'I am to go into exile, and I certainly don't expect you to come to Meknes with me. And it's unlikely that Moses will remain in Córdoba, given all the circumstances. So there's nothing to hold you here – and it's Deborah who needs you now.'

He longed to acknowledge the truth of this but fear still held him back. 'Surely this is not right, my lord. I can't simply cast aside my duties here.'

'You have many duties, my son. First to God, the All-Merciful, then to yourself. I tell you that I give no credence to these rumours and I'm confident that Moses, like me, will free you from all obligations to him. If you don't find Deborah and comfort her now, it will be a heinous betrayal of your duty to her. If you don't go to her now, you'll regret it for the rest of your life.'

Mahmud and Hassan were summoned to escort Yehuda back to the city. As they walked into the Royal Courtyard from the palace they saw Yusuf ibn Tashfin, Commander of the Muslims, riding through the Great Gate with an escort of Almoravid cavalry. Ibn Tashfin, his tunic stained with blood and sweat, was mounted on a white stallion, holding his sword aloft. Clerks and porters scattered as the horsemen rode towards the mounting block in the corner, where the queen mother was still standing. Ameira stood steady and calm, her face veiled but looking fixedly at Yusuf, who reined in his horse directly in front of her. They confronted each other in silence. As he looked into Ameira's eyes, Yusuf's agitation and anger appeared to subside; he glanced down to sheath his sword and when he looked up again there was a slight smile in the queen mother's eyes, to which, much to his own evident surprise, he responded with a smile himself.

'Greetings, my lord,' Ameira said. 'You look a little thirsty. May I offer you some water?' She gestured towards a blue-glazed water butt that stood beside the mounting block. 'I'm afraid it's not as cool as it should be – we made the mistake of using a glazed butt. Unglazed clay would have kept the water cooler.'

Yusuf responded courteously, 'Yes, my lady, some water would be welcome, whether cool or not.' Ameira reached behind her and a servant placed a silver goblet in her hand. Stepping down from the mounting block, she dipped the goblet in the water and offered it to Yusuf.

*

At Moses's house that evening Yehuda was greeted by Zipporah, Moses's wife. She was even more nervous than usual, nodding and cooing like a startled dove. Yehuda could never quite get used to the incongruity – Zipporah, a small, shy woman, the wife of Moses ibn Ezra, the great poet and leader of men.

Her greeting was almost breathless. 'Oh, Yehuda, I'm so glad to see you. Come in, do come in.'

He followed her into the *majlis*, where she rearranged the cushions on the *martaba* and invited him to sit while she stood, twining and untwining her fingers.

'Rabbi Moses is in his private chamber. I'll go and tell him you're here.'

She didn't move, however, but remained standing in front of him, looking down at her hands. She started pulling at the sleeves of her *thawb*, first one, then the other. The *thawb* was elegant, a flowing black robe embroidered in crimson and gold, but it seemed to hang awkwardly on Zipporah's hunched shoulders. At the sound of a crowd shouting in the street outside the house, she flinched and turned. Yehuda hadn't seen her face clearly before, but now it was lit by the oil lamp in the alcove. He was shocked at how haggard and blotched it looked.

'What's the matter, Aunt Zipporah?'

Still saying nothing, Zipporah squatted on the *martaba* beside him. Though the sound of the crowd faded into the distance, Zipporah remained tense. He leaned forward and took hold of her hands. 'Don't worry, Auntie, there's a lot of noise and brawling, but they aren't going to come for us – Ibn Tashfin has promised to protect the Jews, just as the amir did.'

Zipporah turned and looked at him vaguely, as if he was speaking a language that she didn't quite understand. Gradually, she focused on him again, gently freeing her hands from his and patting at her hair, as she often did. 'No, no, Yehuda, it's not that, it's Moses, it's…'

He realised then what the problem was. 'Is he in his black humour again, Aunt Zipporah?'

'The worst I've seen, Yehuda. He's been sitting there for hours. He won't eat, he won't talk, he hardly moves. Maybe you should go in – if anyone can speak to him, it's you.'

'I will go in to him, yes, but first can I do anything for you? Perhaps an infusion of valerian to calm you?'

'Thank you, Yehuda, but no, it's Moses who needs your help. He's in very low spirits just now. It's terrible to see him like this. But he's always glad to see you.'

Zipporah reached out to put her hand on his cheek. 'Oh, Yehuda, your face is so solemn – the caring physician listening to the woes of this silly woman. You're growing up so fast. I can't believe it was only two years ago that you came to Granada, a brilliant child. And now look at you!'

'Well, Aunt Zipporah, if I am growing up, it's thanks to you and Rabbi Moses.'

Zipporah exhaled, calmer now, a half-smile lighting her face. 'You're quite the physician now! And such a poet too. We're so proud of you. So go in, go in – see if you can help him.'

*

Stepping through the low door to Moses's room, the first thing Yehuda noticed was the smell, the familiar smells of parchment, glue and ink solvent overlaid with something unfamiliar and unpleasant – traces of sweat and bad breath, an odour of decay. Only one lamp was lit and the fretwork shutters of the *mashrabiyya* were closed, making the room gloomy and stuffy. Moses's study was always untidy, but this morning the clutter was worse than normal, torn pages and discarded quills scattered on top of the usual heaps of books and documents. Moses sat in the far corner, hunched over a writing board, his beard and hair unkempt.

'Master?'

Moses didn't move. Yehuda waited.

'Master?'

He started as Moses thumped his fist on the writing board. 'What do you want, boy? What do you want this time? Why are you always interrupting me?'

'I'm very sorry, Master. I've come from the amir's palace. He's leaving Granada tomorrow. I was concerned for you, wanted to know if there is anything you need me to do.'

Moses glared at him. 'Yes, Yehuda, I need you and everyone else to leave me alone. If you must play the doctor, do it with Zipporah – she's looking terrible. Go and look after her.'

'She's just worried about you, sir. She sent me to you.'

'Yehuda, you claim to have some insight into how people think, so tell me, why can't people understand me when I tell them that I just want to be left alone?'

Yehuda was used to Moses's black humours, but he still found it hard to confront him, as he knew he must do. Taking three steps across the room, he knelt in front of him, forcing himself to stare, unflinching, into those blue eyes.

'Because you are miserable and they want to help you. Because they love you. Because you are the head of your household and can't abdicate from that. Because, Rabbi, you're a leader of the community and the amir, protector of the Jews, is about to go into exile. Because…'

'Stop it, you fool, be silent!' Moses hissed, 'Do you think I don't know all that? Do you dare to teach me my duty? There will be time for that, and I will do what I have to when the time comes. Right now, I need to finish my last poem.'

Yehuda flinched. 'Your last poem?'

Moses almost smiled. 'Oh, don't be stupid, boy. Do you think I have lost my mind? The last poem I intend to write, the real truth, before I give up writing poetry forever.'

Yehuda sat back on his haunches. A pair of crows cawed at each other in the alleyway outside the *mashrabiyya*. 'May I hear it?'

Moses picked up the paper on the writing board. 'Very well, Yehuda Halevi, but you won't like it. It's a poem for the Days of Awe.' He spat out each line as if challenging an enemy. The poem began:

> *Her name is 'Earth'*
> > *And of no worth*
> > > *Are all her ways*
> *A garden green,*
> > *But in her trees*
> > > *Are poisoned leaves.*

And it ended:

> *Suck not the sap*
> > *Her nipples drip;*
> > > *Press not her breast.*
> *How I have come*
> > *To hate this life*
> > > *And all its arid ways.*

The silence was broken by the repeated caw of the crows outside and the flutter of wings as they chased each other out of the alley-way. Yehuda leaned forward and adjusted the wick of the lamp, which had begun to flicker. 'If that's the real truth, Master, then what are we to make of your poem, the one I first encountered before I even came to Córdoba?

> *Caress a lovely woman's breast by night,*
> *And kiss some beauty's lips by morning light...'*

Moses interrupted with a snarl. 'That's naive rubbish, boy. Even you must see that – it's just vacuous sensuality.' He picked up the new poem again, looking at it for a long time, tracing the lines with his finger. He rubbed the back of his neck and looked up at Yehuda, his anger transmuted to melancholy. 'And this poem is vacuous too, for that matter. It's falsehood too. Indeed, all poems are lies.' When Moses was in this humour it was impossible to tell whether he was absorbed in the argument or just playing games. He could have been referring obliquely to the troubles he and Yehuda were facing, but Yehuda knew that there was still no way he could directly raise the subjects he had come to speak about, anxious as he was to confront him. He had to play the game as Moses was playing it. 'What are you talking about, Master? Good poetry, great poetry like yours, is the essence of truth, truth through metaphor. The divine truths can only be conveyed through metaphor – it was you who taught me that.'

'Nonsense, boy. Metaphors are not truth; on the contrary, by their very nature they distort truth. As Ibn Hazm said, the *truth* expressed in verse is ludicrous; it's always bad poetry. Don't you remember his exquisite example of a poem that tells only the truth, pure truth and nothing else?

Day is day, dark is dark;
Dove is dove, lark is lark;
Mouse is mouse, louse likewise;
Both are rather small in size.'

By now Yehuda was desperate to bring the discussion round to the urgent issues of the real world, but he could still see no opening that Moses would accept. In any case, Moses had caught him in his snare. Young and ardent as he was, he couldn't resist the temptation to argue. He took the poem from Moses's hand and glanced at it.

'Rabbi,' he said, 'if metaphors, images, symbols are indeed falsehoods, then what does the Torah mean by saying that men were created in the image of God?'

'Men and women, Yehuda, not only men: "God created the human in God's own image… *male and female* God created them." How many times do I have to tell you that you must be precise in your citations?' Moses snorted, leaning forward and staring at him. 'But don't you see how absurd that is! Created in God's own image? They had only one single, simple commandment given to them, and they couldn't obey even that. They tasted the fruit. That is how little we resemble God, my boy.'

This seemed to be the opening he had been waiting for. Moses had given him an oblique opportunity to ask the questions that he had come to ask, but he had no idea whether or not it had been done deliberately. He could still keep the discussion abstract, or steer it towards confrontation. His pulse quickened and he took a deep breath. He couldn't turn back now.

'They tasted the fruit,' he said. 'You condemn them for that, Rabbi? And us, now that we have this terrible knowledge of good and evil, what forbidden fruit do we dare to taste?'

Moses, his eyes wide, raised his hand as if to strike Yehuda, but he stopped, flung aside the writing board and rose to his feet. 'What do you mean, boy? Why are you here? Not to discuss *Genesis*, I think. Enough of this. Say what you came to say and then get out.'

Still on his knees, Yehuda looked down at his hands, twisting the ruby ring on his finger. He spoke quietly. 'Master, I come before you lost in confusion. I don't know what to say. I don't know what to do. There are rumours, rumours about you and your brother Isaac, about Deb…' He faltered, looked up and saw how his master's eyes had narrowed. Before Moses could speak, Yehuda pressed on quickly. '… about a scandal. Even now, when everyone is terrified about what will happen to us, what Ibn Tashfin will do, people still gossip in corners, smirk and point as I pass by, ask me where my Master is and what he's up to now. What am I to say to them, Rabbi? You must tell me what happened in Córdoba.'

Moving across to the *mashrabiyya*, Moses pulled the shutters open and looked up at the darkening sky. The sun had already set, but the wispy clouds still carried scarlet and gold traces of brilliance. The smell of roasting meat drifted into the room from the courtyard. '"The Angel of God camps around those who fear Him and rescues them / Taste and see how good is God." Taste and see, Yehuda, we are commanded to taste and see.'

Yehuda clenched his fists – was this man incapable of talking directly about anything? 'Yes, Rabbi, we are commanded to "taste and see" but the psalmist is addressing those who fear God and know the limits.'

Moses raised his head and laughed, startling Yehuda yet again. 'Oh, Yehuda, you're so young, I keep forgetting that you're still so serious, so certain. For you, everything is either black or white, yes or no. How can I stay angry or melancholy when I have my little rabbi-poet to amuse me?' His tone changed abruptly again. 'I wasn't starting another theological debate, you bumpkin, I was answering your question. I have answered your question, and that is all the answer you are going to get. Now let's stop this and go and eat the evening meal. Suddenly I feel hungry again. Do you know what Zipporah has prepared? Smells like lamb.'

'But, sir…'

'But nothing. You want to know the reason for my dispute with Isaac and whether Deborah is involved in that, but I have taken an oath, and will not, cannot, say more on the subject, now or ever. Let the matter drop.'

Yehuda rose from his knees, not knowing whether he dare push Moses any further. As he stood up, they were startled by a crash and a scream in the alleyway. A second crash was followed by shouts and running footsteps and the sound of something being dragged into the street. Moses slowly closed the shutters. Seeing Yehuda move towards the door, he said, 'No, Yehuda, don't go outside. There's nothing we can do. We can only wait here until the madness subsides.'

'And then what, Rabbi? Even if it does subside, what should we do? Are you going to stay in Granada?'

'Well, as you so tactfully reminded me not five minutes ago, I have my duties to my community, so I can't leave yet. We've been through this kind of thing many times before. Tomorrow, or the day after, the chaos will abate and Yusuf ibn Tashfin will install himself in the palace. But he won't stay long. He's a restless conqueror, that one, and he'll move on to "purify" more cities. He's not going to get soft like the previous Masufa Berbers. So I'll stay until calm is restored, however long that takes, and I'll do what I can to ensure as just a regime for us as possible for our people. And then... Well, I don't know yet where I'll go. Not to Córdoba – as you know, Isaac is planning to move and, anyway, he will... Well, I can't go to Córdoba.'

He reached out and put his hands on Yehuda's shoulders, looking into his eyes. 'And you must not stay with me. No, don't protest. I know you want to go your own way, and I think I know where that is. It's time for us to part. I've taught you much poetry and Torah, and Rab Abraham tells me that you're now becoming a skilled physician. There is more, so much more, that I would dearly love to teach you, but now I have to let you go.' He sighed.

'This is the way it has been since the Temple was destroyed: our relationships are never stable, always fragmenting.

'You must make your own way now. You can't stay in Granada either, or Ibn Tashfin will conscript you as a physician in his army. Go to Seville – I'll give you an introduction to Rab Meir ibn Kamniel, an excellent physician there, who also acts as one of the administrators for Al-Mutamid, Amir of Seville and Córdoba. You'll probably come across Isaac and Deborah there, though I don't know how long they'll be staying. The Almoravids are in Seville at the invitation of Al-Mutamid, but it might not be long before they turn on him also.'

Turning to the scattered heaps of papers, Moses scrabbled among them, his back to Yehuda, searching for something. 'Ah, here it is.' He picked up a book and gave it to Yehuda, folding Yehuda's hands in his. 'Anyway, this is my parting gift, a new copy of *The Song of Songs*. The great Rabbi Akiva said that all the Writings are holy, but this is the holy of holies. He said that the whole world is not worth more than the day on which *The Song of Songs* was given to us. From time to time, when you read of the lovers and the mountain of spices, think of your old master. But for now, come, let us join Zipporah and eat together.'

'Thank you, Master,' Yehuda said. 'Thank you for everything.' Moses nodded, turned and took a long time adjusting the catch on the *mashrabiyya* shutters. The interview was clearly over. His cryptic answers and the choice of a gift of the great, sacred love poem were the only indications Yehuda would ever get from him of what had happened in Córdoba, or how he felt about it. It was time for him to go. Head bowed, holding *The Song of Songs* between his hands, Yehuda left the study and walked through the dark courtyard to the *majlis*.

3

DISILLUSIONMENT
SEVILLE, 1090-91

Rabbi Eliezer ben Jacob declared, 'When a person suffers affliction, they must express gratitude to the Holy and Blessed One. Why? Because it is their afflictions that draw them to the Holy and Blessed One.' Indeed, the Torah itself cannot be acquired except through affliction.

Midrash Tanhuma, Tetze 2

Yehuda made his way to Seville by a roundabout route, using byways and sidetracks. The main roads, never free of bandits and highwaymen, were now also overrun with soldiers discharged from the defeated armies.

He never knew, when he saw armed men ahead on the road, whether they were soldiers still in service or discharged soldiers or bandits. He soon learned how to behave to minimise the danger. These men weren't barbarians, not even the bandits; they rarely engaged in cruelty for its own sake, and they knew that a poor, lone Jewish scholar would not be worth robbing. Yehuda was carrying his physician's bag as well as his travelling pack, and this proved to be a further protection: there was always someone wounded or suffering from dysentery or diphtheria, so he was welcomed and treated kindly as he tended to them. He learned a lot about field medicine on that journey! He also heard about conditions in the warring *taifa* states as he sat with the men around their campfires in the evening. Fighters were constantly being discharged from one army and recruited into another, and a rapid network of intelligence connected these men, who always knew who was prevailing in the constant warfare and who was losing.

By the time Yehuda arrived in Seville, Isaac ibn Ezra and his family had already reached the city, but they were preparing to leave for Toledo, where Isaac had strong business connections. Yehuda would love to have gone with them, but Isaac advised him to remain in Seville. The Christian north was still unstable and Isaac was not certain that his family would be able to remain in Toledo. Yehuda had Moses's letter of introduction to Meir ibn Kamniel in Seville and Isaac urged Yehuda to take up the opportunity of a place with him. So Yehuda called at Rab Meir's house and was shown in to see him.

Rab Meir had an air of authority like Rabbi Moses, but in every other way he was his opposite. Where Moses was tall and thin, Meir was short and plump; where Moses was dark and melancholy, Meir was light and cheerful – light in complexion as well as in demeanour, though his eyes were a warm, sparkling hazel where Moses's were steely blue. Meir received Yehuda in the *majlis* of his house, full of sunlight and opulence – Armenian rugs, the like of which he had seen only in the house of Isaac ibn Ezra in Córdoba, cushions of shimmering brocade and inlaid tables of ebony and ivory on which stood silver bowls full of grapes and pomegranates and sweetmeats. The rosewater sherbet that Meir had ordered for them arrived as Yehuda handed him the letter from Moses.

He read the letter slowly, sipping the sherbet and nodding to himself, then looked Yehuda up and down. Although Meir was still smiling, Yehuda felt as if he was being dissected under his gaze.

'So, young man,' he said at last, 'you flee the Almoravids in Granada only to meet the Almoravids in Seville, though for the moment at least they are here as our allies rather than conquerors. Will you remain in Seville or move on again?'

Sensing Yehuda's hesitation, Rab Meir added, 'You are of course very welcome to stay here in Seville. I can instruct you in medicine and also in the arts of administration. If you wish, you can stay with me and my family. I'd be glad of your help. Rabbi Moses speaks highly of the skills you already have as a physician and I could use an assistant – my apprentice, Jacob Albaz, has just been taken off to serve as a medical orderly in Ibn Tashfin's army.' He sighed and looked again at Moses's letter. 'But I'm afraid you won't find much poetry here in Seville. There are plenty of people here who can instruct you in Torah. But poetry? Well, this certainly isn't Granada or Córdoba or even Málaga. Amir Al-Mutamid is a great Arabic poet, as is his friend and vizir, Ibn Abbas. But the Jewish community here in Seville don't really have much to do with literature. Or even scholarship. We're mostly humble merchants, focused on making money more than on making poetry. You are, as I said, most welcome to stay, though you may pine a little for the culture of Granada and Córdoba.'

*

The next day Yehuda moved into Rab Meir's house. As they were sitting in the *majlis* discussing the programme for Yehuda's apprenticeship, a servant announced a visitor. Deborah had come to say farewell – she was to leave for Toledo with her family later that day.

'May I go out and see her, sir?' Yehuda asked.

'Go out and see her, my boy?' Meir laughed. 'Certainly not – she must come in here. Any friend of yours is an honoured guest in this house and should be received in the *majlis*... I'll go and fetch her.'

Yehuda was about to demur, but Meir held up his hand to silence him. 'Just wait here,' he said.

A few moments letter Meir ushered Deborah into the room and quietly withdrew.

Deborah watched him go, then turned to Yehuda, her eyebrows raised. 'He's very tactful, your new master.' She took a step towards him. 'With all the activity around our family's travel arrangements, this is really the first chance we've had to talk.'

'Yes, indeed, Deborah. I...' Yehuda, to his surprise and embarrassment, found himself lost for words. Deborah, as beautiful as ever, was wearing an immaculate blue and white travelling *thawb*, trimmed with lace at the sleeves and hem. She seemed to command the space in which they stood, and Yehuda was a little awed by her elegance and her air of self-assurance. She had grown into full womanhood, while he still thought of himself as a boy.

Deborah, smiling, broke the silence. 'So, young man, are you going to invite me to sit?'

'Oh yes, I'm sorry. Let's sit here.'

Once they had settled on the cushions, Yehuda recovered his confidence, offering Deborah some sherbet from the tray beside them, which she accepted. 'So, Deborah, I hope you will have a safe journey to Toledo. My journey from Granada was dreadful – over a week on foot, always encountering bands of soldiers and brigands.'

'Yes, so I heard. I'm glad you got here safely in the end. It could be a long, dangerous ride for us to Toledo. It certainly won't be as easy as coming to Seville from Córdoba – Al-Mutamid rules both kingdoms, of course, so we didn't encounter any trouble. And the Almoravids are not threatening him.'

'Not yet,' Yehuda said.

'What do you mean?'

'Well, my master Abd Allah was also an ally of the Almoravids, until Ibn Tashfin turned against him. It may only be a matter of time for Al-Mutamid. The Malikite judges…'

Deborah held up her hand to silence Yehuda. She took a sip of sherbet. 'Yehuda, fascinating though it is to discuss the stability of alliances in Andalucía, I can't stay for long. So let's talk about what we need to talk about.'

He hesitated, knowing exactly what she meant but unable to broach the subject. Deborah put her beaker down hard on the tray, spilling sherbet and making Yehuda jump. 'Come, Yehuda, are you going to play the tongue-tied poet still?'

'That's just not fair, Deborah. Why are you being so aggressive?'

Deborah let her shoulders drop and took a deep breath. She leaned forward and put her hand on his cheek, looking into his eyes. 'I'm sorry, Yehuda, this is hard for both of us, but harder for me.' She took her hand from his cheek and adjusted the skirts of her *thawb*. 'I'm the one that people are whispering about. I'm the one, frankly, that Father is worried about. Quite unnecessarily, as it happens.'

'Quite unnecessarily?' Yehuda said, with a dawning sense of relief.

About to give a sharp reply, Deborah caught his eye and laughed. She actually laughed.

'Very well,' he said, exchanging a warm smile with Deborah, 'let's talk about what we must talk about, then.'

'Oh, Yehuda,' she responded, leaning back, 'it's so good to be with you again, with someone I feel will not judge me or jump to conclusions. I'm so sorry for my first response; it was indeed unfair. So, we're ready to discuss Uncle Moses, and what happened or didn't happen with him?'

'Of course. Please.'

'What you really need to know is that absolutely nothing happened between Uncle Moses and me. There were some uncomfortable moments when we were alone together, but he never actually made any inappropriate suggestions, nor did he ever do anything wrong.'

Yehuda had little time to relish the quiet joy that he was feeling. He saw Deborah's troubled look and wanted only to reassure her. 'I'm very glad to hear that, Deborah. But it's not, I have to say, a surprise to me. I never believed that there was any truth in the rumours. How did they start? What did the gossips have to go on?'

Deborah laughed again, a rather bitter laugh this time. 'Gossips never need much to go on, Yehuda – certainly not in this case. You remember how careless he was about leaving drafts around? Well, one of the times he was staying with us, Rebekah found a manuscript in the courtyard. Not knowing whose it was, she gave it to Father. It was a poem by Moses, a very sensuous poem about… well, you can imagine. And at a crucial point the man says to the woman in the poem *"If you go with me, I will go; but if you do not go with me, I will not go."* Which…'

'Which is what Barak says to Deborah in the book of Judges!' he exclaimed. 'Really? Just because of an obscure reference to the prophetess Deborah everyone thought he had…'

'It wasn't only that. There were already suspicions, so Father and everyone else leapt to the wrong conclusion. I don't blame them entirely. Do you remember what Moses said in Córdoba about illicit feelings? "We never follow the desire into action, but we must celebrate its divine origin." Well, I was never convinced about that even as a principle, and it can certainly lead to misunderstandings if you keep saying it – especially when, as in the case of Uncle Moses, you've made enemies by letting fools know that you think they're fools.'

She paused and drained her beaker of sherbet. 'It didn't help that Moses refused to defend himself at first. Nobody believed me when I denied that he'd done anything wrong, and some people even implied that it was my fault – even though there was no "it" to be my fault. Then Moses got really angry on my behalf, and that made people even more suspicious. "Why is he so passionate in her defence?" they would ask. "There must be something there." Only Mother believes me, only she trusts me. She's almost persuaded Father to believe me, or at least to give me the benefit of the doubt. We'll have to wait and see.'

Seeing the tears welling in her eyes, Yehuda leaned across and took Deborah's hands in his. 'It must be truly terrible for you. I'm so sorry I wasn't there to support you through this. I had no idea of what was happening.'

Deborah sniffed and straightened her shoulders. 'Yes, maybe I should have mentioned it in our letters, but I assumed that the rumours must have reached Granada and that you didn't want to confront the issue.' She sighed and looked down, withdrawing her hands from his.

He reached over and took her hands again, forcing her to look up at him. 'Deborah, Deborah, if I'd known of course I would have confronted it, I'd have offered to help. But nobody would tell me anything about it until the end.' He sighed. 'In any case, I don't know how much help I could have been.'

Seeing the distress on his face, Deborah offered him a reassuring smile. 'Well, my friend, you could have been a great deal of help. There is no one whose good opinion I need more than yours. So I am delighted that we've cleared matters up now.'

Yehuda shook his head. 'Now, you say. Now? We've had hardly any time to share anything with each other, and now we must part again.'

They both fell silent, holding hands. After a moment, Deborah looked at the fruit bowl on the tray beside them. 'Very well,' she said, smiling, 'at least we can share this pomegranate.'

Yehuda laughed. 'All right, Deborah, that will have to do. As it happens, you've chosen my favourite fruit!'

He picked up a knife and cut the pomegranate in two. As he handed half of it to Deborah, some of the juice spurted onto her *thawb*. Yehuda was horrified. 'Oh, I'm so sorry, your beautiful gown.'

He reached over to pick up a kerchief, but Deborah held his arm to stop him. 'No, Yehuda, there's no need to try and clean it. I will treasure the stain – it will remind me of you while we're apart. Now, let's share our pomegranate.'

*

As Rab Meir had told Yehuda, while Córdoba and Granada were centres of government and of culture, Seville was essentially a centre of trade, a rich city of merchants and craftsmen. Its vast olive and fig plantations supplied Andalucía, North Africa and the East, as did its high-quality cotton and a range of other products from safflower to horses. The *Wadi al-Kabir*, a great river navigable to the sea, brought merchant ships from all over the Mediterranean. Between the great ships the waterways were always bustling with ferries and small trading vessels.

Walking through the commercial districts to the north of the Alcázar palace, Yehuda was bombarded by the sounds, sights and smells of the markets – the clanging of hammers from the smithies and the rasp of saws from the carpenters' shops; the sunlight glowing on colourful cloths and glinting on fine glass and pottery; the rich aromas of flowers and fruit gradually superseded, as he approached the factory areas, by the smell of rancid oil outside the olive oil refinery and, eventually, overwhelming all else, the stink of the tanneries in Salmat Almasafi.

Yehuda's task that summer morning was to deliver invitations to a party at Meir ibn Kamniel's house. In this case, most of the guests were to be prominent merchants and craftsmen in the Jewish community, so Yehuda spent an hour picking his way through the workshops and showrooms to reach their houses.

The following evening, the guests gathered in Rab Meir's spacious garden, which reminded Yehuda of Isaac ibn Ezra's lovely garden in Córdoba. Now, however, the guests lounging on the divans and cushions were not poets and scholars, but merchants like Saul ben Shimon, who dominated the olive oil export trade, and craftsmen like David Alnajar, one of the most admired furniture makers in Seville. The discussion over the wine, sesame cakes and fruit was not about the poetic structure of a *ghazal* or the topics suitable for a *muwashshah*, but about the difficulties of importing goods from Egypt during the summer season of westerly winds, or the trustworthiness of the Almoravid dinar coin.

During a lull in the conversation, Saul ben Shimon shifted on his divan and turned to Yehuda. His fine, flowing robe did little to hide the obesity that was reputed to result from over-consumption of his own olive oil. Lifting yet another sesame cake to his lips, Saul paused and said, 'Well, young man, you look rather bored.' He put the cake into his mouth and added, spitting out crumbs as he spoke, 'Not interested in the conversation of old men, eh? I suppose you'd prefer the company of young women? Or boys?'

Meir, who was sitting close enough to hear Saul, caught Yehuda's eye and slowly shook his head. Yehuda swallowed the sharp response he was about to deliver and lowered his eyes. 'No, sir, it's not that. It's just that I don't know much about trade.'

'So I understand,' Saul said, brushing the crumbs off his robe. 'I hear you have a reputation as a poet as well as a budding physician. I don't have much time for poetry and that kind of stuff myself – too busy working for money to feed and clothe my family. Like David Alnajar here.' He gestured to David, who was sitting behind him – in contrast to Saul, he was a lean, muscular man dressed in plain linen. 'But he also manages to make enough from his joinery to support scholars and poets like you. He's a great craftsman too – sometimes we call him Bezalel. So perhaps he appreciates the craft of poetry. Not me. I prefer practical crafts like his.'

As Yehuda hesitated, David cut in, 'Oh, leave the lad alone, Saul. He's actually here as an apprentice physician, as you say, which is a perfectly honourable profession – and one of which you'll have sore need if you don't lose some of that fat!' Saul held up his hand, grinning, and David continued, 'As it happens, he is indeed also an extremely talented poet – I've seen and heard some of his poetry and it's outstanding. We're not all indifferent to poetry like you.'

Saul grunted. 'Like most of us, you mean. Seville's too busy with real life to bother with poetry.'

'Tell that to our ruler, Al-Mutamid, who is a poet renowned throughout Andalucía, and whose Vizier is if anything an even greater poet.'

Hearing this, others joined the conversation, which, to Yehuda's relief, turned to a discussion of Al-Mutamid's increasingly precarious hold on Seville – the Almoravids had taken Córdoba in the spring and the merchants agreed that it was only a matter of time before Ibn Tashfin moved against Seville.

*

The merchants were right: Al-Mutamid was able to hold out for a couple of months in Seville but by the beginning of September his troops were overwhelmed by the Almoravid forces. On 9 September 1091, Ibn Tashfin's brother-in-law, Syr ibn Abu Bakr, entered the city. The Almoravids had become accustomed to life in Seville while stationed there during the years when Al-Mutamid and Ibn Tashfin were still allies. Ibn Tashfin, himself an ascetic who shunned wealth and luxury, had been unhappy with the heavy taxes that supported the 'pomp and vanity' of Al-Mutamid and his court, but was not inclined to punish the merchants for their luxurious lifestyle, distasteful as he found it. There were fewer purges of sinners than in other cities. By the time of Rosh Hashana, the Jewish New Year, three weeks after the conquest, the city was calm and the Jews were able to celebrate the High Holy Days in peace and go about their normal business.

Although the fall of Al-Mutamid meant that Meir ibn Kamniel no longer had administrative duties in the court, he remained a respected court physician, having successfully treated Syr ibn Abu Bakr for a nasty bout of dysentery.

One evening a few weeks after Rosh Hashana, Meir was sitting in the *majlis* of his house waiting for Yehuda to return from treating a patient. In his hand was a long Hebrew poem that Yehuda had completed the previous day, with its ominous superscription:

He starts by condemning the people of Seville, and ends with praise for the exalted leader, Rab Meir ben Kamniel

As he read through the poem again, he heard Yehuda coming in from the street and greeting the servants. 'Yehuda,' he called, 'I'm here in the *majlis* and have some fine wine waiting for you.'

Yehuda soon came in from the courtyard, looking tired and flustered. 'Are you well, Yehuda?' Meir asked. 'You look as if you have been having a difficult day.' He poured a beaker of wine and handed it to Yehuda, who nodded gratefully and took a long draught.

'Yes, Master,' he said, frowning. 'It's very frustrating. I treated three patients this afternoon and two of them were just suffering from bad digestion and constipation. The usual story – their reward for a dissolute life with too little exercise and too much wine and rich food.'

Meir held up the poem in his hand. 'You make your position clear in this poem, my friend.' Shuffling through the pages he read from the poem:

Time passes round the cup of Paradise to men,
…they savour its taste and say to me it's honey,
but I sip it and taste the dregs of bitterness
They think that money grows on trees, yet
they are afraid to go near the tree of knowledge…
A man cannot live in the company of madmen
without turning mad himself.

Meir lowered the paper and looked at Yehuda. 'You really don't like these people, do you, Yehuda?'

Uncertain how to interpret Meir's expression – was he annoyed or was he amused? – Yehuda stammered. 'No, I… yes, I… I mean, I…' He stopped, took a deep breath, and looked down at his hands. 'No, Master, I don't,' he whispered.

Meir remained silent. After a while, Yehuda looked up. Meir, his face still solemn, gestured for him to continue.

'It's true,' Yehuda said, 'I find the ways of Seville hard to live with. They worship only wealth and trade. I've begun, God forgive me, to see the people of Seville – Jews and Muslims – as the Almoravids see them, wallowing in their worship of wealth. In my

dreams, I see Yusuf ibn Tashfin on the balcony at Córdoba, fulmin-
ating against "all luxury and vanity, the snares of Satan", and as I
wake, I feel a guilty sense that I understand why he might despise
these pretensions.' To his own surprise, Yehuda found that he was
trembling. Holding his hands together to stop them shaking, he
looked up at Meir. 'For me, you are the one beacon of sensibility
in this whole grubby community.'

Meir leaned across and put his hand over Yehuda's. 'Yes, my
son, so you said in the poem. What was it?

I would have despaired if Meir was not there
to restore my spirits with his love and playfulness.'

Smiling, he leaned back again and took a sip of wine. 'And you
say many other kind things about me, Yehuda. But you need to
find a way to be kinder to others as well, and also to yourself.
I know how much you've suffered. You're still very young, you
haven't seen your mother at all since you left Tudela, and your
father only once. The glorious life of learning, poetry and friendship that you found in Andalucía has been shattered, apparently
forever, leaving you lonely and forlorn. It's not surprising that
you're angry.'

Yehuda remained silent, wiping a tear from his eye with the
back of his sleeve.

Meir stroked his beard. 'So, my friend, what am I going to do
with you? You'll never make a good physician if you can't control
your reactions to people.' He held up his hand, forestalling Yehuda's interruption. 'No, just a minute. I'm serious, we need to do
something. Let me think.'

Meir closed his eyes and lowered his head a little, rolling his
shoulders and then letting them drop. Yehuda had seen him do

this many times, and every time, a stillness seemed to suffuse his whole body as he entered a state of silent prayer. One could do nothing but wait and watch. After a long time, Rab Meir breathed deeply and raised his head. His eyes were still closed, but now there was a faint smile on his lips. He muttered, '*Baruch Hashem* – blessed be the Name of the Eternal' and opened his eyes.

'Let me tell you a story,' he said, smiling again. 'You may be familiar with it. Do you know the stories of Shammai, Hillel and the proselyte in the Talmud?'

'No, Master, I don't know them.'

'Well, in the first one a heathen came to Shammai and said to him, "You can make me a convert provided that you can teach me the whole Torah while I stand on one leg." Shammai drove him off with the builder's yardstick that was in his hand. When the heathen went to Hillel and asked the same question, he told him to stand on one leg and he said, "Do not do to your neighbour what is hateful to you. That is the whole Torah. All the rest is commentary. Go out and learn."'

'That's fascinating,' Yehuda said. 'Shammai was a builder and drove the man off with his builder's cubit: isn't the Aramaic word for a builder's cubit *emet*, which, of course, also means "truth"?'

'Exactly – what a student you are! And that's precisely the point. He drove the heathen off with the truth. This and the other stories all point in the same direction. Every time the heathen asked Shammai a question, Shammai thought "What is the *truth*?" Hillel did not think that way: every time the heathen asked Hillel the same question, Hillel thought, "Who's asking the question?" And he answered in a way that the questioner could understand. That's why Hillel was the greater of the two.'

By now Yehuda was well used to his teachers reaching their destination through an oblique chain of parables and proverbs, but he was puzzled as to what this story was saying about him. There seemed to be no option but to play along with Rab Meir.

'I'm not sure what you mean, Master, but in any case, if Hillel wanted to do what the heathen asked, why didn't he give him what Rabbi Akiva called the essence of Torah, from Leviticus, "Love your neighbour as yourself"?'

'Another good question, my boy, to which there are two answers. First, Hillel didn't know if the heathen was just mocking him or if he genuinely wanted instant instruction in the whole Torah. Hillel's answer was the right answer in either case: if the heathen was mocking him, then Hillel's answer was an appropriate rebuke – don't do to me what would be hateful to you; if the heathen was a genuine searcher, Hillel was showing him the way to the Torah.'

'But he didn't talk about love as the way of the Torah. Why did he give such a pedestrian answer?'

Rab Meir smiled again. 'You think only sparkling answers will do? Well, Hillel knew better – he recognised that he couldn't talk about love immediately. You can't *command* another person to love, but if they learn to have care and respect for their neighbour, they may then come to love their neighbour. That's where Hillel was leading the proselyte. And that's why I am telling you the story.'

As Meir finished, the voice of the muezzin at the Begum Mosque drifted through the *mashrabiyya*: '*Allahu Akbar. Allahu Akbar.*' Before Yehuda could ask any more questions, Meir stood up and crossed the room to open the latticed shutters of the *mashrabiyya*. The setting sun cast a golden light into the *majlis*, its shadows dappled by the leaves of the myrtle in the courtyard. They heard the crowds moving in the street as the Muslims went to their evening prayer in the mosque and the Jews moved towards the synagogue for theirs.

'Actually, Yehuda, the Sufis understand that very well, better than anyone. You may not be ready for it yet, but one day you'll need to learn what they have to say – one day you should study closely the work of the great Sufi scholars like Abu Hamid al-Ghazali, the Persian. But perhaps not quite yet. Anyway, will you come to the synagogue for the evening prayer tonight, Yehuda?'

'If you're going, Master, then yes, I will come with you.' Yehuda tried to keep the exasperation out of his voice. 'But have we finished the subject? What did you want to say about me?'

'About you, Yehuda? I have been talking about you. Perhaps I should have told you the first of the three stories, in which Hillel shows the proselyte that he needs to trust his teachers! What I am saying, my boy, is that you need to go and study the Talmud.'

'What? The Talmud? What do you mean, Master?'

'Are you really surprised, Yehuda? Don't you think you need to learn the Talmud?'

'Well, no, I mean, yes, but I don't understand why you say this now, or, for that matter, what it has to do with Hillel and Shammai.'

'Don't you?' Meir frowned, but then relaxed. 'I'm sorry, Yehuda. I was about to rebuke you but that's not fair. You deserve a clearer explanation from me. So listen.' He sat again on the cushions and took a deep breath. 'Shammai was a very wise man indeed, Yehuda, far more learned than almost anyone in the Talmud apart, of course, from Hillel and Akiva. But let's be honest, he was a prig, and with a very harsh view of his fellow human beings. A bit like you are becoming, I'm afraid, my son.' Yehuda started to respond but Meir held up his hand again. 'No, I'm not condemning you, Yehuda – you haven't reached that stage, not yet. You are young and you haven't yet learned the difference between having judgement and being judgemental. Some people never learn that but you, Yehuda, you have the seeds of greatness in you, so it's very important that you learn that. Absolutely important.'

Yehuda closed his eyes and took a deep breath. When he opened them, he saw that Rab Meir was watching him serenely. 'What does this mean, Rab Meir?' he asked.

'There are two things you need to do to prevent the hardening of your heart, Yehuda. The first is to fall in love – but I can't control that, and you may yet be a little too young for it. The second is to learn the Talmud under a true, enlightened master. Fortunately, such a master is close at hand, and he is calling for you.'

'Calling for me?'

'Well, not for you specifically, but God moves as God moves.' Meir reached across to his writing tablet and picked up a letter. 'I recently received this from Rabbi Yitzchak al-Fasi, the head of the yeshiva at Lucena. He's looking for a secretary and asks me if I know of anybody suitable. I now realise that you are just the right person for him, and he's just the right person for you. He's probably the greatest Talmud scholar in all Andalucía. Go to Lucena and learn from the great Al-Fasi and his colleagues what is the true purpose of scholarship.'

4

REAWAKENING
LUCENA, 1091

A thing can be explained only by what is more subtle than
itself; there is nothing subtler than love – by what, then,
shall love be explained?

Summun al-Muhibb (Baghdadi Sufi, c. 900)

Yehuda dismounted as soon as he entered the city, happy to stretch
his legs and lead his horse through West Gate Square, a spacious
plaza surrounded by inns and elegant merchant's houses – even the
warehouses were clean and well-maintained. There were no longer
any signs of the disruptions of the previous year, when Lucena
had revolted against Abd Allah and surrendered to Ibn Tashfin.
The Almoravids were now in control of Lucena but were leaving it
largely in peace while they focused on new conquests in Andalucía.

Yehuda threaded his way carefully through the crowds of people
hurrying home to prepare for the afternoon prayers. To his delight,
he could see as many scholars as merchants and craftsmen among
the crowds. A young scholar, about Yehuda's age, brushed past him,
carrying what looked like a whole tractate of the Talmud bound in

leather – carrying it carelessly, as if it were no more than a pamphlet, or a bag of raisins. His robe was of fine linen: Yehuda noticed that most of the scholars were as well dressed as the merchants and the craftsmen – and almost all of them, scholars, merchants and craftsmen, were Jews! Córdoba, Granada and Seville had large Jewish communities, but Lucena was a city founded and dominated by Jews. The suburbs had mixed communities, but the walled city was almost exclusively Jewish.

Lucena was also famous throughout the Mediterranean as a centre of learning – famous, indeed, beyond the Mediterranean and as far as the Ashkenazi lands of France and Germany. Among the familiar gowns of the scholars, Yehuda noticed here and there the coarse woollen jackets and trousers of strangers from Ashkenaz. They had come to learn in the yeshivas of distinguished teachers in Lucena, first among them being that of Yehuda's prospective master, Rabbi Yitzchak al-Fasi.

Alongside the melodious Arabic of the Sephardi scholars, Yehuda heard the harsh sounds of the German and French languages, of which he understood hardly a word. Sometimes the Ashkenazis would even try Latin, their second language, but very few people in Lucena knew that either. The only common language was the Hebrew of the Torah or, for the serious scholars, the Aramaic of the Talmud.

Having secured lodgings at a small inn in the corner of the square, Yehuda was in no hurry to go and introduce himself to Master Al-Fasi. The master would be leading the *Mincha* service in his synagogue and would then preside over the afternoon *shiur*, guiding the learning and disputations of his students. So Yehuda lingered at the door of the inn, fascinated by the comings and goings of the scholars, especially the Ashkenazis, whom he had rarely seen before. Their features seemed rather flabby to him, but that was perhaps because of the paleness of their skin, especially that of the women: a few Ashkenazi rabbis, like some in Andalucía, allowed women as well as men to study the Talmud, so women were among the travellers drawn to Lucena.

Yehuda was already enchanted – this was the cosmopolitan life in a new form, bound together not by poetry and wit, but rather by a devotion to the study of the Talmud. He began to think that he could learn to value disputation and the law as much as he already loved poetry and medicine.

Turning to go back into the inn to unpack his valise, he paused as he noticed a group of Ashkenazis riding through the West Gate. Their horses were shambling, heads low, sweat running down their dusty coats. It had clearly been a long, hot journey, and the riders looked as drained of energy as the horses – all the riders except the last one, a young lady on a grey stallion. Her seat was perfectly straight and her head held high. As she came through the gate, she removed her black velvet cap and – O Heavens! – her red hair tumbled around her shoulders. Raising her hands to the back of her neck, she swept up the hair to loosen it. To Yehuda, the movement looked like the flame rising from the altar in the book of Judges. 'And it happened when the flame went up from the altar to the heavens, the angel of God went up in the flame of the altar.' He stood transfixed, staring like a country bumpkin. She looked around and caught his eye. The embarrassment! There was he, a lad of sixteen, and she must have been five or six years older than him. Blushing, he dropped his gaze immediately, but glanced up again to see her smile slightly as she rode on towards an inn on the other side of the square. The party dismounted at the inn yard and lifted their packs from the horses before the ostlers led the horses away.

Yehuda went to his room to get his papers to take to the yeshiva, but before leaving he spent a while writing to his beloved

Deborah to tell her of his safe arrival. He included in the letter a poem that came to him as he watched the young Ashkenazi woman entering the square:

The evening when the young beauty revealed to me
The heat of her cheeks, the braids of her hair
Gleaming carnelian red and veiling
Brows of fresh pearl, the likeness of her form –
She was like the sun blushing as she rose,
Like the flame of the clouds in the radiant dawn.

As he set out for the yeshiva after handing the letter to the innkeeper for despatch, it occurred to him that it may have been unwise to write to Deborah in such terms about another woman – and one he had not even met. He was sure, however, that Deborah was never plagued by jealousy – and would indeed acknowledge that the poem was a good one. He let it go and went on his way.

At the *bet midrash*, the study hall next to the synagogue, Yehuda found the room still full and the *shiur* still in progress, so he went up to the gallery to wait and observe. The small windows of the hall let in little light; the *bet midrash* was lit by a forest of candelabra. The ordinary members of the community had gone home after *Mincha*, leaving the hall to Al-Fasi's disciples, who were sitting on cushions round the candelabra in pairs or groups of three, bent over manuscripts or bound volumes. Some were reading passages out loud while others were arguing about the text in a sing-song tone, as if they were performing a ritual rather than engaging in a dialogue. Yehuda guessed that the text that many of them were studying was Al-Fasi's own great compilation of religious laws and rules, the *Sefer Ha-halachot*.

When a group of three scholars sitting immediately below the gallery stood and moved towards the left of the hall, Yehuda saw, for the first time, that Rabbi Yitzchak al-Fasi was sitting on a dais there. To Yehuda's surprise, the rabbi was not sitting on cushions, like everyone else, but in a high-backed wooden chair in the French style, decorated with carvings and ivory inlays. A table by his right hand was covered with manuscripts and books, while a young amanuensis sat on his left, taking dictation.

Only when the rabbi put a book on the table and leaned slightly towards the amanuensis, did Yehuda realise why he sat in a chair and why he needed an amanuensis to do his writing for him. His movements were slow, and he trembled slightly; Yehuda remembered that Al-Fasi was said to have been born in the year that the inhabitants of Madinat Al-Bira founded Granada, which would mean that by now he was seventy-eight years old. His movements were clearly those of an old man, though it was difficult to believe that he was nearly eighty. Yehuda muttered a verse from the Psalms, 'The days of our years are seventy years or, given the strength, eighty years, but the best of them are trouble and grief.'

The group that had been sitting below the gallery approached the Master to show him a passage in the book they were studying, and a lively discussion ensued. They were arguing fiercely but seemed to be enjoying the dispute – one of the students was smiling and wagging his finger. After a few minutes, the amanuensis, who had been listening to the argument in silence, stood up, took one of the books from the table and read out a passage, upon which Al-Fasi and the three students burst into laughter. Clearly the amanuensis had settled the argument – or proved its absurdity. The laughter stopped abruptly as the five of them looked towards the main door of the *bet midrash*, which was immediately below the gallery in which Yehuda sat. He soon saw that what had distracted them was a party of half a dozen Franks moving into the hall towards the Master. At the rear of the party walked the young lady with the red hair. The men in front of her stood aside and the lady curtsied before the Master.

One of the Franks spoke, evidently introducing the lady, though Yehuda could not hear what he was saying. Rabbi Yitzchak rose from his chair and stepped unsteadily off the dais, supported by his amanuensis. The whole student body gasped as the Master, gingerly and with much effort, knelt before the young lady. Looking into her face, he reached out to take her hand and spoke briefly to her. She responded with a nod. Sill kneeling, Rabbi Yitzchak raised his voice and addressed the yeshiva, in Aramaic so that she would understand. 'I have the great honour to welcome to our yeshiva Rachel bat Shlomo, daughter of Rabbi Shlomo Yitzchaki, known as Rashi, the greatest Torah scholar of our generation, possibly of all generations.'

Rachel gestured to the amanuensis, who helped her to raise the Master to his feet as she replied, in elegant Aramaic, 'The honour, Rabbi Yitzchak, is entirely mine. I would venture to suggest that as long as you live – may God grant that you live to a hundred and twenty years – my father would refute your suggestion that he is the greatest scholar of our generation.'

Acknowledging the compliment with an amused shake of his head, the Master led Rachel bat Shlomo and the Frankish party towards the door at the back of the *bet midrash*. The study session was over; the students gathered up their scrolls and books and started to leave the hall.

*

As Yehuda descended from the gallery, the amanuensis reappeared from the back of the *bet midrash*, heading for the main entrance. A tall, handsome fellow of about Yehuda's age, he seemed very relaxed, strolling across the hall with a light step as if it were his living room. Yehuda ventured to speak to him.

'Good day, sir.'

The amanuensis looked curiously at Yehuda's dusty robe and battered saddlebag. 'And good day to you, my friend. How are you? You look as if you've ridden a long way.'

'I have, from Seville – I arrived just this afternoon.'

The young man's eyes widened and he grinned. 'From Seville?' he said. 'Are you by any chance Yehuda ben Shmuel Halevi, sent by Rab Meir? If so, we've been expecting you.'

'I am, Yehuda ben Shmuel at your service. I have a further letter from Rab Meir.' Fumbling around in his bag, he pulled out the letter and was embarrassed to find it crumpled and dirty. He tried to smooth it out but only succeeded in pulling the seal away from the edge of the paper. The amanuensis put his hand on Yehuda's shoulder and gently took the letter from him.

'It's good to meet you, Yehuda. My name is David bin Avram, by the way. I'll take the letter to Rabbi Yitzchak – I'm his amanuensis.'

'Yes, I know. I saw, I was in the gallery.'

'What, just now? Then you must have seen the arrival of that extraordinary Frankish girl!'

'I did. Is she really the daughter of Rashi?'

'Yes, and she's come to study with the Master. They'll be engaged for some time now, so let's get something to eat and we can gossip about her! I'm not taking you to the yeshiva refectory, though: the food is so terrible there that you'd head straight back to Seville! There's a *funduq* nearby that does excellent lamb, so let's go there.' He took Yehuda by the arm and guided him into the street. 'I'm delighted to see you, my friend – Rab Meir has given a fulsome account of you. And, what's more important, now that you're here I can hand over my duties to you and get ready to leave.'

'To leave – where are you going?'

'A long, long way, to Fez – I have a post at the new school there, but I couldn't leave until you came to replace me. That's why I'm glad to see you! Where are you lodged?'

'At the inn next to the West Gate – I was too tired to look for anything nearer.'

'That's fine, we'll get you proper lodgings tomorrow morning. Watch out for the innkeeper there, though – he's a rogue and he'll try to overcharge you outrageously.'

They made their way through streets crowded with scholars returning to their lodgings or meeting friends in the city gardens. Yehuda felt again that this was a place where he could feel at home, a place where learning was respected above wealth and luxury. David paused at the head of an alleyway from which drifted the enticing smell of charcoal smoke and braised lamb.

'This is it, as you can obviously tell.'

'Yes, indeed, the smell reminds me of the wonderful stuffed lamb they cook in Granada for the Sabbath.'

'We have exactly the same dish here, but we eat it on any day. There's an old Arabic saying, "Of the good things of this world the Muslims enjoy sex the most, the Christians money, the Persians status, and the Jews food." I think there's a lot of truth in that.'

Though a little shocked by David's frankness, Yehuda returned his smile, recognising that he was being tested. He was determined to show that he had the sophistication to fit into this new world. David led the way down the alley and they took their seats in the small, crowded *funduq*, where David was evidently well known. The serving girl and several of the guests nodded to him.

'You'll take the lamb, then?' he asked. 'Try it with the white Cairo beer – this is the only place in Lucena you can get it.' Yehuda nodded and David told the servant to bring two beers and two portions of lamb.

'So, Yehuda, you were in Granada before the Almoravids took it?'

'Yes, indeed – and since you're going to Fez, you'll probably see my old master. The former Amir of Granada, Abd Allah ibn Buluggin, is exiled near there.'

Shocked, David held up his hand and looked around to check if anyone had overheard them. Seeing that Yehuda was puzzled by his reaction, he leaned forward and whispered. 'Be careful how you bandy that name about in Lucena, my friend. You must surely know that he's hated here. Lucena was the first city to rebel against Ibn Buluggin when the Almoravids invaded, and he put down the rebellion with cruel force.'

'Oh yes, I'm sorry, David, I forgot. I should be more tactful. But I'm no politician and he was very good to me. I was apprentice to his physician and the amir treated me very well indeed.'

'Ah, what contrary times we live in, Yehuda. But we can talk about that later. Now I want to know what you know about that Frankish girl.'

'Nothing at all, really, I just saw her at the West Gate when she arrived in town and then in the *bet midrash*. That's all I know. I didn't even know Rashi had a daughter.'

'He does, three of them in fact, and what daughters! Let me tell you about them.'

While they ate the meal, David told Yehuda about Rashi's daughters: Joheved, the eldest and most learned; Miriam, the practical one; and Rachel, the wittiest. All were beautiful, it was said, but Rachel was the most beautiful: she was known as Bella – not, David added, from the Hebrew *baleh*, or worn out, but from a word for beautiful in French or in Latin, he wasn't sure which.

Rashi taught all three daughters the Talmud, and it was said that they even prayed with phylacteries strapped to their arm and head; for a woman to do that was unheard of in Andalucía.

'Thank you, David,' Yehuda said as they finished the meal, 'the lamb tagine was as delicious as you promised, but I'm not so sure about the white Cairo beer. I'm grateful for the introduction, but I think I'll stick to wine. Now I understand why there are scores of references to wine in the Torah but not a single reference to beer!'

David smiled as they rose from their cushions. 'Yes, I suppose it takes some getting used to: I've grown to like it.'

When they left the *funduq* David returned to the yeshiva and Yehuda to the West Gate inn. They had agreed that the next morning David would take Yehuda to his permanent lodgings and arrange an interview for him with Rabbi Yitzchak in the afternoon.

*

Yehuda couldn't stop thinking of what David had told him about Rashi's daughters, enchanted to learn that there were other women who, like Deborah, could hold their own in the world of learning without compromise. He even dreamt of Rachel that night. He felt a little guilty when he woke but told himself that he was not betraying his beloved Deborah. Rachel, after all, was utterly beyond his reach – a Frank, the daughter of the most famous rabbi in the West and, above all, a cultivated woman, who would certainly see him as the insignificant adolescent that he felt he was. Even David, who was much more sophisticated than him, clearly held Rachel in awe.

After attending the rather desultory morning prayers at the inn and paying his account – exorbitant, as David had warned him – Yehuda made his way to the yeshiva. He left his bags in the porter's lodge and followed the old porter through the *bet midrash* to a door at the side. The great hall was already filling with students, settling down in pairs or small groups to pore over weighty volumes of the Talmud. More volumes were stacked around the walls. Yehuda had never seen so many books in his life, not even in Amir ibn Buluggin's library.

The porter opened the door at the side of the hall and waved him into the room. 'This is Rab David's room, sir. I expect it will be yours soon if all goes well this afternoon. Just wait here for Rab David. I'm sure he'll be along shortly. Let me know if you need anything at all, that's what I'm here for. My name is Joshua, by the way.'

'Thank you, Joshua. Tell me, how long have you been a porter here?'

'Well, sir, I started as an under-porter the year the Amir Al-Mu'tadid conquered Hueva, so I'll have been here forty years come the end of this year.'

'In that case, Joshua, you must know more about how the school functions than almost anyone except Rabbi Yitzchak, so you can be sure I'll be seeking your advice on all sorts of issues. Thank you.' Yehuda bowed to him.

'No, thank you, sir.' Almost blushing, the old man bowed, turned and walked back across the hall.

David's room was small but comfortable, with plenty of cushions in a rich, though rather faded, brocade. The low table was covered in books and manuscripts, many of which had slipped to the floor. The smell of dust, parchment and ink reminded him of the study of his former master, Moses ibn Ezra. Moses had once said to him, 'The most important person in any organisation, after the ruler, is the porter, the gatekeeper. Get on the right side of him and you can't go wrong.' Yehuda had taken his advice and seemed to have got off to a good start here with Joshua.

Through the latticed window Yehuda saw David striding across the central courtyard towards the study. As he entered, he greeted Yehuda warmly. 'Welcome, my friend, you're very welcome – Joshua told me that you'd already arrived.'

'Yes, I woke early – the noise in the West Gate Square seems to start even before dawn.'

'Indeed it does, but don't worry, we'll find you much better lodgings today in a quieter part of the city. Before we do that, however, let's discuss what Rabbi Yitzchak will want to ask you this afternoon, and what your duties will be if the Master agrees to appoint you.'

They had not been talking long when there was a knock on the door. David called for the visitor to come in and Rachel bat Shlomo entered the room.

'David, I wanted to ask you... Oh, I'm sorry, I'm interrupting, I didn't realise you had a visitor.' She turned her green eyes on Yehuda and smiled. He managed to return the smile without looking as flustered as he felt, overcome by her beauty and by the fresh perfume of apples and grass that she had brought into the room. David got to his feet and Yehuda followed suit, knocking several manuscripts off the table as he did so.

'You're not interrupting at all, Lady Rachel,' David said. 'It's a good opportunity for you to meet the young man who will succeed me as the Master's secretary. Rachel bat Shlomo, please allow me to present to you Yehuda Halevi of Tudela.'

'Yehuda of Tudela? I know that name – there's a poet of that name. Moses ibn Ezra sent some of his wonderful Hebrew poems to my father. I especially liked one about the stars. What were those lines? Let me think. Ah, yes, I remember. "The star of the East has come to the West; / He has found the sun among the daughters of the West." So evocative. Are you related to that poet?'

'That poem is by me, my lady.'

'What? By you?' He nodded. 'But that was three years ago! You can hardly have been old enough to have... Oh dear, now I'm rushing to judgement and being inexcusably rude, as usual. Please forgive me!' She smiled and bowed gracefully.

David, seeing that Yehuda was tongue-tied, rescued him from his embarrassment. 'Yes, my lady, Yehuda is…'

'Bella, please call me Bella, David. Let's not be formal here in your own study.'

'Well, yes, Bella, Yehuda is indeed a poet – Rab Meir ibn Kamniel was Yehuda's patron in Seville and he sent us a package of Yehuda's poems a couple of weeks ago. Now, where are they?' Before Yehuda could stop him, David rummaged through a sheaf of manuscripts and handed four or five to Rachel.

'Thank you, David. Shall we all sit while I look at these?'

Yehuda hesitated. His poetry was a success within a small circle of Andalucían scholars, but Rachel was from a totally different world. He would be devastated if she dismissed his work or, even worse, laughed at it.

Sensing his discomfort, Rachel smiled. 'Don't worry, Yehuda, I'm sure I'll love the poems, and even if I don't, I promise to be kind!'

They all sat on the cushions – Rachel arranging herself so that the light from the window flattered her profile. She read through the poems, brushing a strand of hair behind her ear in a gesture that reminded Yehuda of Deborah. But Deborah and Rachel were as different as dusk and dawn. Deborah's olive skin had the glow of polished mahogany, while Rachel's pale, freckled skin had only the faintest patina, like damask; Deborah's face was framed in flowing black locks, while Rachel's auburn hair seemed to float about her like a veil; Deborah's perfume was of musk and cinnamon, Rachel's of orchards and meadows. Yehuda had thought that nothing could be more disconcerting than Deborah's eyes – sapphires in a setting of amber – but Rachel's green gaze combined a penetrating intelligence with a constant twinkle of amusement.

When she had finished reading, Rachel glanced only briefly at Yehuda before turning to David. 'So, David, what did you make of these poems?'

David, like Yehuda, had been staring at Rachel while she was reading; he was startled at being addressed but soon recovered, smiling at Yehuda before turning to Rachel. 'Well, Bella, I'm a Talmud scholar, not a poet, but I think they're brilliant. The Hebrew is elegant, the images beautiful, the biblical references intriguing.'

She didn't respond at once, apart from a slight nod, but turned to look at Yehuda for what seemed to him a very long time. 'I agree, David,' she said, still looking at Yehuda, 'these poems have the same freshness and clarity as those that Moses ibn Ezra sent to my father. But rather like them, these poems seem somehow… *comment dit-on?* … somehow incomplete. Wouldn't you agree, Yehuda?'

Having no idea what she was talking about, Yehuda felt deflated. He looked at David, who just shrugged. 'I suppose all poems can be improved,' he said to Rachel, 'so in that sense all poems are unfinished, apart from the Psalms, of course.'

She replied quietly, 'And *The Song of Songs*, Yehuda, don't forget *Shir ha'Shirim* – that is as near perfect a poem as is possible.'

He recalled Rabbi Moses telling him when they parted in Granada that Rabbi Akiva had taught that all the world is not worth more than the day on which *The Song of Songs* was given to us. 'Yes, Bella, but I'm not comparing my little verses to *Shir ha'Shirim* or the Psalms!'

'Of course not, but I believe that your poetry could be great, very great indeed, Yehuda. You have extraordinary talent; but I think that you still have a lot to learn.'

'Yes, I know I'm still young in learning,' he protested, 'but that's exactly why I'm here at the yeshiva.'

'I'm not really talking about that kind of learning, Yehuda. I'm talking about experience.'

Was she just trying to be provocative? Yehuda responded rather sharply, 'Well, of course I lack experience, I'm only sixteen!'

Rachel realised that she had been unkind. While she admired his skill, she had been quietly amused by his immaturity and by his evident attraction to her. She should have been more sympathetic to the confusion she was eliciting in him. She leaned forward and put her hand on his. He'd expected her touch to be cool, but it was surprisingly warm.

'Please excuse me, and don't misunderstand me,' she said. 'Maybe my Aramaic is a little blunt. I mean no disrespect. Even though I know you only from these poems, I have the greatest respect for you. What I'm trying to say is that these poems, well, they...' She picked out one of the shorter poems. 'Look at this one, for example, so short but so exquisite:

> *By the life of our bond, my love, and by your life*
> *And the life of the love that shot its dart at me,*
> *Truly I have become the slave of love: it has*
> *Pierced my ear, it has split my heart in two.'*

'Yes,' David broke in, 'that image about the pierced ear – I wondered about that until Yehuda explained that it referred to the law about a slave who doesn't want to be freed at the Jubilee.'

'Indeed,' said Rachel, 'it's in Exodus: "*But if the slave declares 'I love my master, and my wife and children: I do not wish to go free', his master shall take him before the court. He shall be brought to the door or the door post and his master shall pierce his ear with an awl; and he shall be his slave forever.*"' David and Yehuda glanced at each other – how many scholars in Andalucía, let alone women, would have known that passage by heart? And her accent, which made her Aramaic sound rather formal, seemed perfectly suited to the Hebrew.

She turned to Yehuda and held up the poem. '"It has pierced my ear; it has split my heart in two." That's brilliant, Yehuda, the poet's heart is split because he is a slave forever, yet he himself has chosen that servitude.'

'But if you understand that, then I don't see the difficulty.'

She studied him for a long moment, then drew in her breath and said, 'Look again at these poems. Can you see why I think there is something missing?'

She handed the poems to Yehuda, who read them all, even though he already knew them by heart. Each of them seemed to him as complete as they could be. What did the woman mean? He shrugged and looked up at her in some bewilderment. 'Tell me what's missing.'

'What strikes me when I read these poems is that every single one of them is about the poet's response to his love for the beloved. They are all about how the poet feels about how the poet feels! There's almost nothing about the relationship with the beloved. More than that, there's nothing at all about the beloved herself.'

Seeing the disappointment in his face, she added, 'Don't worry about this, Yehuda. It will change. I'm to be married when I return to Troyes, so although I'm older than you, we are in the same position. All we can know of this kind of love is what we see indirectly. Words become slippery here – both Aramaic and Hebrew fall apart at this point – but what I'm trying to say is that you know of love only through your imagination.'

Yehuda looked down, trying to disentangle his feelings. Seeing his embarrassment, Rachel wondered whether she should end the discussion there. She looked at David, but he just shrugged – she had taken the initiative and it was her decision what to do now.

She decided that she could and should continue. She moved a little closer to Yehuda.

'Yehuda, look at me when you are ready.' When he looked up, she said. 'I want to try something. Give me your hand.' He hesitated. Amused by his blushes, she added, 'Don't worry, we have David here as our chaperone and I'm not going to do anything my father or Rabbi Yitzchak would disapprove of. Just give me your hand.'

He let her take his hand and she turned it so that the back of his hand was in hers, palm upwards. 'Now close your eyes.'

He did as Rachel asked, becoming aware again of the scent that she brought with her into the room and of the warmth of her hand.

'Tell me what you feel,' Rachel said.

What was he to say? How could he tell her how he felt at that moment? He was overwhelmed by her presence, by her closeness, but he could hardly tell her that!

'I feel… I feel confused. I…'

Rachel quietly interrupted, 'I didn't ask *how* you feel, Yehuda, but *what* you feel. Tell me what you feel, the physical sensations that you're experiencing, not your reactions to them. Dismiss everything else from your mind for now. Keep your eyes closed. Take your time.'

Doing as Rachel bid him wasn't easy: he was unsettled by her authority as much as by her beauty, the more so since David seemed so at ease with her. He did as Rachel asked and tried to focus on the physical sensations. He found, to his surprise, that he could dismiss the other thoughts buzzing around in his head and pay attention to what he was immediately experiencing.

After a short time, he spoke. 'Your hand holding mine, its warmth, a faint pressure on either side of my hand. Your scent, like apples and grass, and behind that, the smell of the room, parchment and dust – and the smell of fruit, which comes from the fruit bowl that I know is to my left. An itch in my right leg.'

'Excellent,' Rachel said. 'Keep your eyes closed, Yehuda. Now, David, please continue to be silent, but pass me that. No, not that one. Yes, that one… Thank you. Now, Yehuda, I am going to put something in your hand. Describe it without opening your eyes.' Rachel's sleeve brushed his arm as she put an object in his hand.

'It's round and dense, smooth, but with a rough patch at the bottom against my palm – why, it's a pomegranate! Oh dear… I…' He found himself unable to continue, overwhelmed by a piercing sense of loss.

Rachel's quiet voice broke into his confusion. 'Open your eyes, Yehuda, when you're ready. Take your time.'

When he opened his eyes, he saw that Rachel was looking intently at him – her expression more one of curiosity than of sympathy. 'What happened then, Yehuda?' she asked gently.

He gave the pomegranate to David, who put it back in the fruit bowl. 'It was the pomegranate,' he said, 'it brought so many memories – of my teachers Rabbi Moses in Granada and Rab Meir in Seville, of…'

'Of someone else?'

'Yes, of someone else.'

'Is she someone dear to you?'

'She? How did you know it was a woman?'

'Is it not a woman?'

'Yes, but how did you know?'

'That's not important. We're talking about you. Why did her memory make you so sad?'

He told her about Deborah, about how hard it had been to keep in touch with her through all the troubles and disruptions of the Almoravid and Christian incursions. The last time he had seen Deborah was in Seville, when he had shared a pomegranate with her before they parted. He remembered how he had opened it clumsily, spurting some juice on her blue *thawb*. Yehuda had been horrified but Deborah made light of it, saying that the stain would remind her of him while they were apart.

'Oh, Yehuda, I'm so sorry to have evoked that memory. I know how hard such separation is. But you said, "While we're apart..." That means that she expected you to be together again?'

He lowered his eyes. 'Yes, I suppose it does.'

'When did you last hear from her?'

'She wrote to me from Nava Hermosa on the border with Toledo. I haven't heard from her since.'

'When was that?'

'Almost a year ago – I've written many times but had no reply. These days it seems almost impossible to get letters through to the Christian north.'

'You must find her, Yehuda, you must find her,' Rachel said.

David, who had been watching in silence, now interrupted, 'But Yehuda, you're now in exactly the right place! Where you were, in Seville, was a different story. Here in Lucena we have many contacts with Toledo – there are former students of Rabbi Yitzchak teaching there, and one or two are even in King Alfonso's court. They use the royal messengers to communicate with us in the yeshiva. We can help you to find your Deborah.'

Yehuda gasped, his heart suddenly filled with hope again. 'Really? I had no idea! That's wonderful. I must write again as soon as possible.'

'I'll find out when the next emissary is going to Toledo. We can give him instructions before I leave on Monday, Yehuda.'

'Thank you, thank you so much. I dare to hope that I can find her again.'

'I'm so very pleased for you, Yehuda,' said Rachel. Picking up the pomegranate from the fruit bowl, she continued, 'Meanwhile, we must finish our work. Did you notice what happened – what happened when you stopped thinking about *how* you feel and started focusing on *what* you feel?'

He was reluctant to return to the strange lesson that Rachel was conducting, wanting to sit with David straight away and write the instructions for the Toledo emissary. He made himself calm down and re-focus on the lesson: there would be plenty of time before the emissary left. He took a deep breath, trying to recapture the sensations.

'It was surprising how quickly I was able to dismiss everything but the immediate physical sensations and how vivid and – I don't know how to say it – how pure, how uncluttered those sensations were when I paid attention to them instead of… instead of…'

'Instead of reacting to them,' said Rachel. 'This is all about experience. Without paying attention to our direct experience, we cannot understand the world – the physical world or the divine world.'

'Aha!' said David, flinging up his hands. 'This is Ibn Sina!'

Yehuda was rather envious to see the radiant smile that Rachel gave David, but then she turned her smile on him also. 'The great Abu Ali ibn Sina, yes, whom our Latin translators call Avicenna. He taught the importance of direct, physical experience. He said that you can know by reason that fire burns but knowing it in that way is infinitely less than the direct experience of fire warming your hand. It's like the psalmist says, "Taste and see that God is good."'

These were the very words that Moses ibn Ezra had quoted to Yehuda when he last saw him! He began to understand where Rachel was going, but David was ahead of him and eager to impress her. 'This is what the Sufis call *dhawq* in Arabic – taste or sensation, Yehuda – which Ibn Sina classifies with all *mushahada*, perceptions. Reason gets us only so far – we need to experience and then build upon that experience.'

Yehuda took up the theme. 'Yes, I see what you mean. It's like that Sufi saying, "There is a world of difference between talking about the taste of wine and tasting the wine." But' – he turned to Rachel – 'what has this got to do with my poetry?'

As soon as he had said this he blushed deeply, because as soon as he had said it he knew exactly what it had to do with his poetry.

'I think you know the answer now, Yehuda,' Rachel responded, 'but let's be clear about it. Let's talk about this pomegranate.' She picked the pomegranate up from the fruit bowl and smelt its skin. 'Do you remember the description in the Torah of every detail of the robes of Aaron, the High Priest? Oh, how I love that passage! Especially the hem.' She closed her eyes and chanted slowly, as if savouring every word:

And you shall make on its hem pomegranates of indigo and purple and crimson, on its hem all around, and golden bells within them all around. A golden bell and a pomegranate, a golden bell and a pomegranate, on the hem of the robe all around.

After a pause, she looked at Yehuda again. 'The Torah says that the golden bells are there so that the sound is heard when the High Priest goes into the Sanctuary and when he comes out, that he may not die. By the sound he is recognised by God when he enters the Sanctuary and by the people when he leaves.'

Yehuda nodded. 'The bells, yes, but the Torah doesn't say why the pomegranates are required. What's their purpose?'

'My father says that they represent the world. Look at this pomegranate. Outside it is smooth, simple and actually rather dull.' Reaching for a knife she cut the pomegranate and broke it in two, spilling its red seeds onto a brass plate and releasing the delicate perfume. 'But inside, it's wonderfully complex, a honey-comb of inedible white filled with little miracles of sweetness, each with a nutty little core. It's like the world we live in: what you see is a simple whole, but when you look inside, it's a glorious web of little miracles.

'The golden bells are the songs of the world. You hear them far off as they come to you. But the pomegranates are the world itself, with its hidden wonders, the ones you have to split and peel and pick at. When they wove the pomegranates for the robe from blue and purple and crimson threads, they must have used many complex twists and knots.'

She looked up from the plate and saw the enchantment in his face. She concluded, almost whispering, 'The pomegranate is the world, Yehuda, but you, you are the golden bell.'

*

As secretary to Rabbi Yitzchak, Yehuda often had dealings with Rachel bat Shlomo while she studied at the yeshiva, but there was no repetition of their first encounter, no more lessons about experience and pomegranates. He was puzzled at first by her reticence, but he gradually came to understand that Bella knew how he felt about her and was holding back partly to protect him from the temptation to commit an indiscretion, which could only have ended in embarrassment and humiliation for him. The loss of intimacy saddened him, but he still relished their encounters. She taught him much about the Jews of Ashkenaz and their way of life, and about her father's work on his great commentary on the Torah and the Talmud, which was already renowned in Andalucía as well as Ashkenaz.

5

REUNION
LUCENA AND TOLEDO, 1094

It is good to know the truth and speak it, but it is better to
know the truth and speak about palm trees.

Arab proverb

For the next three years, Yehuda was busy with his duties to
Rabbi Yitzchak and with refining his medical skills at the
yeshiva clinic. His reputation as a poet was also continuing
to grow: he devoted as much time as he could to his poetry,
which was becoming ever more sophisticated as he matured,
while also immersing himself every day in Talmud studies. As
yeshiva students had done for hundreds of years, he sat in the
bet midrash with one or two colleagues, poring over the text
of the Talmud, arguing fiercely about the meaning of obscure
passages, about the interpretation of every kind of law from
those on murder to those on the observance of festivals. At first,
he couldn't see the point of it; he couldn't understand why Rab
Meir had thought he needed to come to Lucena to master this
dry, esoteric discipline.

One day, at the end of the afternoon session, Yehuda approached Joseph ibn Migash, a fellow student a little older than him who had become a *chaver* of his, one of a number of colleagues with whom he studied the texts. Joseph was gentle and patient, a rigorous scholar, but one who, in the words of the *Pirkei Avot*, always greets others with a cheerful countenance. Joseph had risen from his place near the dais, and had begun, along with other senior students, to gather the volumes of the Talmud in order to return them to the shelves. Yehuda offered to help and Joseph accepted with a nod.

Each of them carried an armful of books to the back of the hall. Yehuda loved carrying the big Talmud tractates and the feel of their solid heft and the smell of the leather binding. As they put the volumes on the shelves, he said, 'Please tell me, Joseph, what benefit today's session is likely to be in my life. We've spent the whole afternoon studying the laws on shaving. My group became fixated on the debate between the rabbis on whether or not tearing one's hair out in anguish contravenes the prohibition on shaving with a naked blade and about whether the rule applies to a woman.'

'Yes,' said Joseph, 'my *chaver* and I spent some time on the same topic yesterday.'

'Why? Why are we doing this? It seems unlikely that I'll often want to tear my hair out in anguish. And if I do become a rabbi, I'm equally unlikely to be asked by a member of the congregation if it's permissible for them to tear their hair out. In any case, the rabbis don't even agree on an answer, there is no consensus – so we don't even know what God's law is! We follow the School of Hillel not because his argument wins, but because we always follow Hillel when there's no consensus.' Yehuda sighed as he bent to put a volume of the Talmud on the bottom shelf.

When Yehuda straightened up, Joseph looked at him with a gentle smile. 'Yes, Yehuda, I know exactly what you mean. I used to think that way myself, but over the year or so I've been here, I've gradually come to realise that what we're learning is a way of thinking. It's a way of arguing.' They started walking towards the side door – where the smell of meat was drifting in from the refectory. 'The mental discipline of the argument is as important as the subject we're arguing about. So it doesn't matter if it's about tearing your hair out or about something real like marriage or food.'

Joseph paused as they reached the doorway to let a couple of students pass them on their way into the hall. Yehuda nodded to them, while Joseph greeted them both by name.

As they walked along the corridor, Joseph said, 'There, did you notice that? Do you know who we just passed?'

'Yes,' Yehuda replied vaguely, 'one of them was Shmuel Hacohen, and the other one was… I think it was Eli ibn Rafael…'

Joseph stopped dead. Not expecting this, Yehuda walked on a couple of steps before he realised, turned and went back to Joseph, who was frowning. 'What's the matter, Joseph?'

Joseph didn't answer immediately but closed his eyes, head down, and rubbed his chin. After a while he sighed and looked again at Yehuda. 'How do I put this? I don't want to offend you.'

'Please, go on – say what you need to say, Joseph.'

'Very well. As you know, Rabbi Akiva said that the supreme commandment in the whole Torah, at the centre of everything, is "You shall love your neighbour as yourself". Our Master Yitzchak has explained that you can't love your neighbour unless you are here, present when you meet your neighbour, aware of your neighbour and responsive to him or her. It wasn't Ibn Rafael who passed us just now with Shmuel, it was Gideon ben Zomar.'

'Oh yes, perhaps it was. I didn't notice.' Yehuda couldn't understand where this was taking them.

'You didn't really see either of them,' Joseph said gently, 'so how could you love them as yourself? Don't misunderstand me, I'm not trying to put you down – we all get this wrong some of the time. That's why we all need to learn how to be more attentive. All the commandments that govern us every moment of every day – from morning prayers to the prayers before sleep, from dietary laws to those of charity – they are there to teach us the discipline of constant attention – *constant* attention. We have to learn how to be here, really here, at all times, to be present, aware of what we're doing and who we're meeting. Only that way can we be in a position to love whichever neighbour we happen to meet, whenever we happen to meet them.'

Yehuda took a step back and stared at Joseph, his eyes wide. 'Wow! Oh yes! … Thank you, Joseph, thank you. That hadn't even occurred to me. One of the joys of studying with people like Rabbi Yitzchak – and you! – is that every now and again it's as if you open a door to a bright new room full of treasures, full of light.'

Joseph shook his head, his eyes twinkling. 'Come, Yehuda, I like being flattered, but there's no need to overdo it!'

'But it's true. I see it now. Talmud study gives us the discipline of the mind that you're talking about. It helps us to be here, present, aware of what we're reading and what we're thinking about it. We need to take the same disciplined focus into our daily lives.'

Joseph was clearly delighted that he had found a way to make the point and that Yehuda had grasped it so quickly. He put his hand on Yehuda's shoulder. 'Yes, Yehuda, you have it exactly! So tomorrow you can argue about the laws relating to mixing linen and cotton in a garment and you'll fully understand that this argument is the work of Heaven! Now, let's go and have some dinner.

It smells as if the cooks may not have ruined the meat today, which would be another miracle.'

After this conversation, Yehuda threw himself into his Talmud studies with less reluctance, and Rabbi Yitzchak permitted him, indeed encouraged him, to extend his medical studies, working under the guidance of the physicians in the central Lucena infirmary.

Rabbi Yitzchak also encouraged him to continue writing his poetry, though he gently chided Yehuda for writing only love poems, suggesting that he should try liturgical poems. 'Yehuda,' he would say, 'you have no intimate knowledge of women; you have, perhaps, rather more acquaintance with God, if not directly then through God's works. At least I hope that's the case! So why don't you write poems about things you know more about, instead of fantasising about women?'

The rabbi had a light touch, but it was always clear when he was being serious, so Yehuda obeyed. Yet one more task to fit into the day! But Yehuda now found that he could manage, indeed enjoy, the many tasks assigned to him and still find time for reading and writing. As he put it:

The slaves of Time are slaves of slaves;
the slave of God alone is free.
And so, when everyone asks for their portion,
I say, 'No portion but God for me.'

Meanwhile, the yeshiva emissary had found Deborah and her family, who had indeed reached Toledo and settled there. Deborah's father, Isaac ibn Ezra, had three brothers: Yehuda ibn Ezra, the oldest, was already in Toledo and Joseph, the youngest, moved there from Seville; but Moses ibn Ezra had not joined them in Toledo. The emissary brought Yehuda a letter from Deborah and one from her father and they began to correspond regularly. He still longed to see her, but the letters were some consolation.

One day, after he had finished taking the early morning dictation from Rabbi Yitzchak and was gathering the papers together, the Master said, 'Stay a moment longer, Yehuda, I want to talk to you.' That wasn't unusual – this was the time when he normally asked about Yehuda's Talmud and medical studies or made some gentle enquiries about how the yeshiva students were feeling. He called Yehuda his 'spy', but they both accepted that it was useful for Yehuda to tell him if there were issues his friends were concerned about but reluctant to bring to the Master or the other teachers.

That is how they began on that day, but after a while Yitzchak fell silent and rubbed his palms together, his head bent and his eyes downcast, in the way he did when asked a difficult question about Talmudic interpretation, though Yehuda had asked no question. Yehuda assumed that he was wondering how to broach a new subject. He knew better than to interrupt him, so he waited. After a while the Master looked up and said, 'I know that David bin Avram, before he left, helped to put you back into contact with Isaac ibn Ezra and his daughter – her name is Deborah, isn't it?'

'Yes, Master, it is Deborah.'

'Good, good.' He turned and looked behind him. 'Can you see the wine flask? The servants seem to have forgotten to bring it.'

Yehuda was used to Rabbi Yitzchak's vagueness. His extraordinary mind was sharp and fast despite his great age, but he was like a child when it came to the routines of life. He never seemed to remember where anything was, yet he got confused if anything was moved.

'No, sir, they didn't forget the wine,' he said, 'they moved it across to your left. You asked them last week to do that because you were concerned about knocking it over onto the manuscripts on this side.'

'Ah, yes, I remember now. Would you mind pouring me some – and for yourself too if you want it.'

Yehuda was surprised. The Master himself rarely drank wine this early in the morning, and he had never offered wine to Yehuda before. Yehuda said nothing but filled two brass beakers from the flask and gave one to Rabbi Yitzchak. It was a fine wine from Rioja and the spicy scent began to permeate the room. Rabbi Yitzchak settled back in his chair and took a sip of the wine, waiting for Yehuda to resume his seat in front of him.

'I've been thinking, Yehuda, that it's time to consider your future,' he said.

'My future, Master? But I've been here barely three years.' He was becoming a little alarmed – was the rabbi going to dismiss him?

'No, don't misunderstand me. Your father is dead, may his memory be a blessing, and he had no brother or sister, so I feel a duty to take some responsibility for you, now that you're with us.' He paused. 'It's time to start thinking about marriage.'

'Marriage?' Yehuda blurted out. 'But I'm only just nineteen!'

'Well, yes, I thought you might say that.' He was teasing Yehuda, as he sometimes did; Yehuda wished he wouldn't do that. Other teachers did the same thing. It was infuriating.

This time Rabbi Yitzchak saw that he'd upset him and relented. 'Yes, you're very young, though plenty of men marry at nineteen. I'm sorry, I'm not suggesting that you marry now, however. I certainly don't want a married amanuensis! But in two or three years' time you'll be ready to move on, either here or elsewhere. So now is the time when we should start looking for a suitable wife for you. No?'

'Yes, Master, if you say so.'

The glimmer in Rabbi Yitzchak's eyes made Yehuda dare to believe that the conversation was moving in the direction that he dearly wanted it to move. The Master continued, 'My contacts in Toledo tell me that Isaac ibn Ezra has successfully transferred his business interests to León-Castile and that he's well off. And this daughter, Deborah, is not yet betrothed. I assume that this is good news as far as you're concerned?'

'Yes, indeed, sir, it is the best possible news – though it's not news to me.'

'Well, my friend, you know Deborah a lot better than me. She's said to be a formidable young lady – being married to her is likely to be… an interesting journey. And she, I am informed, is very well disposed towards you.'

'I…' He found that he couldn't speak – it was as if his heart, full of joy, had expanded in his chest and emptied his lungs. Rabbi Yitzchak smiled, waiting patiently. Eventually, Yehuda was able to say, 'I hardly dared hope that she would want more than to be a friend.'

'It seems that she does want something more, and I'm very glad about that. My suggestion is that I write to Isaac ibn Ezra immediately and propose a meeting between the two of you. After that we can discuss a betrothal.'

*

A few weeks later, Yehuda entered Toledo across the Alcántara Bridge. Rabbi Yitzchak had sent him on a mission to take paper, books and some letters to the yeshiva in Toledo, and had arranged for him to visit Deborah and her family at the same time. He deposited everything at the Great Synagogue as soon as he arrived and found lodging at a nearby inn. He couldn't sleep that night, thinking about his meeting with Deborah and her family the next day. Eventually, giving up the idea of sleep, he dressed and left the inn, walking to the gardens behind the synagogue, next to the city wall. He sat on a bench among the trees: the moon was almost full and the trees were brightly lit, but without colour – the myrtle, the ash, the cedar and even the banks of flowers were all rendered black and grey upon grey in the moonlight.

It was a long time since he had seen Deborah. What would she be like? Would she still take his breath away? What would she think of him? Rabbi Yitzchak had said that she was 'well disposed', and her letters were friendly enough, but they were reticent. She wouldn't have been permitted to send them without her father reading them first, so her reticence was only to be expected. After an hour or so of anxious thought, which led nowhere, he left the chill of the night garden, returned to the inn and was able to sleep at last.

He was woken, for the first time since his early childhood in Tudela, by the sound of church bells instead of the familiar call of the muezzin. When King Alfonso VI had occupied Toledo ten years earlier, he had left the Muslims and Jews in peace, but he had converted many mosques into churches, including the church next to the inn. To Yehuda the bells sounded harsh and intrusive compared to the haunting call of the muezzin.

He set off on foot to find Isaac's house, following the directions given by the synagogue porter. It was the day of the weekly fair and he had to pass through the Plaza del Conde where the main market was being held, noisier and more colourful than the markets in Córdoba or Granada. In the corner of the square a crowd was listening to minstrels. He couldn't resist lingering a while to hear their song and the sound of their rather crude lute-like instruments. Their song was one of romance and battle, but he found it hard to follow their Spanish dialect, so he didn't stay

for long. It was time to face his anxieties and confront Deborah
and her family.

Their house was as large and grand as he had expected, a solid
building in the northern style, with a small garden and orchard
but no courtyard. The lime whitewash was fresh and clean, and
it was clear that the family had prospered in Toledo. When the
servant showed Yehuda into the guest hall Isaac, his wife Leah
and Deborah's brother and sister rose to greet him warmly,
but Deborah was not there. Leah said to the servant, 'Michael,
kindly go and tell her ladyship that our guest has arrived and
that she's keeping him waiting. We would all be honoured if she
would deign to grace us with her presence.' Clearly nothing had
changed: Deborah was still as wilful as ever and her family still
treated her behaviour with amused irony.

They had only just completed their formal greetings when
Deborah appeared in the doorway. As soon as their eyes met, all
his doubts and concerns fled. She had been beautiful before, but
her beauty was now complete. She was of course taller, almost as
tall as Yehuda, and as elegant as a gazelle. Her eyes, that penetrating blue, were smiling and melancholy at the same time. He felt
almost assaulted by her beauty – her lovely skin, her black hair
tumbling to her shoulders, her figure, now fuller than before. Ah,
her figure! Yehuda recalled the Shulamite woman in *The Song of
Songs*: 'Your stature is like a palm tree, and your breasts are like
clusters of grapes.'

Isaac coughed gently. Deborah and Yehuda both blushed,
realising that they had been staring at each other and had forgotten the others in the room, but their embarrassment didn't last
long. Everyone sat and exchanged news over figs and poppy-seed
cakes. Thanks to Leah and Isaac's tact and sympathy, it seemed
as if nobody noticed that neither Deborah nor Yehuda was fully

engaged in the formalities of the conversation. Eventually Isaac said, 'It's good to see you again, Yehuda. I'm delighted to hear that you are learning so much with Rabbi Yitzchak al-Fasi. Come into my library and tell me about it – and you can take a look at the books I've acquired recently. I'm sure that the others can spare us for a while.'

After a few minutes showing Yehuda a tract on Merkabah mysticism that he had just bought, Isaac put the ancient volume aside and said, 'So, Yehuda, I'm sure you know why I wanted to speak to you. As Rabbi Yitzchak has told you, he and I have been discussing you and Deborah. He said that you are fond of her. Is that right?'

'Yes, indeed, sir, I am,' Yehuda responded, aware that he was blushing deeply again.

'Let me tell you, then, how these things are dealt with, at least in our family. First, I should make it clear that I think you an admirable young man and that if you wished to ask for Deborah's hand in marriage, I would be very happy to give my consent.' He paused and reached for his beaker of rosewater.

Yehuda was overwhelmed with joy. 'Thank you, sir, I…'

Isaac gently interrupted him, holding up his hand while he finished drinking. 'But I am not the one who matters here. Deborah must, of course, consent to the match. That would apply to any woman in our family – even one less, um… less assertive than my beloved daughter. Are you sure you know what you'd be taking on if you were to marry Deborah?'

Yehuda wasn't quite sure what Isaac meant – was he talking about her personality, as he seemed to be, or was he referring to the rumours about her and Moses ibn Ezra and their effect on her reputation? The first was exactly why he loved her, and that was why the second would not deter him.

'Yes,' he said, 'I do know, and there is no doubt at all in my mind that marrying Deborah is what I most dearly want in this world.'

'Well, that's very clear, my son, so there's no more to be said until you've spoken to her. If she consents, then we need to talk about the terms of the betrothal; in the absence of your late father, may he rest in peace, you and I may need to discuss matters directly, aided by Rabbi Yitzchak. There will be plenty of time – I am assuming that you will wish to wait a couple of years before the marriage.'

'Wish to wait, no – resigned to waiting, yes.'

Isaac returned his smile and moved towards the door. 'Very well. All that remains now is for you to talk to Deborah. Wait here and I'll send her to you.'

He left, and within a few minutes Deborah entered the library, her eyes downcast, more subdued than usual.

Yehuda also felt a little awkward but thought that it was for him to start the conversation. 'So, Deborah, here we are,' he said. 'Shall we sit?'

'Yes indeed, Yehuda, let's do that,' Deborah responded, echoing Yehuda's formal tone. She gestured to two chairs on either side of the heavy oak table. 'Please sit here, and I'll sit on this side.'

As they settled into their chairs, Yehuda said, 'This is a different world from Córdoba, Deborah – we're sitting on chairs at a table rather than cushions on a *martaba*.'

'Yes, and the food's different too. I've come to like roasted beef, though I do rather miss lamb tagine.'

'And this morning I was awakened by church bells rather than a muezzin.'

After a moment of awkward silence, it was Deborah, as always, who first abandoned the formalities. 'Yehuda, here we are, as you said, finally face to face. I'm so glad to see you, and now we're in a much better state than when last we met, torn apart by the horrible rumours about Uncle Moses.'

'Yes, we are. Where is he now? Do you know? While I was in Seville we corresponded for a while, but I lost touch after he left Valencia.'

'Father also lost touch with him and, indeed, made very little effort to find him. But now they are writing again: Moses moved to Girona and has a post in the yeshiva there – but he's thinking of leaving there and coming to Toledo for a while, to join Father and my uncles Yehuda and Joseph.'

'And Zipporah? How is she?'

'Aunt Zipporah was very ill for a while, but she seems to be better now. They're settled in Girona, but I think they both want to be with the family again.' Deborah paused and looked out of the window at the orchard. He waited. Soon she sighed and turned back to him.

He reached across the table and took her hands in his. 'So now let us think about the future. That's why I'm here. You know – I'm sure you know – that I have loved you since we first met. I was a child then and I'm still only on the threshold of being a man. But of this one thing only I am certain, that we belong together. Being parted from you is a constant pain in my heart. As the song has it, "*I am worthless and poor when parted from my glory, and I become like a shadow.*"'

'Not "the song", Yehuda, but your song – it's your lovely Hebrew translation from the Arabic, which you sent me from Seville.'

'Yes. You remember it!'

'Of course I remember it – I've kept every letter and every poem you sent me, and I treasure them all. Our letters may not have been private, but the meaning of your poems was very clear.'

'And you felt... feel the same way?'

Deborah's eyes widened in surprise for a moment. 'Do you doubt it, Yehuda?' She got up, moved around the table and sat in the chair next to his.

'No, I don't doubt it now,' he said. 'I dared to hope while we were apart, but now it's not just hope, it's certainty.'

Deborah leaned towards him and stroked his cheek. He hesitated, but then he put his hands on her shoulders and drew her to him and, for the first time, they kissed. She had never kissed liked that before, and neither had he. As their lips parted, she murmured:

Let him kiss me with the kisses of his mouth,
For your loving is better than wine.

Yehuda leaned back, smiling wryly. 'Well, Deborah, that is indeed a first… Normally it's me who starts quoting from *The Song of Songs*.'

*

During the remaining time that Yehuda served as secretary to Rabbi Yitzchak in Lucena, the Master, with his usual tact and kindness, sent him on several missions to Toledo, giving him the chance to spend some time with Deborah. Their love rekindled and their friendship grew in those two years, but when Yehuda was finally able to move to Toledo and marry Deborah, the marriage brought a new intensity and joy to their relationship.

The wedding was a big occasion, the Ibn Ezra brothers being prominent people in the kingdom. Moses ibn Ezra joined his three brothers in Toledo; the old rumours and suspicions were by then forgotten or put aside and everyone was delighted to see him again during the period before the wedding. The ceremony was held in the gardens by the Tagus River, in the very place where Yehuda had sat in the moonlight on his first night in Toledo before reuniting with Deborah. The gardens were crowded for the *nisuin*, the final part of the wedding ceremony, almost exclusively with Deborah's family, but Yehuda and Deborah hardly noticed the crowd. When Deborah came under the brocaded wedding canopy and walked in silence seven times around Yehuda, he was conscious only of her presence, her perfume, the outline of her face behind the chiffon veil as she passed in front of him, and Deborah was conscious only of Yehuda's gaze.

Finally, he lifted the veil, took her hand in his to place the ring on her finger and uttered the ancient formula, 'Behold, I betroth you to me according to the laws of Moses and of Israel.' The dry phrases sounded like a song to them and even the reading of the marriage contract passed like a dream. They heard the technical language as if it were a coded poem, a transmutation into real life of the spirit of *The Song of Songs*. During the chanting of the seven matrimonial blessings first Deborah and then Yehuda drank from the same wine cup. Their eyes met and he was sure that she, like him, was remembering their first kiss.

After the wedding feast, the couple spent their first night in a summerhouse in that same garden, among the myrtles. Deep in the night, they heard the horses of the night guard as they crossed the Alcántara Bridge. Deborah quoted the horsemen among the myrtles in the vision of the prophet Zechariah, the ones sent out by God to roam the earth, who 'answered the angel who was standing among the myrtles and said, "We have roamed the earth, and the entire earth is still and quiet"'. Not long afterwards, Yehuda wrote:

The lovers stand among the myrtles,
  Their love-myrrh ascending to perfume the void.
The myrtle, desiring their succulent odour,
  Spreads its wings like a cherub around them.
The myrtle seeks to envelop their fragrance,

But their joy overwhelms its scent.
That joy was a constant blessing of their lives together.

*

Moving to Toledo, Yehuda had been accepted, on Rabbi Yitzchak's recommendation, as an assistant to Joseph ibn Ferruziel. A renowned physician and scholar, Joseph was also a man of great sympathy and discretion. He taught Yehuda the best of Arabic and Greek science, not only from the texts but also by the way he treated his patients: they studied together the theories of the great Muslim scholar Ibn Sina on how body and soul are united – and in practice Joseph never dealt only with the physical disease, but also paid close attention to the mind and soul of the patient.

Unfortunately, Yehuda and Deborah were to experience these skills at first hand because a year after the marriage Deborah had a miscarriage that left her weak and in low spirits for a long time. She sat for hours in the *majlis*, holding a book in front of her but reading very little of it; she picked at her food at mealtimes, eating hardly anything; and when friends and neighbours came round she was polite enough, but did not engage enthusiastically with them as she always had before. Yehuda was desperately worried, but he was unable to get close to her – she rarely responded to his attempts to console her. He even tried occasionally to provoke her into one of their heated arguments on some point of politics or theology, which had always engaged and enlivened her in the past, but Deborah would just shrug her shoulders and change the subject. Joseph ibn Ferruziel attended to Deborah throughout this period and played an important role in helping her to recover, both in body and in spirit. It was Joseph who noticed Deborah's growing interest in Yehuda's medical books and who persuaded her to train as a midwife, arguing that she could turn what she had learned from her dreadful experience into something positive.

After a few months, Deborah began to regain her zest for life. Her Arab neighbours told her that a miscarriage was not such a disaster because a miscarrying woman is quick to conceive again, and Deborah did indeed become pregnant within a year. She and Yehuda were elated, rejoicing in their good fortune and returning to the lively and loving relationship they had enjoyed before the miscarriage. Yehuda was becoming a respected physician and widely admired poet. Deborah found that she was highly skilled as a midwife and enjoyed the work, and now they could look forward to starting a family.

Tragedy struck the couple a second time, however, when Deborah was successfully delivered of a daughter, Rachel, who was weak from birth and died of dysentery after only three months; Joseph was once again a comforter of both parents, and this time the tragedy brought Yehuda and Deborah together in mourning for their lost daughter instead of coming between them as the miscarriage had. A year later, they were blessed with a beautiful, healthy daughter, Miriam.

During this time, Joseph's medical practice was increasingly focused on the royal court, and Yehuda become familiar with the ways of the Alcázar palace, which were much more formal than those of the courts of the amirs in Andalucía.

6

THE ROYAL COURT

TOLEDO, 1099

Wherever the art of medicine is loved, there is also a love
of humanity.

Hippocrates, *Aphorisms*

Claudia, the Lady of the Bedchamber, burst into the room where
Joseph and Yehuda were sorting a new shipment of herbs.

'The queen! The queen! Come quickly, she's sick.'

'What is it, Lady Claudia, what's happened?' asked Joseph.

'The queen has a fever. It's very bad – please come quickly.'

As he began packing his medicine bag, Joseph said to Claudia,
'Yes, we're coming; tell us what happened.'

'The queen fell in the garden on Tuesday morning and cut her
leg on a stone,' Claudia replied. 'It was a small wound and didn't
seem serious, so she said there was no need to call you. We just
bound the wound with a kerchief. But now there's a bad abscess
over the wound and the queen has a high fever. It looks serious.'

'Yehuda, bring the instrument box and I'll bring the medicine
bag,' Joseph ordered. The three of them ran through the palace to

the royal apartments. It seemed that word of Queen Bertha's illness had already spread, so in this case their haste was not seen as a breach of etiquette. As they ran, Claudia told them that young Princess Urraca was at the queen's bedside with the ladies-in-waiting – the king was out hunting but had been sent for.

When they reached the queen's bedchamber the shutters were closed and the candlelight seemed to be absorbed in the dark tapestries on the walls and the brocaded dresses of the ladies-in-waiting, creating a gloomy atmosphere.

'Your Royal Highness.' Joseph bowed to Princess Urraca, who was standing at the foot of the bed, tying back the bed curtains.

'Ah, Ferruziel, you're here at last.' The princess held out her hand for Joseph to kiss her ring and nodded curtly to Yehuda. 'Please attend to the queen, we're worried about her.'

Joseph bowed again and they moved to the bedside. The queen was lying propped up on pillows, wearing a heavy bed gown stained with sweat, her eyes closed and her face flushed. Joseph put his hand gently on her brow – she did not stir, and her eyes remained closed. He turned to the princess and said, 'I'd be grateful if you could have the shutters opened, Highness, so that I can examine Her Majesty. And if I might suggest, it would be a good idea to clear the room for the time being until we know what we're dealing with.' The princess nodded and Claudia opened the shutters while the other ladies left the room.

As Joseph was examining the queen, King Alfonso strode into the room with his squire. 'What's going on?' he started to ask, but the princess gestured for him to keep his voice down.

'As you can see, Father, Ibn Ferruziel is here. I've sent for Mother's doctor to examine the queen along with him.'

Yehuda was the only person who noticed Joseph stiffen. Urraca's mother, Constance of Burgundy, had brought a Frankish physician with her as part of her entourage when she married King Alfonso, and the physician stayed on after Constance died. The new queen, Bertha, was more inclined to consult Joseph on medical matters, but Urraca continued to consult the Frankish physician, Guy de Clamency, still calling him 'Mother's doctor'.

Completing his examination, Joseph washed his hands in the bowl on the chest of drawers and dried them carefully on the towel handed to him by Claudia. The king moved to the bed and looked down at his motionless wife. 'So, Joseph,' he said, his eyes still on the queen, 'what's your diagnosis?'

'Your Majesty, the wound on the queen's calf has become infected, badly infected, and that is causing the fever. The abscess has developed very fast, but it's not too late to heal it. We shall apply a poultice, with your permission.'

Once Joseph and Yehuda had cleaned the wound and applied a hot poultice, the swelling almost immediately started to reduce. As they were putting on a fresh poultice, Guy de Clamency bustled into the room, nodded rather curtly to the king and the princess and gestured to Joseph to step aside. He removed the poultice and pushed his finger into the wound. The queen cried out in pain and briefly opened her eyes before falling again into a swoon.

'Majesty?' he said to her, but the queen did not answer. De Clamency bent down and studied the wound again, then put his hand on the queen's forehead. He turned to the king. 'I am very sorry, Your Majesty, but I have to tell you that the queen's life is in danger. The wound in her leg is disrupting the humours through-out her body. She can be saved only by amputating the leg.'

Princess Urraca and Claudia gasped.

'No, you can't mean that. You can't,' the king cried as he turned to Joseph. 'Joseph, do you agree?'

Joseph glanced at de Clamency and looked back at the king and Urraca. 'Well, Majesty, the infection is indeed causing the fever, but the infection can be reduced.'

'But even if that were possible it will be too late,' de Clamency insisted. 'No treatment can work fast enough.'

'But, sire, the formula for the disinfectant poultice we are using is one recommended by the great Greek scholar Discorides – I've used it before and it does work quickly, I assure you.'

'Discorides?' Guy was almost shouting now. 'Discorides? This is nonsense. Your Majesty, are you putting your faith in a Jewish doctor using Arabic medicine drawn from a pagan Greek writer? As a Christian doctor, I am asking you, do you want your queen to live with one leg or die with two?'

The king hesitated, but Urraca spoke up. 'Father, we cannot take a chance. Let the doctor do as he says he must. You can see that the queen is dying!'

The king moved to the bed and took the queen's hand in his. After a long time, he turned to Guy de Clamency, tears in his eyes. 'Very well, doctor, do what you have to do.'

Horrified, Yehuda was about to speak but Joseph put his hand on his arm to restrain him. 'It's decided,' he whispered. 'We can do nothing to stop this.'

On de Clamency's instructions, Claudia went to summon a knight to come with a well-sharpened battleaxe. The bedcovers were removed from the bed and a wooden block placed under the queen's leg. When the knight arrived, de Clamency instructed him to strike a sharp blow to cut cleanly below the knee. The initial blow did not sever the leg, so the knight struck a second time as blood and bone marrow spurted from the open wound onto the silken bedcovers. The king and Claudia cried out in horror, while Princess Urraca turned aside, covering her face with her hands. Joseph and Yehuda rushed in to work with de Clamency to stem the flow of blood, but their efforts were futile. Within a few seconds, de Clamency and Joseph pronounced Queen Bertha dead.

*

That evening, Joseph and his wife Hannah came to dine at Yehuda's house, with Joseph's son Solomon ibn Ferruziel, so that they could discuss the implications of the death of the queen.

Miriam, the daughter of Yehuda and Deborah, now five months old, was awake when everyone arrived and she was allowed to stay with the adults for a while. By common consent, no one spoke about the tragedy during the meal: Miriam was the centre of attention until Deborah went to put her to bed while Yehuda offered the visitors the marzipan and crystallised fruit that concluded almost every meal in Castile.

As Deborah came back and sat down at the table, Yehuda turned to Solomon to open the discussion. 'So, Solomon, what do you think this means?'

Solomon, a tall, handsome man in his late twenties, a little older than Yehuda, was becoming established at court as a counsellor to the king. He said, 'The death of Queen Bertha is not only a tragedy for the king, it could also be very bad for us as well.'

'Why?' asked Hannah. 'Why should it be bad for us? It was Guy de Clamency who overruled Joseph's advice. It was he who ordered the fatal blow to be struck. He's to blame, not Joseph or Yehuda.'

'Yes,' said Solomon, 'but the situation is delicate. Things are getting more and more complicated here as the king moves ever closer to the Roman Catholic way of doing things.'

'Well, it's not surprising that he's doing that,' said Deborah. 'First, he marries Agnes of Aquitaine, then Constance of Burgundy, and then the Italian Bertha. Whenever a Catholic queen dies,

a new Catholic queen succeeds, and building after beautiful building is demolished to make way for an ugly Romanesque one.'

'Deborah, Deborah!' Hannah said, looking around as if she
thought somebody might be eavesdropping. 'You really need to be
careful how you speak of their majesties.'

Much as Yehuda loved Deborah, he still found it hard to accept
her habit of deliberately provoking people. They all knew that
Hannah was a staunch loyalist and also as nervous as a bird, and
Deborah must have realised how she would react to her outburst.

Yehuda therefore intervened before Deborah could respond.
'Yes, it is difficult and delicate, Hannah, as Solomon says – and
it's not just the buildings, Deborah, as you well know. The Frankish influences are everywhere, and Frankish priests and monks
are gaining ever more power in the kingdom. Many Christians in
Castile and León resent the introduction of Roman Catholic rites.
They still love the Mozarabic liturgy of St Isidore that's been here
for centuries. When Princess Urraca was married to Raymond of
Burgundy four years ago, he brought yet more Catholic priests to
Toledo and made no secret of his distaste for the old rites, not
to mention his contempt for the old Castilian aristocracy.'

'So you agree with me?' Deborah said. 'And they haven't changed
just the church services – they've even replaced the old Visigothic
script with the Carolingian one! People don't like that either.'

'That's what I'm trying to say, Deborah,' said Solomon,
the gentle diplomat, attempting to introduce a more measured
discussion. 'It's not really a question of whether we like the new
buildings or not, and it's not for us to concern ourselves with
how the Christians pray, or how they write Latin for that matter.
What worries me is the way these changes affect the attitudes of
the Christians, to each other and to our Muslim neighbours and
to us Jews.'

'Yes,' said Deborah, 'Yehuda said the same thing this afternoon, but I still don't understand why. As Hannah said, it was de Clamency who made the fatal mistake.'

'Perhaps I can explain, since I share Solomon's concern,' Joseph intervened, having listened in silence until then. Solomon gestured to his father to continue.

Joseph held up the dessert plate. 'Look at Deborah's perfect Toledo marzipan,' he said. 'Hannah, try some, you haven't had any yet.' He passed the plate to his wife, who took a piece, looking rather bemused, and tasted it.

'Yes, Deborah,' she said, 'this is excellent, a particularly delicate flavour. You must give me the recipe.' Deborah smiled and nodded: it seemed that peace was restored between them, at least for the time being.

Joseph continued, 'Toledo is now famous throughout Europe for its marzipan, but it wasn't always that way. People had been growing almonds in Castile for centuries, but they knew virtually nothing about sugar. They never made marzipan. When the Arabs came they brought the knowledge of how to grow and use sugar cane. Marzipan is the marriage of Castilian almonds and Arabic cane sugar!'

Deborah realised where Joseph's argument was heading and took up the theme. 'Yes, I see what you mean, Joseph. It's like the exquisite knives that you gave us for a wedding present.' She picked up one of the knives with which they had cut the marzipan. 'It's the same story as the new swords. Toledo has always made strong steel but it was the Arabs who taught the Castilians to temper the steel perfectly and make the finest, sharpest blades.'

'King Alfonso has always understood that,' added Hannah. 'After he took over Toledo he turned some mosques into churches, but he also protected the Muslims as well as us Jews, and he even struck coins with Arabic inscriptions.'

'And took a Muslim mistress!' said Deborah.

'Deborah!' Hannah and Yehuda exclaimed at the same time. Hannah blushed and shook her head.

This time Deborah had the grace to see immediately that she had gone too far. 'I'm sorry,' she said, 'that was… indelicate of me. Actually, I was thinking of the whole story of how Princess Zaida came to be in Toledo, and of Ibn Ammar and the chess set.'

'The chess set?' said Hannah.

'Yes,' Deborah replied. She turned to Solomon and smiled. 'Solomon told me about it, didn't you?'

'Yes,' he said, 'I heard it from Ibn Feria, the almoner. It's a legend among the Muslims. Apparently, when Alfonso was embarking on yet another of his campaigns against Andalucía, Al-Mutamid, Amir of Seville, sent his friend and counsellor, the great poet Ibn Ammar, to negotiate with Alfonso. One day they were playing chess with a beautiful Persian set owned by Ibn Ammar. They agreed that if Alfonso won he'd keep the chess set and if Ibn Ammar won he could name his own prize. Ibn Ammar won and he demanded that Alfonso should spare Seville. Alfonso kept his word, at least until Al-Mutamid stopped paying his tribute!'

'It's a good story,' said Deborah, smiling, 'and even if it's not true, the point is that the Muslims think of Alfonso as a fearful enemy, but honest and chivalrous. So, when the Almoravids took Seville and sent Al-Mutamid into exile, it was naturally to Toledo that his widowed daughter Princess Zaida fled. And then she and the king became…'

'Yes, quite, Deborah,' Joseph interrupted, seeing Hannah blush again. 'Certainly, Zaida was… well, she felt at home here. King Alfonso has always respected and to some extent followed the Andalucían way of doing things, so she was comfortable at court. But Queen Constance hated Zaida, for obvious reasons.'

'Well, Father, not just because she…' Solomon saw his father shaking his head and hesitated. 'Well, anyway, the other problem was that both Queen Constance and her daughter Urraca despised the Andalucían ways, as do Urraca's husband Raymond and the Catholic Bishops and Cluniac monks that Constance and Raymond have brought to Spain.'

'And that doesn't go well with the nobles or the ordinary people here,' Deborah said. 'As Yehuda said, most Castilians and Leónese resent these Frankish influences, and I'm not surprised. The Franks are barbarians. They have no learning, they know nothing of Greek or Arabic sciences and their medicine is primitive. Even I know more about Discorides than they do!'

'I'm sure you do, Deborah, I'm sure you do!' Joseph took another piece of marzipan and a candied apricot. Yehuda noticed that he was eating more, as he always did when anxious, though he was trying to disguise his anxiety that evening.

'It would be funny if it wasn't so sad,' Joseph continued, his eyes downcast. 'Discorides, the Father of Pharmacy. He wrote his great work, *On Medical Substances*, almost a thousand years ago. A hundred and fifty years ago, the Byzantine emperor sent a copy of it from Constantinople to Córdoba as a gift for Abd al-Rahman III, Caliph of Córdoba. The caliph was delighted with it, and had it translated into Arabic – his Jewish court doctor and a Benedictine monk worked together on the translation. That's the world that the Franks hate – where a Muslim caliph has a Greek pagan text that he got from the Orthodox Byzantine emperor translated into Arabic by a Jewish physician and a Catholic monk!'

'These Franks have very little Greek and no Arabic, as you say, Deborah,' said Solomon, 'and they're only just getting Discorides translated into Latin, and likewise Hippocrates and Galen and even Aristotle and Plato. And—'

'This is all very interesting, everyone,' Hannah interrupted curtly, 'but what's it got to do with us? I still don't understand why all this is dangerous for Jews. You said that Queen Bertha's death is bad for us, but when I asked why, you launched into stories about marzipan and chess and Discorides. Why is it dangerous?'

Joseph got up and went across to sit next to Hannah, putting his hand on her knee. 'It's not dangerous for us yet, my love, but it might become so,' he said gently. 'When Guy de Clamency made the king choose between a *Christian* doctor and *Arabic* medicine administered by a Jew, he meant a *Frankish* Christian doctor and *Andalucían* medicine. An Andalucían Christian doctor such as Manuel Abuduram would have done exactly the same as we did. Nevertheless, Princess Urraca supported de Clamency. Her mother Constance, like Queen Bertha, knew how to strike a balance between the incoming Franks and the Mozarabic Christians, even when introducing Catholic ways. Urraca isn't like that; she's much more like the other Urraca, the king's sister. Both of them, and Raymond of Burgundy, believe in divide and rule. They're trying to set everyone against the Muslims and the Jews to distract them from the tensions between the Franks and the native Castilians.'

'Exactly – which is not surprising,' Yehuda added. 'Many Franks hate both Muslims and Jews and they believe they can turn León-Castile against us. Among the Frankish crusaders who've just conquered Jerusalem there are many who think that they should kill all "infidels" for the sake of their souls.'

'Whose souls,' Deborah asked, 'the crusaders' or the infidels'?'

'This is no joke, my love. Many, many Jews and Muslims have indeed been massacred, in Ma'arra, in Jerusalem, everywhere.'

'I'm not joking,' Deborah responded, frowning. 'Friends in Acre write to me that the Western crusaders include some wicked people, and some stupid people who simply don't understand what the Crusade is about. The Pope, and especially the Cluniac monks who are preaching the Crusade, keep saying that killing Jews is forbidden. But these people believe that it's more about killing infidels than capturing Jerusalem.'

Solomon, who had been silent for some time, said, 'And on the other side some Almoravids think that killing infidels – Christians and Jews and even heretical Muslims – is what their *jihad* is about. Unfortunately, we Jews are infidels to some people on both sides. Alfonso and the more enlightened Almoravids understand the damage that this hatred can do to their kingdoms – we can only pray to God that they prevail.'

*

After Queen Bertha died, Princess Zaida of Seville, King Alfonso's mistress, converted to Christianity, taking the name Isabel, and she was married to the king. They had already had a child, Sancho, the king's only son: their marriage made him legitimate and the king's heir.

Alfonso's daughter, Princess Urraca, appeared not to be upset that Sancho had displaced her as heir, but she continued to favour Frankish and other Roman Catholic priests, courtiers and doctors. The incompetent Guy de Clamency was dismissed, but Urraca and Raymond brought in other doctors trained in Paris and in Italy. Those doctors were less dismissive than Guy of the Greek texts that the Arabs had preserved, and they continued to have the texts translated into Latin. But they were still hostile to the 'Arabic' doctors (whether Muslim or Christian) and, of course, equally hostile to the Jews. Alfonso insisted on keeping Joseph ibn Ferruziel as a court physician, and Solomon as an adviser, but the king was growing old, and his protection was becoming less certain.

That was one of the reasons why Yehuda had left the court to set up a practice on his own, along with his desire to spend more time advising on religious cases in the Jewish community, since he was also expanding his learning in Jewish law and philosophy. Over the next few years, Yehuda's medical practice flourished and his fame as a poet spread throughout Andalucía. Their daughter Miriam grew to be a healthy and vigorous child, a delight to both her parents, but Deborah was unable to bear another child.

When Deborah expressed her sorrow that she had not given him a son, Yehuda found no way to assuage the pain. He had pointed out that it was wrong to say that *she* had not given him a son – it was God who gave and took away life, and though Yehuda was a good physician, neither he nor any of his colleagues, nor any of the classical texts could fully explain infertility or miscarriages or infant deaths. When he said this, it just seemed to add irritation to Deborah's sadness: she told him emphatically that a scholarly answer about God or medicine didn't help at all.

Deborah had resumed her practice as a midwife soon after Miriam was born. She was an excellent midwife and enjoyed the work. But Yehuda was aware that occasionally, and particularly when she was tired, delivering a boy child reminded her of their lack of a son – especially when the family, as they always did, expressed their great joy that the child was a boy.

Yehuda tried to tell Deborah that he was content with Miriam and didn't long for a son, but she just brushed that aside. It was one of the few subjects that they found it difficult to talk about. Yehuda had even started to keep his business letters from her, since many ended with the conventional formula that the writer prayed that God would give them 'male children studying Torah and fulfilling the commandments'.

7

DISQUIET
TOLEDO, 1106

The wisdom of the Torah is divided into two parts. The
first aims at the knowledge of practical duties and is the
wisdom of external conduct. The second deals with the
duties of the heart, namely its sentiments and thoughts,
and is the wisdom of the inward life.

Bahya ibn Paquda, *Duties of the Heart* (1040)

'So, Deborah, you don't need to work tomorrow!' Yehuda said as
he entered the kitchen. Deborah and Miriam were wrapping up
the bread dough in a damp cloth ready to be taken to the bakery,
while Abigail, their servant, was putting on her outdoor cloak.
'Good morning, Miriam,' he added. 'Have you been helping to
make the bread?' This was rather obvious, given that Miriam's little
hands, face and tunic were covered in flour.

'Yes, Daddy, I've been helping Mummy and Abigail.' She
brushed the hair away from her face, thus adding white streaks to
the dusting of flour already speckling her curly black locks.

'You've been a big help, darling, thank you,' said Deborah.

'Perhaps if we can get you clean,' Yehuda added, 'you can go with Abigail to the bakery and see the bread being baked in the big oven.'

'Yes, yes, please, Daddy!' Miriam hugged her father, who gently extricated himself and brushed the flour off his *jalaba*.

Abigail waited patiently while Deborah and Yehuda cleaned Miriam up as best they could and changed her tunic.

As Abigail took the package of dough and crossed the courtyard to the front gate, with Miriam skipping beside her in the sunshine, Deborah washed her hands. 'What was that you said about tomorrow, my love?'

'There's a new moon tomorrow, a new month, so it's Rosh Chodesh, a day of rest for women. You don't need to work.'

Yehuda expected a smile – how he loved her smile! – but instead her face fell. 'What's the matter?' he asked.

'Yes, I'd forgotten, tomorrow's the first of Elul.' She looked down at her hands. 'I'll be thirty on the fifth of Elul.'

'Indeed you will, my love. Why does that trouble you?'

Deborah sighed. 'I think you know why, Yehuda. I'll soon be reaching an age when I can no longer safely bear children, and I still haven't given you a son. I haven't been able to give you a proper family at all.' Putting her towel on the rail, she sat on the stool by the kitchen table, her hands on her knees and her head bowed.

Yehuda knelt in front of her, taking her hands in his and kissing them. They still carried a trace of the yeasty smell of the dough. 'Deborah, my dearest friend, we do have a proper family. We have each other, and I still adore you as I always have. Nothing in the world gives me more happiness than our love for each other. And God has given us Miriam, a beautiful treasure. She's a wonder. She's full of joy and curiosity and intelligence – why, she's only six, but she's already starting to read and to enjoy learning. We have a lot to be grateful for.'

Deborah was not consoled. She kept her hands in his but looked away. 'Yes,' she said quietly, 'but I have still not given you a son.'

Kissing Deborah's hands again, Yehuda said, 'No, we haven't been blessed with a son, but you have given me so much, my darling. Your love means everything to me.' Kneeling before her, he recited:

You have captured my heart, my sister, my bride,
You have captured my heart
With one glance of your eyes,
With one jewel of your necklace.
How beautiful is your love, my sister, my bride,
How much better is your loving than wine,
The fragrance of your oils than any spice!
Sweetness drops from your lips, my bride,
Honey and milk are beneath your tongue
And the scent of your robes is like the scent of Lebanon.

'Enough, enough.' Smiling a little, Deborah wiped her eyes with the back of her hand. 'This section goes on for another five or six stanzas and Solomon ibn Ferruziel sent a message to say he was coming to see us this morning. What will he think if he finds you kneeling in front of me reciting sensuous passages from *The Song of Songs*?'

'I imagine he'll think that I am still in love with you, which I'm sure he already knows. You're cutting me off before one of the best passages in the poem, but if you don't want to hear about pomegranates and henna and myrrh and springs of fresh water, so be it.'

As Yehuda got to his feet, Deborah said, 'Yes, you're right, Yehuda, we have a lot to be thankful for. But that doesn't mean that we should deny our troubles. You keep quoting Bahya ibn Paquda about the importance of feeling and thought, but you talk as if his *Duties of the Heart* was telling us that we must always be happy and thankful. He doesn't say that at all. He says that we should be mindful of all our feelings, that we should know ourselves in our sorrow as well as our joy, in our anger and our compassion, our pride and our humility.'

'What's this about pride and humility?' Solomon ibn Ferruziel was standing at the door of the kitchen. 'I'm sorry to interrupt, but the gate was open and no one answered when I knocked.'

'No, it's we who should apologise, Solomon,' Yehuda responded. 'There was no one to greet you because Abigail took Miriam to the bakery and the other servants have gone to the market. You're very welcome – let's go to the reception room. Do you want anything to eat or drink?'

'No thank you, Yehuda, I don't need anything.'

Deborah lifted the plain muslin cloth from an earthenware jug on the table. 'Not even some of our fine *'aqid*? Abigail mixed the curds in water just now, before she left for the bakery, so it's very fresh. Come, taste it! We have honey to sweeten it as well, if you wish.'

Solomon smiled. 'Thank you, Deborah, that's very tempting.' He leaned over the jug and breathed in the sour aroma of the drink. 'These wonderful milky concoctions have converted me to your Andalucían tastes. But no, thank you, I really don't need anything to eat or drink.'

'Very well,' said Deborah. 'Let's go through.'

As the three of them settled on the chairs in the reception room Solomon said, 'My apologies again for disturbing you, but I'm here on a rather delicate matter. Queen Isabel wants to see you. She asks if you can come to the Belvedere Gate this afternoon.'

Deborah and Yehuda exchanged glances. This was not the first time that he had been asked to come to the queen, even though he now had his own practice and was no longer formally a court servant.

'Oh dear,' Yehuda said to Solomon, 'this is indeed delicate. I'm not sure it's wise for me to keep doing this.'

'Yes, Yehuda, I understand, but the queen is desperate to see you. She may have become a Christian but she won't abandon everything Andalucían, including your medical science. She consulted Joseph, but he's afraid of upsetting the other doctors. More importantly, he thinks that your knowledge is more appropriate than his in this case.'

'My knowledge? Why? What's the problem?'

'I'm sorry if I didn't make myself clear,' said Solomon. He stood and went to close the door of the reception room. As he came back, he said, 'Did you say everyone is out?'

'Yes,' Deborah said, 'everyone is out of the house. Why? What's the mystery, Solomon?'

'Well, when I said that the queen wants to see you, I didn't mean just Yehuda. I meant both of you. She's... well, apparently she's pregnant.'

'What? Pregnant?' Deborah jumped to her feet. 'She's older than me. She must be in her late thirties! This could be dangerous.'

'Exactly,' Solomon agreed. 'It's unusual for a woman of her age to bear a child at all. That's why Joseph thinks that your experience as a midwife will be as important as Yehuda's as a physician. I know that this won't be easy for you, Deborah, but it's important that we help Zaida.'

'Yes, I understand, Solomon.' Deborah smiled. 'The very fact that you, a Jewish courtier, still refer to Queen Isabel as "Zaida" illustrates just how dangerous the situation can be.'

'Oh heavens!' Solomon exclaimed, returning Deborah's smile. 'You're right, I did. That was a stupid slip – if I did that at court I'd be in serious trouble.' He paused. 'So, will you do it? Will you go to the queen?'

Deborah looked down at Yehuda, who was still sitting, watching the two of them with a solemn expression. He had not taken Solomon's slip of the tongue as lightly as she had. 'You're being uncharacteristically silent, Yehuda,' Deborah said. 'What do you think? Should we go?'

'I'm not sure. I'm willing to do it – I've seen the queen in private before. But I don't want to put you in danger.'

Deborah's eyes widened and she took a step towards him, half angry, half amused. 'Oh, Yehuda, you are incorrigible – you "don't want to put me in danger". Like I am your child or your donkey and you want to make the decisions about what's good for me and what's bad for me! If you're going, I will go. That's my decision, not yours. To be honest, we both know that we don't have a choice. We must go. That's the Jewish law – saving a human life, *pikuach nefesh*, is the highest law.'

'Yes, yes, but…'

Deborah held up her hand to silence him. 'And even if it were not the *din*, Queen Isabel is our main protection against the enemies of the Jews now that King Alfonso is growing less strong. We must help her.'

'Very well, so be it.' He turned to Solomon. 'We'll come.'

'Excellent. If you both come to the Belvedere Gate after the palace watch changes this afternoon, I'll ensure that you're admitted to the women's chambers.'

'Good, that's settled. Do you have to go back now or will you stay a while?'

'I'm in no hurry. It won't take long to arrange your admission and there's nothing much happening at the palace while the king and the court are out hunting. Perhaps I could take some of that *'aqid* after all?'

'By all means,' said Deborah. 'I'll go and get it. Yehuda, do you want some?'

'Yes please, my love.'

Deborah went to the kitchen, returning with the jug, a bowl of honey and three cups.

'Honey, Solomon?' she asked, as she sat at the table.

'No thank you, Deborah, I like the *'aqid* as it is, fresh and sour, please.'

'We take it like that as well,' Deborah said, pouring out the drinks. 'So, Solomon, how's Aviva and how are the children?'

'They're very well, thank you, and we're all looking forward to seeing you at our house on Friday night, especially David. He loves playing with your Miriam. But what was it you were saying when I arrived, about knowing ourselves in our joy and in our sorrow? It sounded interesting.'

Deborah shifted in her chair. 'Well, it wasn't exactly an academic discussion.' She looked at Yehuda, who nodded slightly. 'We were talking about how I feel about not having had a son.'

'Oh dear, I'm very sorry, I didn't mean to...'

Deborah shook her head, smiling at Solomon. 'No, no, don't apologise, don't feel bad. You did nothing wrong at all. You're a dear friend, and I know that you understand how I feel. I only mention the subject to explain why we were talking about the need to be mindful of our feelings.'

'Ah, yes,' said Solomon, 'Yehuda keeps telling me about this. Isn't it something called *Duties of the Soul*? It sounds very intense, probably too difficult for me.'

'No, Solomon,' Deborah replied, 'it's called *Duties of the Heart*. It's by Bahya ibn Paquda. You really should read it. It's not all that intense. His message is very simple and, at least to a woman, rather obvious. We spend a lot of time thinking about what he calls the duties of the body – the actions we can see like giving charity, eating kosher food or keeping the Sabbath. But we don't think enough about the duties of the heart, our feelings and our thoughts, the inner life.'

'Really?' Solomon smiled. 'That sounds pretty intense to me. In any case, surely what matters is what we do, not what we feel? Apart from the commandments to love our neighbour and love God, there's not a lot in the Torah about what we feel. It's our actions that matter.'

'Bahya would disagree,' Deborah replied. 'He says that if you give charity without love, or pray without attention, if you're not mindful of what you're doing, then you're not really fulfilling the commandments.'

Solomon looked down at his hands, clearly uncomfortable.

'You don't look very convinced!' Deborah said.

'No, I'm not… well, I mean, it's a bit…' He looked up at Yehuda and Deborah. 'I mean, I don't want to start an argument. You're my friends, quite apart from the fact that you've just agreed to do a big favour for me and the queen.'

'Solomon,' said Yehuda, 'it's because we're friends that you can be honest with us! What's the problem?'

Solomon still hesitated. Deborah leaned across and put her hand on his. 'Please, friend, you are obviously concerned. Tell us why.'

Solomon took a deep breath. 'Well, this all sounds very Sufi to me. That's dangerous for us. Thanks to Urraca and her clique, the tensions at court and in the city between the old and the new Christians, between them and the Muslims and between all of them and us Jews are getting worse. I'm worried about us being seen to adopt Muslim ideas, especially Sufi ideas that even many Muslim leaders don't like. It's not just this Bahya and his writings. Yehuda also quotes Muslims like Ibn Sina and Al-Ghazali all the time, and not only in discussions with Jews. It's dangerous, as I said.'

'How can it be dangerous?' Yehuda said. 'There's no harm in learning wisdom from Muslims, especially from Sufis. They have a deep understanding of the mind of human beings. As Al-Ghazali said, if men and women are created in God's image, then if we want to understand God, it might be useful to start with understanding people.'

Solomon waved his hand as if to brush aside what he was hearing. 'Yes, yes, so you say, but where's the authority for this to us as Jews? We need to stick to the Torah and the Talmud, to our own traditions, or we'll be lost.'

'This is in our tradition, Solomon. It's very much part of our tradition. We *are* commanded to be mindful of our experience. As the psalmist says, "Taste and see that God is good." Taste and see. And by the way, talking of taste and see, you haven't tasted your *'aqid* yet.'

'Indeed I haven't.' Solomon smiled, relaxing a little, and they all took a sip of the cool, sour milk. 'Delicious!' He raised the cup to Deborah, who nodded in acknowledgement.

'And if you want the authority of the Talmud,' Yehuda added, 'there's that passage in *Pirkei Avot* where Rabbi Yochanan agrees with Rabbi Elazar ben Arach that all virtues originate in a good heart.'

Solomon was still not convinced. 'Surely, Yehuda, Deborah, it's our mind, our mental faculties, that take precedence, not our feelings. That's what the philosophers teach us – to use rational argument to understand the world and to know how to act.' Solomon winced and rose from his seat. 'Ow! What happened?'

'I stamped on your toe, that's what happened,' said Deborah. 'How did you perceive that experience? Through your mind or through your body? How did you react? With your mind or with your feelings?'

'That was very unkind, Deborah!' said Solomon. 'But I think I see what you mean. Or rather I feel it.' He sat down again and rubbed his toe.

'That's why Al-Ghazali attacks the refusal of the philosophers to value experience,' Deborah continued, nodding at Yehuda. 'He says that what's most peculiar to Sufis can't be learned. It can be attained only by direct experience and inward transformation. The drunken man doesn't know anything about the definition, causes and physiology of drunkenness, yet he is drunk, whilst the sober scholar may know all about drunkenness in theory, but he has no idea what it actually feels like to be drunk.'

Solomon had stopped rubbing his toe and was listening intently. He took another sip from his cup. 'So, you seem to be going a step beyond experience and emotions – this may also relate to revelation, to experience of the divine?' He looked at Deborah and grimaced. 'Not that stepping on someone's toe is necessarily the best way to demonstrate revelation!' Deborah stuck out her tongue and he grinned.

'Yes,' Yehuda said, 'Al-Ghazali was attacking the *filasaf*, the Muslim followers of Aristotle. They seek to understand the nature of God only through rational argument, building from one premise to another. Al-Ghazali asserted that understanding in this area comes only from direct experience, from the ecstasy of contact with the divine. Like the drunken man.'

'This is interesting, but I still think it could be dangerous. The Roman Christians won't like it if you attack Aristotle! Anyway, I'd like to pursue this further, but I think it's time for me to be getting back to the palace. So, if you'll excuse me—'

The door was flung open and Miriam burst into the room, closely followed by Abigail. 'Mummy, Mummy, we've brought the bread!' She saw Solomon and stopped running. She even bowed, quite graciously. 'Oh, hello, Uncle Solomon.'

'Hello, Miriam, it's good to see you. I trust you're well.'

'Very well, thank you, Uncle. And I hope you are also.'

'Yes, thank you. What a polite young lady you are. On Friday night you must teach our David some manners.'

Miriam blushed. As Abigail stepped forward to usher her out of the room, Solomon said, 'Good morning, Abigail. I hope you're well too. I was about to leave – perhaps you and Miriam would see me out.' Making his farewells to Deborah and Yehuda, Solomon left with Miriam and Abigail, who closed the door behind them.

*

Waiting in Queen Isabel's antechamber, Deborah and Yehuda were reminded that she had removed Bertha's dark tapestries and replaced them with whitewashed walls. Princess Zaida may have become Queen Isabel, but she retained her Andalucían tastes.

The door to the queen's bedchamber was flung open and young Prince Sancho rushed out, shouting, 'Let's go down to the courtyard! It's almost time for my fencing lesson!' He came to an abrupt halt when he saw them, graciously returning their bows. Sancho was fourteen years old and was happier playing the soldier than the courtier, but he still managed the etiquette of the court with reasonable grace. He was soon followed by Sancho's younger sister, Princess Elvira, and by the governess. She nodded to Yehuda and Deborah and said to the prince, 'No, Your Highness, it's not yet time for fencing. First we must go to Brother Thomas for your Latin lesson.' Both children pulled a face but said nothing as the governess led them from the room.

'The queen will see you now, Magister Yehuda and Mistress Deborah.' Lady Claudia had appeared in the doorway to the queen's bedchamber. 'Please do come through.'

Having inherited Claudia as Lady of the Bedchamber, Queen Isabel had seen no reason to replace her. Claudia was expert in the ways of the court, and the queen relied on her to gently ensure that she knew how to follow the elaborate set of rules that the previous queens had introduced from across the Pyrenees. Princess Urraca's supporters were dubious enough about this convert queen; she did not want to remind them of her status by clumsy breaches of etiquette.

As they entered the bedchamber with Claudia, the queen rose from her cushions. In public, she was totally the Queen of León-Castile, but in her private chambers she felt able to eschew chairs and furnish the room with the rich Damascene cushions and Armenian carpets that she had grown up with in Seville. The scent of sandalwood pervaded the room from a small incense burner in the corner.

The queen was still alluring. Her flawless complexion was warm and dark, the colour of walnut wood. She had the full lips, strong nose and dark, gleaming hair of the most beautiful Andalucían women. Where Deborah's blue eyes seemed to see through you, Isabel's black eyes drew you irresistibly towards her. It was easy to see why she had enchanted King Alfonso.

As Claudia introduced Yehuda and Deborah and they bowed to the queen, she held out her hand for them to kiss her ring. 'Yehuda, I'm glad to see you again. And as for you, Deborah – I'm happy to meet you at last. I've heard so much about you.'

Turning to Claudia, she said, 'Thank you, Claudia, you may leave us now.'

Looking startled, Claudia stuttered, 'But… but, Your Majesty…'

The queen held up her hand. 'I understand your concern, Claudia, and applaud it. But I think Mistress Deborah here will be a sufficient chaperone while the doctor examines me, yes? And I'd prefer to be alone with them, at least while we first discuss my condition. Don't worry, I'll send for you when we're finished and we can discuss it together then.'

Still looking unhappy, Claudia muttered, 'Yes, Your Majesty' and left the bedchamber.

Turning to them, the queen said, 'Claudia's a treasure and serves me well, as she served Queen Bertha. But I'm not entirely sure where her loyalties lie. In this court, it's impossible to know who's discreet and who reports to Urraca and her clique.' Seeing Deborah's surprise, she added, 'Don't be startled, Deborah. I know I can trust your husband and speak frankly to him, even though he's no longer a court doctor. And,' she added, smiling warmly, 'I hope that I can trust you also. I already know your reputation as a midwife and a scholar.'

Instead of bridling at the blatant flattery, as Yehuda expected her to do, Deborah melted before Isabel's smile. 'Yes, Your Majesty,' she said meekly.

'Thank you, Deborah,' the queen replied. 'Now, to business. Solomon must have told you why I wanted to see you.' They both nodded, and she went on. 'I'm sure I must be with child – my monthly cycle is disrupted and I'm frequently sick. I have borne two children to Alfonso and had one miscarriage, but this seems a little more difficult.'

After Yehuda and Deborah had examined the queen and consulted each other, he told her that she did indeed appear to be with child, and in her third month.

'You will need to be very careful, Your Majesty,' Deborah added. 'The strength of your womb will not be as it was, and the pregnancy could be dangerous for you as well as for the child. You'll need frequent rest, certainly for the next few weeks and possibly throughout the pregnancy.' She smiled. 'And you'll not be going out hunting with the king again for some time!'

'Yes, you're right, Deborah. I think the king suspects, because he made no objection when I told him yesterday that I wouldn't ride out with him this afternoon. Well, I'll take your advice – and it looks as if you'll be seeing a lot more of me for a while, if you'll agree to help Joseph and the other doctors to look after me.'

'Of course, Your Majesty, if you wish,' Deborah replied.

Sitting up on the bed, Isabel said, 'Yehuda, would you mind checking that there's no one lurking in the antechamber?'

He went and looked out of the door and confirmed that the antechamber was empty. 'Good. I'm sorry if you think me over-cautious, but I'm worried. I don't know for certain about Claudia, but I'm sure that some of my ladies are not to be trusted. I have borne the king a son, it is true, and Sancho is a strong child, but we're surrounded by enemies, especially now that Sancho is the legitimate heir. Princess Urraca has grown more confident since she bore a son this year, though she hasn't yet challenged Sancho's right to succeed. Nevertheless, Raymond and his Roman Catholic clique are constantly plotting to strengthen Urraca's position further and to draw her closer to Aragon and the Franks. That is why I called for you.

'I really hope that my new child is another boy and that I'll live to protect them both, and Elvira – otherwise I fear for their future. More than that, I fear for the future of León-Castile and of Spain if the new Roman Christians prevail. We must ensure that the succession goes to Sancho, or to his brother if this child proves to be a boy.'

Yehuda and Deborah exchanged glances. None of this was news to them; indeed, they had just been discussing these very issues with Solomon. That, however, was not the same as discussing them here, in the tense environment of the royal court. Deborah shrugged almost imperceptibly. Yehuda understood the gesture: she had no experience of court politics and it was for him to decide what to do or say.

Yehuda decided that, in the circumstances, he had no choice but to be open with the queen. 'Yes, Your Majesty,' he said. 'Every Muslim and every Jew in Toledo is beginning to share your concern for the kingdom and for their place in it. We are the scapegoats for those who are seeking to mollify the Mozarabic Christians.'

They sat in silence for a little until Deborah decided to intervene. 'This may all be true, Your Majesty, but what matters right now is you and the child that you're carrying. I'm not here to look after the kingdom, but to care for you. And you need not only constant rest, but also peace of mind. It's hard, I know, but you must try to stop fretting about Princess Urraca's clique and concentrate on your own health.'

'Thank you, Deborah,' said the queen with a faint smile. 'There speaks the good midwife. As a matter of fact, Claudia has been saying exactly the same thing. She's been telling me to spend more time playing music and hearing poetry and less time worrying about the intrigues of the court.'

'Whatever her motives, she's right,' Deborah said. 'You need to take her advice.'

'Thank you,' said the queen. 'Perhaps, Yehuda, you would fetch Claudia, and the four of us can discuss my regime for the coming months.'

Deborah and Yehuda were frequent visitors to the queen's quarters and they worked with Joseph ibn Ferruziel and the other doctors to minimise the risks to her pregnancy. But in the early months of the following year the queen's condition deteriorated. She died just before she came to full term. The child, had it survived, would have been a boy.

*

After the death of Queen Isabel, the balance of power had shifted to Princess Urraca – whom people called 'the Reckless' – and her husband Raymond of Burgundy. Queen Isabel's son, Prince Sancho, continued to be the heir presumptive and his father King Alfonso still strove to keep the peace between the native Castilians and the Catholic newcomers. The friction continued despite their efforts, however. To distract attention from these conflicts, Raymond and his clique kept stirring up hostility to the Jews and Muslims as a convenient common 'enemy'. They accused the Muslims of being secret supporters of the kingdom's opponents among the Muslim *taifa* states in Andalucía and the Jews of playing each side off against the other.

Matters came to a head after King Alfonso VI resumed his efforts to keep control of those *taifa* states that still paid tribute to him. Solomon ibn Ferruziel was sent by the king on a mission to Seville in 1108, in the hope that the judges there might act as intermediaries with the Almoravid amir.

Yehuda composed a poem to welcome Solomon back to Toledo, but before Solomon reached home he was murdered – Raymond's clique had spread rumours that he was a traitor, and other rumours too, about his relationship with Queen Isabel before she died.

King Alfonso would have none of this, rightly believing that these were lies designed partly to weaken the position of Isabel's son Sancho. The king did what he could to keep the peace between all the factions, but he was growing old and weak. Then Alfonso was defeated by the Almoravid army under ibn Tashfin's son,

Tamim ibn Yusuf, at the battle of Uclés – and, worse still, Prince Sancho was killed in that battle.

There were riots in Toledo after the defeat and the death of Sancho, during which many Jews were killed and houses and synagogues burned. The madness gradually subsided, but then King Alfonso himself died and there were new riots. Yehuda and Deborah decided that they must leave Toledo and return to Andalucía. They moved to Córdoba in 1109.

8

BURNING
CÓRDOBA, 1109

Better to be a fly on a heap of excrement than to be a theologian at the door of kings.

Abu Hamid al-Ghazali

'Abu Hasan al-Lawi? Is that you?'

Yehuda did not at first respond to his Arabic name – he had only just arrived in Córdoba and had rarely used or heard the name in his fifteen years in Toledo. The speaker tapped him on the shoulder and repeated the question. As soon as Yehuda turned and saw his smile, he recognised him as an old friend from his youth in Córdoba.

'Ahmad, it's wonderful to see you again! I hardly recognised you. You have grown so tall and...'

'And fat. Yes, yes, fat. You don't have to say it.' Ahmad pretended to pout, but there was a twinkle in his eye and the familiar dimples showed in his cheeks.

'No,' Yehuda responded, 'I wasn't going to say fat, I was going to say distinguished. You've become so distinguished – and such a fine beard!'

'Abu Umar Ahmad bin Ali bin Hazm at your service,' Ahmad replied in mock solemnity, putting his right hand across his chest and bowing slightly. It was true that there was a distinguished air about him. He had become a little overweight, but his robe was elegantly cut and fitted him well – the linen robe of an *alim*, a scholar, with fine silk trimmings. He carried himself straight, showing off his height. The wiry, over-active friend with whom Yehuda had played and argued when they were thirteen had become a man of substance in every sense, but Yehuda could still see the humour and intelligence that had so attracted him as a boy. Seeing Ahmad's appraising look, Yehuda was also aware of how much he himself had changed, but in a different way from Ahmad – Yehuda was now leaner than he had been as a boy, his face lined and tanned, but his hair a little thinner.

The narrow Calle Juderia was bustling with people hurrying home from the *Zuhr* midday prayers at the Great Mosque, visible at the end of the street, and the two of them had to stand aside to let them pass.

'Have you just come from prayers, Ahmad?' Yehuda asked.

Ahmad glanced around nervously. 'Yes, I have, Yehuda, and something else too.' He hesitated. 'But we can talk about that later. Why are you here? What are you doing in Córdoba?'

'It's a long story. My home is just around the corner, north of the Great Mosque – please come back with me and we can talk. The house is still half furnished – we arrived only a few days ago – so we can't entertain you as we would wish to, and as you deserve. I beg you to forgive us our shortcomings and honour us with your presence. Deborah will be delighted to see you again.'

'Deborah will be delighted to meet me *again*? Deborah? Do you mean Deborah the daughter of Isaac ibn Ezra?'

'Yes, Ahmad, we're married now.'

Ahmad put his hands on Yehuda's shoulders. 'What? Can this blessed news be true? I mean, what I should say is *mashal'lah*, or rather *mazal tov*, that's wonderful news.' He embraced Yehuda warmly before taking a step back. 'But when, where, how?'

'It's a long story, as I said – and I'm sure you have a lot to tell us as well. So, do me the honour, come home and meet Deborah and we can catch up with each other.'

As they walked past the open north-west gate of the Great Mosque a few people were still leaving after the prayers. Yehuda noticed a bustle of activity inside the courtyard by the western gate. Soldiers were carrying faggots of wood to add to a pile near the gate, as if they were building a bonfire.

'What's going on there?' he asked Ahmed.

Once again, Ahmed looked around nervously. Almost in a whisper, he said, 'Something terrible is going to happen here. Let's not linger. I'll tell you when we get to your house.'

A few yards after the gate they left the wide street that ran along the wall of the mosque and turned into Sharie Alhamman, hemmed in by the tall house fronts on either side. As they approached the corner of Harrat Alshaela, Ahmad stopped abruptly.

'Wait a minute,' he said, pointing to the big house on the corner of the lane, 'are we going there? Are we going to that house? Really? Isn't that…'

'Yes, Ahmad, it was house of Isaac ibn Ezra, Deborah's father. After Isaac decided to stay in Toledo, he sold it to a friend of his who lives in Cairo but often came to Córdoba on business. The friend is now spending more time in the East now, so when we thought about moving here, he agreed to sell the house back to us. Let's go inside and we can talk about all this with Deborah.'

As they entered the familiar courtyard, Yehuda could hear Deborah in the kitchen, talking to Miriam and their new servant,

Shulamit. 'Deborah, my love,' he called, 'look who I've brought with me.'

Deborah came out, wiping her hands on a cloth. She stopped as soon as she saw Ahmad and smiled broadly. 'Why, Ahmad, you rascal! You haven't changed a bit. Yehuda, where did you find this reprobate?'

'Just outside the Great Mosque after the *Zuhr* prayers, and he'll be delighted that you think he hasn't changed. He accused me of thinking he was fat.'

'Not quite, Deborah,' said Ahmad. 'He used the euphemism "distinguished". But you, Deborah, you've hardly changed at all – and you're just as radiant as ever.'

Other women would have lowered their eyes at this compliment, but Deborah just laughed and said, 'You're still full of hot air, Ahmad! But it's wonderful to see you again. Come in and we can talk. Our house isn't yet as comfortable as it should be. As Yehuda will have told you, no doubt, we've only just moved here. But you're very welcome to what we have. Maybe a little food after your prayers?'

'Thank you, Deborah,' Ahmad said, 'that would be delightful.'

As they moved towards the *majlis*, Miriam came out of the kitchen to see what was going on. Now eleven years old, she was still as intense and as untidy as ever, and she had flour in her hair and on her clothes yet again. Miriam had inherited her mother's beauty – her olive skin, arresting blue eyes and natural grace – but seemed to have no desire yet to emulate Deborah's poise and elegance. Yehuda never understood how when she and Deborah made bread together, Miriam would end up covered in flour while her mother remained elegant and impeccably clean.

'Ahmad,' Deborah said, 'this is our daughter Miriam. Miriam, this is an old friend of ours from when we lived here before.'

Miriam brushed her hair back from her forehead and bowed to Ahmad, while keeping her eyes on his.

'Why, Miriam,' Ahmad said, 'you have your mother's blue eyes, and are just as disconcertingly observant, I think! I'm very pleased to meet you.'

This time, Miriam did lower her eyes as she blushed and muttered, 'And I'm pleased to meet you, sir.'

'Miriam, please ask Shulamit to bring some *mulukhiya* soup, cold chicken and beans and some sherbet for our guest,' Deborah said as she ushered Ahmad into the *majlis*.

Once they had settled on the *martaba*, Deborah and Yehuda started to tell Ahmad about Alfonso's wars and the death of Prince Sancho at the battle of Uclés.

Their account was interrupted by Miriam, carrying in the tray of drinks, followed by Shulamit with the food. Shulamit was always graceful and unruffled and even Miriam had brushed the flour out of her hair and changed her clothes – as Shulamit had probably insisted, against Miriam's protests that she was fine as she was. The smell of the spicy soup, the chicken and the beans cooked in herbs, filled the *majlis*. As Miriam and Shulamit finished serving, Miriam eyed the newcomer with undisguised curiosity.

Deborah said, 'Thank you, Shulamit, this is just what we need – Miriam, please stay a while to meet Ahmad properly.' Smiling, Shulamit bowed and left the room, while Miriam stood looking at Ahmad.

'So, Miriam,' Ahmad said, 'how do you like Córdoba?'

'Well, sir,' Miriam said solemnly, 'I haven't really had time to make a proper judgement yet. The people seem nice but the food's a bit too spicy.'

'I'm sure you'll get used to the food,' Ahmad said, 'and people are more important than food.'

'Yes, they are, I suppose,' said Miriam. 'Also, I like our house here, especially the courtyard. I can get out of my room to read and play when the weather's nice. It's a bit warmer here than in Toledo, though it seems to rain a lot more.'

'True,' Yehuda said, 'but that means that the trees are greener and the fruit is sweeter.'

'Yes, Father,' Miriam responded, 'we build houses and dwell in them and plant gardens and eat their fruit.'

Ahmad grinned. 'How learned you are, Miriam. Isn't that from your book of Jeremiah?'

Miriam looked pleased. 'Yes, sir, it's from chapter twenty-nine.'

'Well, well,' said Ahmad, 'we have another scholar in our midst!'

Deborah and Yehuda exchanged glances. 'That's true, Ahmad,' Yehuda said, 'Miriam already knows how to read Hebrew and Spanish as well as Arabic. But perhaps that wasn't the most tactful quotation in the circumstances.'

'Why not?' Ahmad asked.

'The verse Miriam quoted is about the exile of the Jews in Babylon, where Jeremiah says of the exile, "It will be a long time: build houses and live in them, plant gardens and eat their fruit".'

Miriam looked a little crestfallen, so her father added, 'Don't worry, Miriam, Ahmad is a good friend and we can trust him, but we don't want to put it about that we see living in Andalucía as living in exile, like Babylon!'

Frowning, Miriam drew herself upright. 'But we do, Father. In our prayers we mourn the destruction of the Temple and we say that we long to return to Zion. Should we lie to strangers?'

'Deborah,' said Ahmad, smiling, 'I see that Miriam is her mother's daughter. She won't be cowed.'

'I hope not!' said Deborah. She gestured to Miriam to come to her and gave her a hug. 'You're right of course, Miriam, but returning to Zion is only a distant hope, especially now that the crusaders have conquered it. It's been a thousand years since the Temple was destroyed and I don't think we're going to get back there very soon. So we need to avoid offending people where we live, here in Andalucía, by saying that we don't want to live among them.'

'Yes, I see, Mother,' said Miriam, mollified, 'and anyway, I think I'll like it here.'

'Good,' said Deborah. 'Now, it's time for you to go and have a look at your Hebrew texts. Your new tutor, Samuel, will be here later today and you need to be ready for your lesson.'

Miriam pulled a face – until she caught her mother's eye. 'Yes, Mother, I will.' Turning to Ahmad, Miriam bowed and said, 'It was a pleasure to meet you, sir.'

As she walked gracefully out of the room, Ahmad exclaimed, 'What a girl! You must be very proud of her.'

'Yes, we are,' Yehuda said, 'and you're right, she is her mother's daughter. Thank God.' Smiling, he took Deborah's hand and she returned the smile.

'Let's get back to what happened in Toledo,' Ahmad said. 'You were talking about Alfonso's wars and the death of Prince Sancho. We heard about that, of course. Córdoba was fighting alongside Granada and other states against Alfonso and our troops also suffered badly at Uclés.'

'Yes,' Yehuda continued, 'but one result in Toledo was that things started to get really bad for Jews and Muslims, culminating in the riots against the Jews this year, which is why we had to leave.'

'So you'll be settling here in Córdoba?' asked Ahmad. 'I hope so, and I'm sure you'll do very well here. My Jewish friends tell me that you're getting a reputation as a great scholar, as well as a physician and, of course, a famous poet!'

Yehuda managed a smile. 'Yes, but we'll keep our house in Toledo, which, fortunately, was not burned down. I can't abandon my community there, so I hope to go back from time to time to resume some of my work when things return to normal, as they must. Urraca, whatever she feels, will need to stabilise the kingdom now that Sancho is gone and she is queen. She's still negotiating her marriage to the King of Aragon, and there are even disputes about whether that should go ahead.'

'Enough of this sad story,' Deborah said. 'Let's hear about Ahmad. Have you had enough to eat, my friend?'

'Yes, thank you, Deborah, it was delicious. But I'm afraid that sad stories aren't confined to Toledo. A tragedy is about to unfold right here in Córdoba, just down the road in the Great Mosque.'

'A tragedy?' Deborah asked.

'Yes,' said Ahmad, 'a terrible tragedy. A book burning.'

Yehuda remembered the bonfire being built in the courtyard of the Great Mosque. 'A book burning? What books?'

'Only one book,' Ahmad replied. 'Al-Ghazali's *Ihya*, *The Revival of the Islamic Sciences*.'

'What?' Deborah and Yehuda exclaimed at the same time. Deborah got to her feet. 'Al-Ghazali of all writers! And the *Ihya* of all works! How can that be? How did this happen?'

'Deborah,' said Ahmad quietly, 'please keep your voice down. Walls have ears, as your rabbis say.'

'I'm sorry, Ahmad.' Deborah sat down again on the *martaba*. 'You're right, of course, but I can't believe this. Al-Ghazali sent scholars to instruct the early Almoravids and supported their cause from the beginning. Why are they burning his books now?'

'Yes,' Yehuda added, 'and why the great *Ihya* of all books – even Jews and Christians admire the *Ihya*.'

'Just as you said about Toledo, it's a long story. I can't...' Ahmad bowed his head, apparently unable to continue.

'Wait a minute,' Yehuda said as he realised the special significance of this for Ahmad. 'A book burning? The last book burning in Andalucía was in Seville fifty years ago, before we were born. Al-Mu'tadid burned the books of Ali ibn Hazm, who was your...'

'My great-grandfather, yes,' Ahmad whispered. 'I never knew him, of course, but he was a huge figure in our family. My grandfather told me a lot about him and about the great dispute. By the time you and I were growing up some of the heat had gone out of the conflict. A group of us studied Ibn Hazm's *Fisal* with his disciple Shurayh al-Ru'ayni, but we still had to keep quiet about it. It wasn't easy.' Ahmad bowed his head again, lapsing into silence.

Deborah poured another cup of sherbet and offered it to Ahmad. 'Here, take this, my friend.' As Ahmad took the cup, she smiled and said, 'I wish I could offer you some wine!'

Ahmad returned her smile and said, 'I wish I could accept it in the circumstances.'

'Yes,' said Deborah, 'it's an awful reminder.'

'It's not just a reminder, Deborah, what we are seeing here is the same dreadful error.'

'Yes, I would think that the issues...' Yehuda started to say, but Deborah held up her hand to silence him. She understood that Ahmad needed to talk about this, not just to debate the issues.

She leaned over to Ahmad. 'What do you mean, Ahmad, the same error?'

Ahmad took a deep breath and then, to their surprise, he smiled. 'Oh, Deborah,' he said, 'you think that things are complicated in Toledo with your Castilians and your Franks, but that's nothing compared to Córdoba and the other *taifa* states. On top of the disputes between and within the different doctrinal schools – the Malikite, the Zahidi, the Shafi'ite – we also have Arabs against Berbers. The Andalucían Arabs despise the Berber Almoravids and think they're barbarians and…'

Deborah held up her hand again, also smiling. 'Slow down, Ahmad! I don't understand. Surely the Arabs here invited the Almoravid Berbers into Andalucía to help them fight King Alfonso?'

'So they did,' Ahmad said, 'but their allies became their masters and now they – I mean we – resent their rule. Especially since they started to weigh us down with non-Quranic taxes.'

'And the Malikites?' Yehuda asked.

'Oh dear,' Ahmad said, 'I wish I hadn't mentioned that. It's very convoluted. Basically, Amir Yusuf ibn Tashfin, whom you encountered in Granada, Yehuda, was a conqueror and a strong ruler, but his son Ali has problems on all fronts.' He counted off each point on his fingers: 'First, down in the Sahara, the Gudala dissidents in Sijilmasa don't like his Lamtuna and Massufa followers, even though they're all Berbers. Second, in the Maghreb the Shi'ite Fatimids are threatening to move west from Egypt to challenge Ali's Sunni order. Third, here in Andalucía, Ali has a disgruntled Arab population to deal with, as I said. There's more, but that will do for now!' Ahmad took a sip of sherbet and put his cup on the tray. 'In Andalucía Ali relies on the Malikite jurists, the *fuqaha*, to support his authority and they rely on him to keep them in power as judges and to enforce their rulings.'

'So the story is repeated indeed,' Yehuda said. 'Wasn't it Malikite jurists who had your great-grandfather's books burned in Seville?'

'You're right, it was. That was the price of their support for Amir Al-Mu'tadid when his position was getting precarious. It's almost exactly the same story, as you say.'

'Yes, and it was also Malikite *fuqaha* who went to Marrakesh with a *fatwa* against the Almoravid amirs and persuaded Yusuf ibn Tashfin to overthrow Abd Allah of Granada.'

'Why the Malikite jurists?' Deborah asked. 'What's their problem with Ibn Hazm and Al-Ghazali? I thought everyone respects Al-Ghazali.'

'I think I know the answer to that,' Yehuda said, looking at Ahmad. 'It's all about experience and the roots of Sharia, isn't it?'

Ahmad was about to answer when Shulamit, who had appeared in the doorway, coughed gently to attract their attention. 'May Miriam and I clear the trays now, please?'

'Yes,' Deborah answered, 'please do, Shulamit.'

'I've finished my revision,' Miriam said as Shulamit gathered up the empty cups and plates. 'Can I stay?'

'Not just now, my darling,' Deborah said, 'we are discussing business.'

Miriam looked crestfallen and Yehuda said to Deborah, 'Miriam will hear all about the book burning and it will be useful for her to learn something of what's behind it. Maybe she should stay a little.'

'Yes, the burning...' Miriam started to say but Deborah interrupted her.

'She's not old enough to follow the arguments and that would make it dangerous for her to talk about it. No, Miriam, don't pout,' Deborah said to Miriam, who was indeed pouting. 'Not everything is open to you, not yet.'

'Well, my love,' Yehuda said quietly, 'I think I know how you might have responded to your father or Uncle Moses if they had said that to you.'

Shaking her head, Deborah frowned at Ahmad, who was smiling, evidently amused at this exchange.

'Of course, you're right, Deborah,' Yehuda went on, 'these are dangerous times, but in this case I think Miriam may be able to learn something useful. May I go on?'

Deborah, still frowning, shrugged and said, 'Very well, if you insist.'

Yehuda held out his hands to Miriam and drew her towards him. 'Miriam, what did I teach you that Abu Hamid al-Ghazali says about experience?'

'What, really?' Ahmad interrupted. 'You're teaching Miriam Islam?'

'Not Islam, Ahmad, philosophy! So, Miriam, what does Al-Ghazali say?'

Miriam paused a moment, gathering her thoughts. 'He says that learning things from books is important, but so is what we see and hear and touch and smell, what we learn from being in the world. And also what we feel. We need to learn from those as well as from the Torah and Talmud.'

'Yes, or in his case the Quran and Hadith. Well done.'

'And he also says that we have to use logic to interpret that experience, but I'm not so sure what that bit means.'

'You have it absolutely right, Miriam!' said Ahmad. 'None of us is entirely sure what that bit means, which is where the trouble begins. Did you know that Al-Ghazali got these ideas from Ibn Hazm, my great-grandfather?'

Miriam's eyes widened. 'Really? Al-Ghazali learned from your great-grandfather?'

'Not directly, of course, he never met him, but he read the works of Ibn Hazm, who first put these ideas forward. But then Al-Ghazali added something else, something the jurists really, really dislike, which is why they are burning his book.'

'That's what I was trying to say before,' said Miriam, with a defiant look at Deborah. 'Shulamit told me that they are burning a book this evening, but she didn't know which one.'

'There you are, my love,' Yehuda said to Deborah, 'it seems our daughter knows more than we think.'

'Indeed,' Deborah replied, 'but that's enough. Miriam, you've heard what we were discussing. Now you can take the other tray and help Shulamit to clean up. I know, I know,' she added gently as Miriam straightened her shoulders and prepared to object, 'you'd love to stay and hear more, but Father and I need to talk with Ahmad and some of it will be difficult even for us to understand. Once we have the whole picture, I promise, I really promise, that we'll come and tell you about it.'

'Very well, Mother. I understand.' Turning to Ahmad she bowed and said, 'I hope that we shall meet again before long, sir', before making her exit.

'I should be going soon, I'm afraid,' Ahmad said after Miriam had left the *majlis*. 'I need to get home and reassure my wife before returning this evening for the book burning. It's due to take place after the *Asr* prayers. We need to be sure that there are people there who dispute the position of the qadi Ibn Hamdin and his party.'

Ahmad started to rise but Deborah gestured to him to sit down. 'Please, Ahmad, one moment. You said that Al-Ghazali added something else to Ibn Hazm's teachings that the jurists really disliked. What was that?'

'Ah, yes. The qadi and the Malikite jurists claim to be the only source of knowledge and authority about what the Sharia is. It was bad enough, Deborah, that Ibn Hazm said that we should actually return to the Quran and the Hadith if we want to understand the laws. In the *Ihya*, Al-Ghazali goes one step further. He argues that there are aims and objectives that lie behind all the individual rules that make up the Sharia. He says that we need to understand what God was trying to achieve in providing humankind with the Sharia, what the purpose of each law is.'

'Which means,' Yehuda said, unable to remain silent any longer, 'that if there are laws that turn out on specific occasions to be harmful or not in tune with the aims of the laws, then they can be overruled and replaced with others. But that is what our rabbis—'

Ahmad broke in. 'I'm sorry, Yehuda, Deborah, I really must be going. But you can see, Deborah, how this totally undermines the position of the judges, if everyone starts to question the purpose of laws! But I must rush.' He stepped off the *martaba*.

'Can I come to the book burning?' Yehuda asked.

'There will be invited notables there. Such as myself.' Ahmed managed a smile. 'But there is a place for others, including non-Muslims. I know that Abraham ibn Ezra is going. If you meet me at the north-west gate before the *Asr* prayers, Yehuda, I'll introduce you to him and you can go in and wait together.' He took a deep breath and turned to Deborah. 'I'm sorry to leave so abruptly, Deborah. It was wonderful to see you again and to meet Miriam. Thank you for the excellent food and the company. It was very much what I needed!'

Ahmad got up and left before Yehuda could tell him that he already knew Abraham ibn Ezra. They had met briefly as boys in Córdoba and had corresponded while Yehuda was living in Toledo. Abraham too was a poet, but by the time Yehuda moved to Córdoba Abraham was becoming known not only for his poetry but also for his work on a great commentary on the Torah.

*

That evening, when they met at the Great Mosque, Abraham was clearly as pleased to see Yehuda again as he was to see Ahmad. After

Ahmad left them to go to the prayer hall, they were admitted into the courtyard by the Almoravid guards, without much enthusiasm on their part, and directed to the stands in the north-west corner where they had a view of the bonfire by the western gate. The pile of faggots that Yehuda and Ahmad had seen earlier in the day had by then grown to a large bonfire, as tall as a house. An enclosure had been cordoned off between the bonfire and the prayer hall for the notables, as well as a pathway from the prayer hall to the enclosure. As they waited, the light began to fade and servants lit lamps on poles all along the pathway and around the enclosure.

The prayers had not finished yet so there were not many people in the public stands, but as soon as the prayers finished the worshippers poured out into the courtyard. The women left by various gates, but most of the men came into the public area. After a while, the notables moved in procession from the door of the prayer hall to the enclosure – rich merchants, scholars (with Ahmad among them), jurists, Almoravid officers and finally the chief courtiers.

Gradually the hubbub of the crowd subsided into an expectant silence, the only sound being the rustle of the evening breeze though the palm trees dotted around the great courtyard. After what felt like a long time, the *muezzin* called from the minaret, his voice a high vibrato as if he was chanting the call to prayer, 'In the Name of Allah, the Most Beneficent, the Most Merciful, let all stand aside and make way for his Highness, the Amir of the Faithful, Ali ibn Yusuf ibn Tashfin, and for the Qadi of Córdoba, Abu Abd Allah Mohammed ibn Ali ibn Hamdin.'

The qadi emerged first, resplendent in a robe of the finest black cotton, his white turban embroidered with flashes of green and yellow silk, his beard neatly trimmed. He was carrying his tall staff of office in one hand and a single scroll of parchment in the other. After a short pause, the young amir emerged, a chilling contrast in his plain blue woollen robe and turban, his face covered in the customary Berber style, showing only his eyes.

Accompanied by four Almoravid soldiers, the qadi and the amir walked slowly down the passageway, stopped in front of the bonfire and turned to face the assembled notables. At a nod from the amir, the qadi handed his staff of office to one of the soldiers and unrolled the scroll.

After pausing for dramatic effect, Qadi ibn Hamdin began to read slowly from the scroll. 'In the Name of Allah, the Most Beneficent, the Most Merciful. All praise and thanks be to Allah. And in the name of the Commander of the Muslims, Ali ibn Yusuf ibn Tashfin.' He glanced at the amir, who remained inscrutable. 'Whereas the muftis of the Grand Mosque of Córdoba have issued a *fatwa* against the heretical work, the so-called *Ihya, the Revival of the Religious Sciences* by Abu Hamid Mohammed ibn Mohammed al-Ghazali...'

As the qadi continued reading, a murmur arose among sections of the notables, beginning with the scholars but gradually extending to others – it was clear that there were many who were not at all happy with what was being done. As the text roundly denounced Al-Ghazali's linking of the science of practice and the science of enquiry and discovery with the science of divinity, the murmurs grow louder. Finally, when Ibn Hamdin read out, 'Anyone who reads or uses the book is denounced as an unbeliever', there were loud shouts of 'No! No!' from the crowd – those on the stands as well as some of the notables.

The amir had been showing some discomfort as the murmurs grew, looking at the ground and shifting from foot to foot, but when the shouting began he straightened up, reached out and took the qadi's staff of office from the soldier and banged it three times on the ground. The entire courtyard immediately fell silent – the meaning of the amir's gesture was obvious. He had made his decision: he would interpret any challenge to the qadi's authority as a challenge to his own, which would not be tolerated.

The qadi finished his reading to the now silent crowd, and declared, 'Bring forth the book!'

From the door of the mosque a line of soldiers appeared. The first six were carrying flaming torches. They were followed by five more soldiers, each carrying three bulky, leather-bound copies of the *Ihya*. Seeing them, Yehuda was immediately aware of the immense time and effort that had been devoted to meticulously and accurately copying the text in each version of the manuscript. Behind the soldiers came two muftis carrying large amphorae.

As each of the leading soldiers reached the bonfire, he thrust his torch into its base. The wood must have been very dry and well-seasoned because it immediately started to crackle loudly as flames crept up the bonfire. Before long, the acrid smell of wood smoke drifted across the courtyard. When the flames reached the top of the bonfire, Qadi Ibn Hamdin took the first copy of the book from the soldier leading the line and held it out to one of the muftis, who poured oil from the amphora onto the book. The qadi flung the book into the bonfire. As it burst into flame a sigh rose from the crowd and some people cried out, as if in pain. This time the amir did not intervene and as each book was doused in oil and cast onto the bonfire, the roar of the flames was echoed in the sighs of the crowd. As more books were thrown in, the notables in the enclosure near the fire covered their faces and started to move away from the searing heat and the sparks, pressing against the barriers that separated them from the public stands.

Yehuda said quietly, 'You may burn the paper, but you cannot burn what the paper contains.'

'What?' asked Abraham ibn Ezra, turning to him. 'What was that you said?'

'These are lines from a poem that Ibn Hazm wrote fifty years ago, when they burned his books in Seville. "You may burn the paper, but you cannot burn what the paper contains, which is preserved in my soul despite you."'

'Ah, yes,' said Abraham, 'I think I read that poem, but it didn't mean much to me until now.' A tall and handsome man with a fine, flowing beard, Abraham was a little younger than Yehuda. He spoke in a quiet but clear voice, as if rehearsing his thoughts rather than announcing them. 'But you know,' he went on, 'I am perplexed by this rejection of the *Ihya*. Can they really be rejecting all striving for understanding?'

Yehuda moved closer to Abraham and responded in a whisper, hoping that Abraham would also keep his voice down. How could he think it was safe for a couple of Jews to be discussing these matters in a mosque courtyard during a book burning? Nevertheless, he could not resist the temptation to pursue the topic. 'Yes, they can indeed reject that striving. Many Muslim jurists are saying that the gates of *ijtihad*, of striving to find new ways of understanding and interpreting the Sharia, are closed. There was a time when *ijtihad* was appropriate, *ijtihad* was indeed required, but now, they say, that time has passed. The canon is complete, and the task of the jurists is only to preserve that canon, not to question it.'

'Yes, yes, Yehuda, I understand that,' Abraham said, now also keeping his voice low, 'but I find it very perplexing, as I said. How could anyone think that? A Jew certainly could never think like that.'

'Don't be so sure, Abraham. There are rabbis who would say something very similar about the Talmud.'

'Yes, my friend, but they would be wrong. Oh! What was that crash?'

'It was just the bonfire collapsing,' Yehuda replied. 'The centre has burned out, but there's plenty of wood left and they still have five more copies of the *Ihya* to burn. What do you mean, wrong?'

'I mean it's wrong to say that we are not obliged to think for ourselves, to *interpret* the writings. That would be disastrous.'

As Abraham's voice rose, Yehuda held up his hands and looked nervously around them. He whispered, 'Please, my friend, keep your voice down.'

Abraham nodded and lowered his voice again. 'Yes, I'm sorry, Yehuda, but this is so important to me, to all of us. Look, the Talmud says that the middle words of the Torah are *darosh darash Moshe* – Moses enquired diligently. At the very centre of the Torah is the word "enquired"! Moses enquired. The essence of Torah is enquiry and study. For us, the gates of *ijtihad* should never close.'

In his enthusiasm, Abraham's voice was growing louder yet again. Seeing the alarm on Yehuda's face, he whispered, 'I'm sorry, Yehuda, you are right, this is not the place to talk. But I'm delighted to see you again and we should discuss these matters further – as it happens, this is currently the point I have reached in my commentary on the Torah, so you can help me out on this! Let's…'

He stopped as the voice of the qadi rang around the courtyard. 'In the name of Allah, the Beneficent, the Most Merciful…' Turning, Abraham and Yehuda saw the qadi standing nearer to the bonfire, which was now burning steadily. 'This,' he shouted, 'is the last copy of the *Ihya* that we have found in Córdoba.' As he held up the book for all to see, the courtyard was totally silent apart from the crackling of the fire. 'As we destroy this haram work of heresy, let it be accepted by all that, in these times, the gates of *ijtihad* are now closed.'

The qadi held out the volume and a mufti covered it in oil. A quiet murmur once again began to build in parts of the crowd, which became a single shout of protest when qadi threw the book into the fire.

The amir once again banged the qadi's staff on the ground. In the silence that followed the amir said, 'It is over. Depart in peace.'

For a tense moment nobody moved and nobody spoke, until the notables started to process along the pathway towards the prayer hall. People in the crowd then turned towards the exits and the quiet murmur of normal conversation resumed.

Abraham turned back to Yehuda. 'I was going to say, let's meet again very soon. Which synagogue are you going to attend?'

'We haven't yet decided which would be best for us. Our house is in the Sharie Alhamman, so we have a lot to choose from.'

'Come to the new synagogue in the Sharie Alhazzarat for evening prayers tomorrow. It's not far from where you live and I think you'll like it. There's a lot of *darosh*, a lot of enquiring, in that community! I'll meet you there and show you round.'

'Fine, I will come soon. Meanwhile, we should leave here. Let's see if we can catch Ahmad on the way out.'

They joined the crowd as people moved, quiet and subdued, towards the courtyard gates. At the north-west gate they stopped and waited for Ahmad.

*

Not long after the book burning, Ali ibn Yusuf returned to Marrakesh, the centre of his Almoravid empire. Meanwhile, in the same year, 1109, Urraca became Queen of Léon-Castile after the death of her father, Alfonso VI. The fears that Yehuda and his friends had expressed about Urraca proved to be justified. Her relish for power was matched only by her hostility to the Andalucían way of life and to Muslims and Jews. Her husband,

Raymond of Burgundy, had died two years before, but Urraca found a fellow spirit in Alfonso I, King of Aragon and Navarre. When they married, their combined kingdom became unassailable in Christian Spain. Alfonso styled himself Emperor of Spain and began a series of successful campaigns against the Muslim rulers of Andalucía, as well as some Christian kings. The climax came in 1118, when the Catholic Church declared a Crusade in Andalucía. Many Frenchmen joined Alfonso, who conquered Zaragoza at the end of that year and went on to achieve more victories, earning the nickname 'the Battler'. Muslims and Jews fared badly in the territories conquered by the crusaders.

Meanwhile, Ali ibn Yusuf also had many other problems to confront, not least a violent rebellion against Almoravid rule by the citizens of Córdoba in 1121, supported by the *fuqaha*, the Muslim judges. Forced to return to Córdoba to deal with the rebellion, Ibn Yusuf reluctantly negotiated a peace with the *fuqaha* and the citizens. He then declared a *jihad* against Alfonso the Battler and his followers. Very soon, however, Ali left his brother Tamim ibn Yusuf in charge in Andalucía and returned to Marrakesh to confront the Almohads. A Berber religious scholar, Muhammad ibn Tumart, had founded the Almohad movement in the Atlas Mountains, to oppose what he saw as the decadence and secularism of the Almoravids. The Almohads challenged Ibn Yusuf and his Malikite scholars in Fez and Marrakesh, but then withdrew to the mountains. Ibn Tumart declared himself the Mahdi, throwing down the gauntlet to challenge Almoravid rule.

9

FLOURISHING
CÓRDOBA 1123

You are a locked garden, my sister, my bride.
a spring enclosed, a fountain sealed.

The Song of Songs, 4:12

Ali ibn Yusuf was less friendly towards the Jews than his father
had been – indeed, under pressure from the Moroccan *fuqaha* Ali
banned Jews from living in Marrakesh, although they were allowed
to come into the city to do business. The situation in Córdoba,
however, was very different. The long tradition of Muslims, Jews,
and Christians living peacefully together remained the norm, and
Jews were able, for the most part, to go about their business and
perform their religious duties as they had before.

Yehuda joined Abraham ibn Ezra's synagogue in Sharie
Alhazzarat and gradually became a community leader there –
teaching, responding to religious questions and arbitrating in
religious disputes. His medical practice flourished, and, like
many doctors, he also made a good living as a merchant trading
in medical supplies, herbs and spices, and even paper. Somehow,

he also found the time to continue writing poetry – love poems, tributes to friends and, increasingly, religious poems – which were becoming famous in Andalucía and beyond.

His daughter Miriam fulfilled her potential as an excellent scholar and also helped her mother in her midwifery practice. As Miriam reached maturity but remained unmarried, however, Deborah started giving Yehuda a hard time about his failure to find a husband for her. In vain he pointed out that it wasn't just a question of finding a husband, but of finding a husband acceptable to Miriam. She had rejected what seemed like scores of perfectly eligible men – some rich, some learned, some handsome, some all three. They all fell short of her standard. Deborah and Yehuda couldn't establish what exactly her standard was, but it seemed to be a combination of worldliness and religiosity, learning and imagination, and seriousness and wit that nobody in the world could attain. Certainly, no biblical character had attained it; Yehuda thought that you'd have to combine King Solomon and King David and Moses and Joseph to satisfy Miriam.

Deborah would often say that Yehuda ought to act like a real father and insist that Miriam should marry this candidate or that. Again, it was in vain that he pointed out that insisting wouldn't have worked with Deborah herself when she was young: no amount of 'insistence' by her father would have persuaded Deborah to marry Yehuda if she hadn't wanted to, and Miriam was at least as stubborn as her mother.

One evening Yehuda came home after a particularly tiring day. He had spent the morning at the Alcázar dealing with the minor ailments of the women of the Almoravid harem; the middle of the day in his own surgery; and the afternoon in the synagogue ruling on some rather complex religious cases.

He had hardly begun his meal when Deborah started again on the old theme. Miriam was out studying with a group of women under the tutelage of Abraham ibn Ezra. Deborah said that it was all very well letting her do what she wanted, but learning wouldn't get her a husband. Miriam was now twenty-three years old and there were hardly any women of her age still unmarried. Yehuda should do his duty as a father and find her a husband.

She carried on in this vein for some time and eventually, tired and exasperated, Yehuda said, 'Very well, Deborah, I swear by almighty God that I will marry Miriam to the very next unmarried man who enters our house.'

At that very moment, Shulamit came into the *majlis* to say that she had admitted a young mendicant who had called at the door: should she feed him in the kitchen or did they want to see him first? Horrified, Deborah and Yehuda stared at each other. He had just sworn a solemn oath – something he almost never did – and now God had called him to account. The man standing in the courtyard, if unmarried, would have to become Miriam's husband, whoever he was.

The man was indeed unmarried, a young wandering mendicant who introduced himself as Solomon ben Joseph. Naturally, they didn't immediately invite him to marry their daughter, but they did invite him to stay with them for a while and study with Yehuda. On that first day he was very reticent, saying virtually nothing about himself and giving answers of only a word or two when addressed. He seemed to perk up a little when Miriam arrived home and she was introduced to him, but he still said very little.

The next day, Yehuda returned from his study in the synagogue a little preoccupied. When Miriam asked what the matter was, he told her that he'd written a long *kina*, an *Ode to Zion*, but was stuck on the last verse. He had written sixteen verses but couldn't find the right four lines to finish the poem. Solomon overheard him and asked to see the draft. He read it through, picked up a pen and immediately wrote a perfect ending, addressing Jerusalem with references to the Psalms and to Ezekiel and to the Book of Daniel. The verse read:

Happy is he who stands and waits, and sees
*   Your light rising as dawn breaks over him, and beholds*
the goodness of Your chosen ones, and rejoices
*   in Your joy when you return to your former state.*

The last line echoes the Book of Ezekiel:

And your sisters, Sodom and her daughters, shall be restored
to their former state, and Samaria and her daughters shall be
restored to their former state, and you and your daughters shall
be restored to your former state... I on My part will recall My
covenant with you in the days of your youth, and establish with
you an everlasting covenant.

Having thus shown the most extraordinary scholarship and poetic skill, Solomon revealed his full name, Abu l-Rabi' Solomon ben Joseph ibn Gabbai. He was a nephew of Abraham ibn Ezra. He had been brought up in Zaragoza but fled the previous year when it was conquered by King Alfonso the Battler and his Mozarabic Christian allies. He wandered as a mendicant for a year before seeking out his uncle Abraham in Córdoba. It was Abraham who had sent him to their house to introduce himself, but they hadn't asked him why he had come and he had chosen not to tell them. He had decided to let things develop at their own pace.

Yehuda often told this story. 'Who can understand the ways of God?' he would conclude. 'I'd foolishly sworn an oath, and instead of punishing me, God sent a man who showed himself to be irresistible to Miriam – tall and handsome, learned beyond his years, a skilled poet, a wit and a trickster.'

Solomon and Miriam were married within a year and a daughter, Hannah, was born a year after that. The poem that Solomon finished, the *Ode to Zion*, is now one of Yehuda's most famous.

10

TRANSITIONS
CÓRDOBA, 1126

The remnants of Zion residing in Spain
Here among the Arabs, there among the Christians,
Trembling, ready to leap forward to the Temple,
yet trusting and calm, like a child at the breast.
Yehuda Halevi (from Ode to Zion)

As Yehuda sat in his study, restlessly arranging and rearranging his papers, Shulamit came to the door with Yehuda's granddaughter, Hannah, now nearly a year and a half old, asleep in her arms. Though Shulamit's hair was now grey, she still stood straight and gracious, a picture of calm assurance. Yehuda's hair was also beginning to turn grey, though he was still lean and vigorous, unlike most of his friends who had turned fifty, like him, but were more self-indulgent than he was.

'Any news?' Yehuda asked.

'No, sir,' Shulamit replied. 'Miriam is still in labour; it could be a while yet. But you have a visitor – Joseph ben Samuel ibn al-Ukhtush has just arrived from Granada. Shall I ask him to come back tomorrow?'

Yehuda put aside the papers and got to his feet. 'No, no, Shulamit, we can't turn Joseph away after his long journey, and in any case, he's not been in Córdoba for a long time, so it'll be good to see him again. Let's go and welcome him.'

Joseph was waiting inside the front gate. He looked tired and a little haggard, but when he saw them approaching, he smiled broadly and straightened his shoulders.

'Yehuda, it's such a blessing to see you again.' He gestured at Shulamit and Hannah. 'And to meet your beautiful granddaughter – Shulamit has already introduced Hannah to me.'

'It's very good to see you too, my friend,' Yehuda replied, embracing him. 'How long has it been? Two years, three?'

'More than three years – I've been so busy trading with Almería and Egypt that I haven't had time to visit Córdoba. Last time I was here was before Miriam was betrothed. Now you have a granddaughter!'

'Yes, Joseph, and another grandchild on the way today if God wills. Miriam has been in labour since noon.'

Joseph took a step back. 'What? I'm sorry. I had no idea. This is a terrible time for me to intrude. Let me go and leave you in peace.'

'Not at all, Joseph, quite the opposite. I'd be glad of your company. I've been trying to work but failing miserably. Please do stay.' He turned to Shulamit. 'Where is Solomon?'

'He's in the *majlis*, sir, and to be honest I think he could do with some company too. He's more than a little anxious, as you might expect.'

'Very well, let's join Solomon in the *majlis*, then. Would you like something to eat or drink, Joseph? I know it's a bit early in the afternoon for wine, but to be honest I'd like a glass. I think Solomon might benefit from some too. Will you join us?'

'Yes, Yehuda, thank you, that would be very welcome.'

'Good – Shulamit, would you please ask the girls to bring wine to the *majlis*, and some olives and bread?'

'Certainly, sir.' She turned to Joseph as she moved towards the kitchen. 'And welcome back to Córdoba again, Master Joseph.'

'Thank you, Shulamit, it's good to be back.'

Solomon was sitting on the *martaba* as they entered the *majlis* – he was shuffling papers distractedly, without much focus, just as Yehuda had been doing earlier.

'Solomon,' said Yehuda, 'at last you get to meet Joseph ibn al-Ukhtush. He's just arrived from Granada. I know we're all a bit preoccupied today, but I couldn't turn him away.'

Solomon stood and came towards them, smiling warmly. 'Of course you couldn't turn him away, Father-in-law, not such a close and distinguished friend.' Turning to Joseph, he put his right arm across his chest and bowed. 'We've corresponded on business so much, sir, and Master Yehuda has told me so much about you that I feel I know you already. It's a pleasure to meet you in person at last.'

As Joseph returned the bow they made an incongruous pair: Solomon, tall and broad-shouldered; Joseph, short and stocky. Solomon's hair was long and blond and his eyes were green, while Joseph had jet-black hair and dark brown eyes.

They sat down as two of the servant girls entered with the wine, olives and bread. While the girls were pouring, the quiet of the house was shattered by a loud shriek from across the court-yard. One of the girls jumped and spilled a drop of the wine she was pouring onto the Persian rug. Her eyes widened as she stared, horrified, at the stain on the rug.

'Don't worry, Judith,' Yehuda said, 'you couldn't help it and it's only a small stain: it will remind us of the birth of the child!'

'Thank you, sir, I'm very sorry,' Judith said nervously as she dabbed at the wine stain with a cloth from the food tray.

'It's all right, Judith, you and Bilah can go now.'

After the servants had left Yehuda raised his glass. 'Welcome again to Córdoba, Joseph.' The rich, spicy aroma of the wine revived them all as much as the drink itself.

'This is excellent wine,' Joseph said, 'I don't think it's one I've tasted before.'

'It's a bobal wine from Murcia – Solomon brought some back with him from a business trip.'

'Well, my compliments, Solomon, on your excellent taste.'

Solomon, his head bowed, was tracing the pattern on the rug with his finger.

'Solomon?' Yehuda said gently.

'What? Oh, thank you, Joseph. I'm sorry, I'm a bit distracted at the moment.'

'I'm not surprised,' Joseph responded, 'it's always a difficult time for us fathers, the labour.'

Solomon smiled. 'But not as difficult as it is for Miriam.'

'I suppose Deborah's delivering the baby?'

'No, not exactly. Deborah is there but Miriam insisted that there should be another midwife present to take care of the delivery itself. She didn't want her mother to be her midwife! So Ruth bat Shmuel is there.'

'Understandably,' Yehuda said. 'I can imagine what tensions it would have generated if Deborah had been the sole midwife! Actually, I feel sorry for Ruth – she was trained by Deborah, who's probably giving the poor woman a hard time.'

Another shriek rent the air, followed by a loud groan. They glanced at each other but said nothing.

After a while, it was Joseph who broke the silence. 'So, last time I was here in Córdoba there was no Solomon. Now here you are, Solomon, married to Miriam, a father once and, please God, soon to have a second child. In Granada we heard a strange rumour about how the marriage came about. You must be aware of it.'

Solomon hesitated, both pleased and embarrassed. Seeing Solomon's discomfort, Yehuda intervened, 'Yes, we're aware of the rumour, Joseph, and if it's the one I think you mean, then it's true. I'd better recount the story in case the rumour has distorted it, if Solomon will permit me.'

Solomon nodded and Yehuda told Joseph the story, rounding off the account with a glowing tribute to Solomon's virtues as husband to Miriam.

Solomon held up his hand. 'Please, Yehuda, you're embarrassing me. Miriam is—' He sat up suddenly and looked towards the courtyard. 'What was that sound? Was that the cry of a baby?'

All three of them heard the cry, the distinct cry of a newborn. 'Praise be to God,' Yehuda said, and Solomon and Joseph responded, 'Amen.'

They waited in silence, but not for long. After a few minutes Deborah appeared at the door, hot and dishevelled. She carried the baby over to Solomon and said, 'Solomon, meet your new son, healthy and handsome. Miriam is also well and happy.'

*

The next day, Abraham ibn Ezra came over for the afternoon meal to meet his new grand-nephew, and Joseph ibn al-Ukhtush was invited to join them. When the visitors arrived, Miriam, Hannah and the new baby were sleeping so they were five for the meal.

Abraham, who was already well acquainted with Joseph, asked what brought him to Córdoba. Joseph explained that, with Alfonso the Battler constantly threatening Granada, he was planning to move to Córdoba for an extended stay. He had come on a short visit to arrange accommodation and various business matters in advance.

'You'll be coming at an interesting time here as well.' Abraham said. 'Ali ibn Yusuf has also decided to move back here after Alfonso defeated his brother Tamim at Arnisol.'

'Yes,' said Joseph, 'I had an interesting journey here, one step ahead of the crusaders! But I'm surprised that Ali is making his base here after the great Córdoba rebellion. I've been wanting to ask you, if I move here from Granada will I be jumping out of the smoke into the flame? Maybe I should move to Cairo! My friend and colleague Halfon ben Nataniel keeps trying to persuade me to join him there. I've sent him some of your poetry, by the way, Yehuda, and he is a great admirer: I'll put the two of you in touch. Perhaps you should come to Egypt with me.'

'I hope to travel to Egypt again one day, if only en route to Jerusalem, which I am increasingly longing to see.'

'Yes, Halfon tells me that he loves your *Ode to Zion* so much that he's had it read out in his synagogue!'

'I don't think you need to worry about coming to Córdoba, though, Joseph,' Yehuda said. 'At first things were rather precarious after the rebellion, when Ali granted peace on condition that the people compensated the Almoravids for destroyed or looted property. But he's now gradually won people around; especially since they've seen how the crusaders behave in the territories that they've conquered. Alfonso the Battler is nothing like the late Alfonso of León-Castile – the Battler's a brutal barbarian. The Almoravids are positively kind and gentle compared to the crusaders.'

'Not so kind to the Christians,' Deborah interjected. 'Ali has ordered the mass deportation of Mozarabic Christians to the Maghreb because some of them allied with Alfonso.'

'Yes indeed,' said Joseph, 'that's one of the reasons I'll be moving here – the exile of the Mozarabs along with the incursions of Alfonso will affect my business. I'll need to be here for some time while new arrangements are completed and things settle down.'

'Always assuming,' said Solomon, 'that the Jews aren't the next victims.'

This started the old debate, one that they had had many times. The Almoravids did not persecute or attempt to convert the *dhimmis*, the people of the Book, Jews and Christians. They were allowed to practise their religion openly, provided they continued to pay the *jizyah*, the Quranic tax on non-Muslims. They weren't in as favourable a position as they had been under the previous rulers, when they had been able to occupy even high office in the courts of the amirs. Those offices were now closed to Jews, but Jews were, on the whole, left in peace and were able to pursue their professions, as Yehuda was – even being engaged as a physician to the Almoravid court. Solomon, however, thought that the position of the Jews was precarious, and that it might deteriorate rapidly, as had that of the Mozarabic Christians. Yehuda and Deborah argued against him, though they recognised the risks as the position of the Almoravids was undermined by the attacks from the crusaders and the rise of the Almohads. Everyone was becoming nervous and uncertain.

The debate was cut short by the arrival of Miriam with Hannah and the baby. The rest of the conversation was devoted to the two children, and to Miriam, who was looking radiant and healthy if, understandably, a little tired.

*

As Joseph and Abraham were leaving, they agreed to meet Yehuda and Solomon at the synagogue for evening prayers. Entering the Alniquabat Plaza on their way to the synagogue, Yehuda and Solomon saw for the first time the impact of Ali's decision to exile the Mozarabic Christians. Outside the Mozarabic church on the north side of the plaza, several dozen people were piling chests and bags against the church wall. In front of the crowd an altercation was taking place between a small group of Lamtuna Almoravid soldiers and some local officials. They were shouting at each other so loudly that Solomon and Yehuda, and the Mozarabs around the church, stopped to listen. The Almoravids wanted to supervise the movement of the baggage, but the officials argued that such movement clearly fell within the remit of the muhtasib as the right-hand man of the qadi and the supervisor of markets and trade.

The citizens of Córdoba were used to such disputes between the local authorities and the Almoravids, which for the most part they regarded with a mixture of exasperation and amusement. On this occasion, however, the Mozarabs were clearly afraid that the Almoravids would turn their anger and frustration against them. Although the Almoravid officer had removed his veil while arguing with the officials, the rest of the soldiers remained veiled and it was difficult to tell just how angry they were becoming. Yehuda remembered the blood of Fuad ibn Said on his face in Granada thirty-five years before, and the many horrors that he had witnessed since then, and he shared the concern of the Mozarabs.

The argument was interrupted by the entry of the muhtasib himself, accompanied by a couple of other officials. Yehuda knew Asim ibn Muhammad well because, like most physicians, Yehuda traded in medicines and paper and often had to obtain licences and permits from the muhtasib – and because Asim's brother-in-law, Sa'id, was the tax collector to whom the Jews paid their *jizyah*. Asim was noted for his sound judgement and quiet authority, and he proved to be just the right person to restore calm on this occasion. As he approached, the local officials appealed to him to back them up, but he waved them to silence and bowed respectfully to the Almoravid officer. He remained with his head bowed until the officer bowed in return, then asked the officer, rather than his own officials, what the problem was.

Somewhat mollified, the officer quietly repeated that he needed to supervise the movement of the baggage.

'I quite understand that, Your Excellency, and of course you will need to supervise the movement of all baggage related to the... ah, to the relocation of these people. But when the Amir of the Faithful announced the deportation, he decreed that those Mozarabic Christians who were to be sent to the Maghreb would have a month to settle their affairs and prepare for the journey, did he not?'

'Yes, muhtasib, he did,' the officer replied.

'You will agree also, I think, that the month of grace still has two weeks to run?'

The officer could see where the muhtasib's questions were leading, but tempers had cooled by now and he affirmed with good grace that the journey would not take place for two weeks.

'In that case,' Asim went on, 'what is happening here is that the Christians are assembling their goods to put in storage before the journey – I assume that they'll be storing the baggage in the church here until they have to leave. The movement therefore seems to be an internal movement that falls under my jurisdiction rather than a movement in compliance with the amir's decree, which will of course be your responsibility. Perhaps we could interpret it that way and work accordingly. But if you disagree, then my officials will of course withdraw and leave the matter in your hands.'

Some of the soldiers clearly wanted just that, but the officer decided that honour had been satisfied and chose to withdraw with good grace. The soldiers therefore left the square and movement of the baggage resumed under the supervision of the local officials. The muhtasib turned to leave the plaza by the Sharie

Alhamman and as he walked past Yehuda, he actually winked at him. Yehuda understood his amusement: it is by playing such games of irony that the conquered reconcile themselves to living under a foreign yoke.

*

Abraham ibn Ezra asked to have a word with Yehuda after the evening prayers. They went to his study behind the synagogue to talk while Solomon went back to the house to be with Miriam and the children. The organisation of Yehuda's study was one of the ways in which his habits diverged from those of his former teacher, Moses ibn Ezra. Even at the best of times, Moses's study was a mess, with books and papers scattered around the floor, but Yehuda's was clean and tidy. Neat stacks of manuscripts and books were carefully arranged on shelves and around the walls of the room, leaving a clear space in the centre for several Armenian cushions and a low table.

A brass tray of drinks had been placed on the table. As they settled on the cushions, Abraham accepted a glass of pomegranate juice from Yehuda. He asked Yehuda about his visit to Isaac ibn Ezra and Leah in Toledo a few weeks earlier, when Moses had also been visiting.

'It was a sad time,' Yehuda said. 'Their brother Yusuf had just died, which was why Moses had returned to Toledo.'

'It was Moses I wanted to ask you about,' Abraham said. 'How did he seem?'

'Rather sad and restless, I'm afraid. He's been drifting around the Christian north. He still isn't on very good terms with Isaac and his other brothers – he came to Toledo because of Yusuf's death but left again soon after I came back to Córdoba.'

'It's strange. In some ways he hasn't recovered from the fall of Granada thirty years ago, and he's almost stopped writing poetry altogether. Yet his zest for scholarship and religion is as fierce as ever. Indeed, he's trying to persuade me to abandon poetry and focus on scholarship – he says that I have a special skill in it.'

'Indeed you do, Abraham – you're always one step ahead of me when we struggle to interpret the Torah – but you also have an extraordinary skill in poetry. You really mustn't give that up, especially at Moses's behest. He's saying the same thing to everyone. He's told me to give up poetry too!'

'Really?'

'Yes, but I don't see why I must give up one thing to do another. One of the joys of living in this world is that we can cultivate many fields – I find it really fulfilling to strive to succeed as a poet, a physician, a philosopher, a Torah scholar, a community leader and a trader.'

Abraham smiled. 'The last, a trader, is one thing that I'll never be. I've tried my hand at business in many different forms and each one of them has been a disaster. I'm sure that if my business was in candles the sun would never set and if I sold shrouds no one would die! My son Isaac is still a boy but he understands business better than me, as does your Solomon.'

'But you're a great teacher, so you'll always be able to support yourself. Maybe Moses is right – not that you should abandon poetry, but that you should spend more time on scholarship.'

'Perhaps. On that subject, Moses has just sent me a fascinating document. I think he may have given you one also. Can I smell sandalwood?'

'Sandalwood? What do you mean? Oh yes, the sandalwood box.' He leaned over and picked up the box that Moses had given him in Toledo, a beautifully carved box from India. Holding it to his nose, he breathed in the spicy aroma, then handed it to Abraham.

'He sent me a similar box,' Abraham said. 'May I open it?'

Yehuda nodded and Abraham opened the box, took out the scroll inside and read the title. 'Yes, it's the same document: King Joseph's story. How typical of Moses to choose an exotic box for an exotic correspondence.'

The scroll was a copy of the correspondence a hundred years previously between Hasdai ibn Shaprut, who was the Jewish vizier to Caliph 'Abd al-Rahman III of Córdoba, and Joseph, the King of the Khazars of Central Asia. The Khazar tribe had converted to Judaism two hundred years before that. In the correspondence, King Joseph told Hasdai the story of that conversion. The then King of the Khazars, Bulan, had had a dream in which an angel appeared to him, praised him for his works and promised him blessings if he would observe God's statutes.

'It's a fascinating story,' Yehuda said. 'I'm thinking of working something around it. Unless, of course, you want to use it,' he added hastily.

'Not me,' said Abraham, 'it's far too exotic for me. When I get fed up with poetry I devote myself to Torah study, and of course the Greek philosophers, with perhaps some mathematics and astronomy too.'

'There you are, you see, Abraham, you are no more capable of sticking to one thing than I am!'

11

RESTLESSNESS
CÓRDOBA, 1137

Looking into the mirror I spotted
a single strand of grey hair
and plucked it out. 'I'm easy game alone,'
it said, 'but what do you plan
to do with my troops close behind me?'

Yehuda Halevi

Old age affects the body but does not affect the soul. On
the contrary, the soul becomes stronger after fifty years,
whereas the body declines.

Ibn Sina (Avicenna), quoted in
Yehuda Halevi, The Kuzari

Yehuda's study of Torah and philosophy continued over the next
ten years, as did his writing of poetry, and his reputation continued to grow. His philosophical essays were well respected, though
not as famous as his poetry. Friends from Córdoba to Cairo hired
scribes to make copies of his poems, sometimes binding them in

single volumes, or *diwans*, which were widely circulated. He was now composing more poems of devotion to God than to women, though his love for Deborah remained as strong as ever. He was also delighting in Miriam and Solomon and his two grandchildren, Hannah and young Yehuda – Solomon and Miriam had given him the honour of naming their son after him.

His medical practice and community duties, however, also continued to expand, consuming more and more of his time and his spirit. Now over sixty years old, Yehuda was finding it difficult to cope with the demands placed on him. He remained lean and healthy and his mind was as sharp as ever, but he tired more easily. He was therefore becoming increasingly resentful of his public duties, which prevented him from devoting as much time and energy as he would like to his own pursuits, especially his studies.

In a letter to his friend Rabbi Habib of al-Mahdiyya he expressed his frustration:

> *I call this place 'Busy' because it keeps me on the run. It makes me the watchman of others' vineyards while I neglect my own, makes me have dealings with healing, diverts me from the words of the prophets...*

> *I wish, I wish, I wish that the Merciful One would restore me to what I was before and bring back my youth! I would go back to studying and achieve a wisdom I failed to achieve before. I would stay among the columns and listen like the students. But what can I do now that the white hairs have overwhelmed the black, tender youth has turned to sunset? Now that the turn of years has altered me, and the seasons made me falter and set me on coals? I have aroused myself and shaken out my clothing*

and rowed hard to get back to the dry land, yet I have failed.
I have searched out my conscience and laid bare my hidden
self; but no vision came, and my meditations brought me no
revelation from God.

Yehuda wrote that he thought himself trapped in a great city
inhabited by powerful men, hard masters whom he could satisfy
only by wasting his days on their whims and using up his years
healing their ills and their quarrels. 'We have tried to cure Babylon, but she has not been cured.'

One day Solomon consulted him about a passage in
Al-Ghazali's *al-Munqidh min al-Dalal* – Deliverance from
Error: 'Declare your jihad on twelve enemies you cannot see
– egoism, arrogance, conceit, selfishness, greed, lust, intoler-
ance, anger, lying, cheating, gossiping and slandering. If you
can master and destroy them, then you will be ready to fight
the thirteenth jihad, against the enemy you can see.' Discussing this again reminded Yehuda of conversations long ago in
Toledo, with Deborah and with Solomon ibn Ferruziel, about
Ibn Paquda and the duties of the heart. He came to realise that
it was not the outer world that was the source of his frustration, but his response to that world. He needed to declare jihad
on his inner enemies, to work on himself, instead of blaming
others for his frustration.

Deborah had indeed been saying that to him for some time,
supported by Miriam, but he had not understood what they were
talking about. Now, he determined to change his ways, to make
more time for his family and his studies and to spend less time
complaining about how busy he was.

His first step, his declaration of intent, was to undertake the
task of tidying and reorganising his study. It was cluttered with

piles of medical notes, business letters, bills of lading, invoices and other trivia alongside written questions and rulings on a host of major and minor religious issues. His room was beginning to resemble Moses ibn Ezra's study in Granada during the first weeks of the Almoravid conquest, redolent of confusion and despair. As Moses had done, he had often promised himself that he would tidy it up but kept procrastinating.

He got to work, gathering all the papers together in order to review them, discard the useless ones and put the useful ones in some sort of order. Moving a pile of particularly old and dishevelled papers, he uncovered the sandalwood box containing the correspondence with the King of the Khazars. He had reviewed it from time to time and had begun to conceive the vague idea of using it as the basis for a defence of the Jewish faith. This time, as he took it out of the box and started to read, he decided that it was finally time to turn that vague idea into action, that a defence of his despised faith could be a focus for his resolution to return to scholarship.

They lived in Córdoba, ruled by Muslims who claimed universality for their faith, and he still spent time in Toledo, ruled by Christians who just as forcefully claimed universality for theirs. Yehuda saw this belief as dangerous, but he knew that it would be even more dangerous to challenge it and fatal to claim universality for Judaism. Reading the Khazar letters, however, he saw very clearly that Jews did not actually claim universality – they had their own particular mission. That mission was given to them directly by God at Sinai, and the truths that they received there were the very basis for those other religions; yet, Yehuda felt, the other faiths scorned the truth of Sinai and claimed that their greater truth had overtaken it. Why, he thought, they had even stolen and distorted the Sabbath day! As Yehuda had written,

They compare – it's just lip service –
their day to my holy day.
Christians push it up to Sunday,
Muslims put it back to Friday.
How can Arab and Christian untruths
fool the People who have the truth?

It's time, he thought, to push back – not to deny the universal truths of their faiths, but to uphold the particular truth of his. He did not, of course, want everyone to convert to Judaism as the legendary Khazars had done, but he did want Jews and non-Jews to understand that Jews stood for an eternal truth, a particular truth to which other traditions owed an important debt. He would use the story of the King of the Khazars to defend that truth.

At the evening meal that day, after Hannah and young Yehuda had gone to bed, he floated the idea to Deborah, Miriam and Solomon, who all thought it a very bad idea – though for different reasons.

Deborah said that Judaism didn't need defending; she thought that Yehuda would be better off reconciling Judaism with Sufism and philosophy, since he was so passionate about all three. Yehuda responded that this was exactly what the work would do, through its 'defence' of Judaism. Deborah looked dubious but said that she would wait and see.

Solomon thought that there was nothing wrong with Islam for Muslims, or for that matter with Christianity for Christians, so what was the point of Yehuda exposing himself to danger by attacking them? Yehuda agreed that it would be both mistaken and dangerous to attack them, but in this work there would be no attack. The king would hear from a Muslim and a Christian before hearing from the Chaver, the Jewish scholar. The king would reject

Christianity and Islam simply because they were inaccessible to him as an outsider. He would find in what the Chaver told him about Judaism an accessible way to serve God. Solomon thought this rather weak, as did Deborah and Miriam, but they agreed that it was safer than a head-on attack on Islam and Christianity.

The most telling critique, however, came from Miriam. 'I remember the manuscript,' she said. 'You showed it to me some time ago. It began with an angel appearing in a dream to King Bulan. The angel praised him for his works and promised him blessings if he accepted God's statutes. Is that right?'

'Yes,' Yehuda said, 'that's how the whole conversion started.'

'But it doesn't work, Father. How many times have you told us that what matters is what we do, how we behave? Being a good Jew is all about practical action; everything else is second-ary. The angel told the king that his works were pleasing to God. If the king's actions were pleasing to God, then the king was already following God's statutes, so why did anything need to change? And if he didn't know God's statutes, then how could he be taking actions that were pleasing to God? In other words, since the king's actions were already pleasing to God, conversion to Judaism was unnecessary!'

The stunned silence that followed this pronouncement was broken by Deborah. 'There you are, Yehuda, my darling – you've brought Miriam up as a scholar and she has defeated you. Maybe your detractors were right to say that you shouldn't have taught Miriam the intricacies of Talmudic reasoning.'

Yehuda reached out, took Deborah's hand and kissed it. 'If that's true, my love, then it's you who are to blame. It's you who insisted that a girl has as much right as a boy to learn the Talmud.'

'This is all very charming,' Miriam said rather curtly, 'but what about the point I'm making?'

'Give me a moment to think about that, Miriam,' Yehuda said. They all waited while he took a pomegranate from the fruit bowl, held it in his palm, looked at it, returned it to the bowl and picked up and peeled an orange. As he put the first segment of the orange in his mouth, he looked up and saw that they were all smiling at him.

'I'm sorry,' he said sheepishly, 'I was a little preoccupied.'

'How unusual,' Deborah said.

'Yes – I mean, no. I suppose it's not unusual. I realise that Miriam is absolutely right. If I'm going to use this story, I'll have to turn it around. What the king should be told by the angel is that although his *intentions* are pleasing to God, his *actions* are not. The king will set out in search of a religion whose way of action is pleasing to God. A key theme must be the importance of action for drawing near to the divine.'

'Perhaps,' said Solomon, 'you should bring in a philosopher to contrast speculation with action.'

'That's an excellent idea, Solomon, although you are perhaps being a little unfair to the philosophers! King Bulan will dismiss the philosopher because the king wants a specific way of serving God, not an objective description of the universe. Then he'll hear from the others.'

So began the work that ended with the publication two years later of Yehuda's great work, *The Kuzari: in Defence of the Despised Faith*.

*

First thing the next morning, the *khadim*, the servant who worked for Yehuda's family on their business affairs, came to say that a shipment had just arrived at the South Gate from Almería, containing goods and correspondence from Alexandria. Solomon agreed to go and see to their part of the shipment: he had by then virtually taken over the management of the trading side of the family's affairs.

Despite his resolution to spend more time on his studies, Yehuda had a full programme that day in Córdoba, which was going through yet another period of instability. Tashfin, Amir Ali's son, had proved a skilled governor after he replaced his uncle Tamim in Andalucía, but he was faced with repeated incursions by the crusaders and with defiance from a number of local Muslim rulers. Some Mozarabic Christians once again supported the crusaders, and Tashfin had just ordered a second mass deportation to the Maghreb. Meanwhile, Almoravid rule in Marrakesh was under threat from the Almohads, under their new leader, Abd al-Mumin, and Tashfin was gathering troops to send across to help his father Ali in the fight against the Almohads.

All these movements of people spread disease and anxiety as well as conflict and disruption to trade. This meant that Yehuda's work as a physician had doubled and his communal duties had become more complex – as he had complained in his letter to Rabbi Habib. On that particular day, he didn't manage to get home between the time he left for morning prayers and the end of evening prayers.

When he reached the house, he found Abraham ibn Ezra there with Solomon – neither of them had been at evening prayers. Abraham's son Isaac had moved temporarily to Alexandria, and Solomon worked closely with both of them on mutual business matters, so Yehuda wasn't surprised to see Abraham at his house. On this occasion, however, Abraham and Solomon both looked troubled, as did Deborah and Miriam – who were bringing in wine and food.

As soon as they had exchanged formal greetings Yehuda asked, 'What's the matter? Is there something wrong with the shipment?'

'Not with the shipment, no,' Solomon said, handing him a letter.

The letter was from Isaac to Solomon. Isaac had been in Alexandria for several months by then and was clearly very happy there. The Fatimid caliphate was much more stable than the Almoravid empire – the Frankish crusaders were occupying the Holy Land, where fighting continued sporadically, but they showed little or no inclination to move against Egypt. The Fatimid caliph in Cairo, Al-Hafiz Il-Din Allah, was a sophisticated and tolerant ruler, who treated Jews and Coptic Christians, and even Sunni Muslims, favourably unless they directly challenged his authority. Indeed, he had recently issued a decree declaring that 'we believe that we should spread wide the mantle of justice and benevolence and embrace the different religious communities with mercy and compassion. Measures to improve conditions should include Muslims and non-Muslims alike, who should be provided everything they might hope for in the way of peace and security.'

This was well known in Andalucía, but the letter made it clear that Isaac's admiration went beyond respect for Fatimid toler-ance. After a few paragraphs on business matters, Isaac went on to describe how he had been drawn to the Daniel Mosque, where there was an alim who was a convert from Judaism. The alim, now named Sabir, was instructing him in the principles of Islamic theology, which Isaac was finding very intriguing.

As Yehuda read this he looked up from the page and saw that everyone was watching him – Abraham, Solomon, Deb-orah and Miriam.

'Intriguing,' he said, 'he's finding Islamic theology "intri-guing". I understand why you are concerned.'

'Yes, indeed,' said Abraham, 'among the papers from Alexan-dria that Solomon has put in your study there is a letter to you from Halfon ben Nataniel. Halfon wrote to me too. I'm sure that he'll be telling you that Isaac's attraction to Alim Sabir's Islam goes beyond academic interest. Halfon says that Isaac is not yet rushing to conversion, but there is a severe danger that he will convert.'

'I'm so sorry, my dear friend,' said Deborah, 'and I know what you are going to say. You are going to tell us that you must go to Alexandria.'

Abraham took a deep breath, his eyes welling with tears. 'Yes, Deborah, I have no choice. The caliph's tolerance goes only so far: it doesn't extend to converts who want to change their minds. If Isaac converts to Islam, then it will be death for him to return to Judaism. I must stop him.'

He straightened up and wiped away a tear with his hand. 'I believe I can succeed. Halfon tells me that he has persuaded Isaac to take things slowly and wait until after the High Holy Days before making any kind of decision. The alim is not pushing him to hurry with a decision. The messengers told your *khadim* that the ship will return to Alexandria as soon as the westerly winds begin in a couple of weeks, so I can catch it and be in Alexandria in good time.'

'Please let us know if there's anything at all we can do to help,' Deborah said. 'Yehuda and I will, of course, support you as much as we can to minimise the disruption, as will Solomon and Miriam.'

'Actually,' Abraham went on, looking at Yehuda, 'this isn't such a disruption after all. As you know, Yehuda, I have been thinking of a journey to the Ashkenazi lands and this just means that I'll have to start with a trip to Alexandria.'

'Really?' Miriam said, perplexed, 'I hadn't heard that. Why would you want to go there? Those lands are full of Frankish barbarians.'

'Maybe they are, but my cousin Moses ibn Ezra tells me that the position of the Ashkenazi Jews is becoming more secure, even while Andalucía becomes less stable. The Jews of Italy and France are developing a taste for the learning of the Arabic world and the

Greek texts that have been preserved by the Arabs. The Frankish Christians are also starting to look at them. I'm tempted to go and share some of our learning with the Jews of Rome and France and perhaps even England. They can't read Arabic and I don't know much Latin, but I'm thinking about writing a Torah commentary for them in Hebrew or Aramaic.'

'You mean like Rashi's commentary?' Miriam asked, looking at Yehuda. He had long ago told her about his encounters with Rashi's daughter in Lucena, and this had stimulated her interest in his commentaries, which were indeed outstanding.

Abraham answered, 'No, not at all like Rashi's. He explains the Torah on the basis of ancient Midrash and uses this to reconcile everything in the Bible with everything else, however contradictory it is. I would apply strict rational standards of accuracy, grammatical precision and reliability. That's what we have learned from the Greeks through the Arabs.'

Deborah smiled and poured some more wine for everyone. 'There you are, Abraham, it seems that you're feeling a little better already. You talk of accuracy, grammatical precision and reliability as if they were to be relished like wine and olives and marzipan.' She raised her beaker. 'Let's drink to your success in talking some sense into your son, and to your new commentary on the Torah – may it be as successful as your poetry.'

They all responded 'Amen' and drained their glasses, and Abraham left the house in a slightly better frame of mind, at least for the time being.

*

That evening, as they were preparing for bed, Yehuda told Deborah for the first time about a plan that he was beginning to form – about his growing desire to go to Jerusalem, to see Zion, perhaps to live there. At first she didn't take him seriously, but as she realised that he was indeed serious she got more and more angry. She pointed out, rightly, that he had hardly travelled outside Andalucía, apart from a few business trips across to Oran or Tangier; that he was over sixty years old and it was a bit late to become an adventurer; that the Mediterranean was becoming increasingly dangerous, riddled with pirates and insane crusaders; that he had responsibilities to his family, not to mention his community; and that there was no way she was going to leave her home and her family to come with him.

Yehuda responded, when he could, that Solomon had made a couple of voyages to Alexandria and reported not only that it was safe there but that he would be welcomed as a famous poet and philosopher; that this was confirmed by Halfon ben Nataniel and others in Egypt, who were urging him to come; that it was a relatively short journey from Alexandria to the Holy Land, which was much less dangerous than it had been now that the fighting had virtually ended; and above all that he felt an increasingly strong belief that Zion was a special place, that the *Shechina*, the presence of God, was focused on Zion and that he must experience that. Maybe he wouldn't decide to live there, but he must at least see it.

Deborah was wholly unconvinced. She said, rather bitterly, that his famous Ode to Zion and similar poems about Jerusalem, like his early love poems, were self-indulgent, as Rachel bat Yitzchak had identified all those years ago in Lucena. It was totally selfish of him to abandon all his responsibilities, and indeed to betray his love for her and Miriam and the grandchildren in order to pursue some vague yearning to see Zion.

They argued for a long time, both of them becoming increasingly frustrated and unhappy. Eventually, exhausted, they agreed to put the whole topic aside and revisit it in a year's time. If he still felt the same way, then they would have to discuss what could be done about it.

They had similar arguments from time to time over the next two years, until the publication of *The Kuzari*, in which, among other issues, he dealt at some length with the importance of the Holy Land as a sacred dwelling of God. By that time, Deborah had come to realise that Yehuda was not to be dissuaded. She allowed him to plan a journey to Egypt and then on to Jerusalem.

Meanwhile, Abraham had succeeded in persuading Isaac not to convert to Islam and had journeyed from Egypt to Rome, while Isaac returned to Córdoba to manage his father's business. By the time Yehuda was preparing to travel, Isaac needed to return to Alexandria on business, and Solomon agreed to accompany him as far as Jerusalem, so the three of them set off together.

PART II

THE JOURNEY (1140-41)

12

YEHUDA'S FIRST LETTER TO DEBORAH

The Sultan's Ship, at sea, approaching Oran,
26 Tamuz 4900 [16 July 1140]

To my darling Deborah, beloved of my soul, greetings

I don't know whether my heart has stopped inside me, or wandered off in search of you, back in Córdoba. Were it not for that emptiness, I could bear the cramped squalor of this ship, the cacophony of creaks and shouts, the endless, queasy motion. Every time I close my eyes to seek some peace, I see you standing on the quay at Málaga with our beloved daughter and grandchildren, then turning away, your head bowed. I don't know how long I can bear this separation.

What doubles the pain for me, as I know it does for you, is that you never seemed to understand why I must make this last journey, why I absolutely must see Jerusalem before I die. You have accepted it because you are you. But you still question how I could decide to abandon you and everything else that I love in order to seek some epiphany in what is, after all, only another place. Only another place – you have said those very words. But that's like saying 'only a poem', or 'only angels' or only, my dearest love, only you.

Only now do I begin to see why you questioned my reasons for doing this. It's not because you did not understand, but because you understand so much more than I will ever know, fool that I am. I used to say that my heart was in the East, while I am at the far end of the West. Do you remember that poem?

> *How can I taste or savour what I eat?*
> *How keep my pledges – while Zion lies*
> *shackled to Christendom and I to Arabia bound?*
> *Giving up the riches of Spain would be as easy for me*
> *as it will be precious in my eyes to feast*
> *on the dust and rubble of the shrine razed to the ground.*

The riches of Spain? What was I thinking? Of course I don't find it hard to give up riches and luxury – well, yes, it is hard to sleep on a bale of hides in a crowded, noisy, stinking hellhole of a cabin, and to eat the muck that they have been feeding us on this ship, but that's not the point. When I wrote that, I was thinking of riches in the sense of fine houses and soft beds and precious jewels. How could I have ignored the jewel of jewels, the giving up of which is the hardest thing I have ever done? The jewel of jewels is you, my love, my fair one, my friend – and my other jewels are my daughter Miriam and my grandchildren Hannah and young Yehuda.

Did I not realise what it would mean for me to leave you, to leave Miriam and the children? Or what my leaving would mean for you and for them? Yes, of course I had a glimmering of it, but I didn't anticipate how painfully it would shred my heart. You saw, you warned me. For you, that was the overwhelming issue. Yet, for all the pain of it, I still know that this is what I must do. Whatever the cost, I must make this pilgrimage to Zion.

The sea is relatively calm as I write this on deck. The moon is glowing in the grey, turquoise and pink of the twilight, casting a sheen on the darkening sea. Preparing for the evening prayers, my book fell open at Psalm 118. 'This is the day that God has made, let us rejoice and be glad in it!' And I do, my love, I do. For all the sorrow and pain, I do rejoice, at where I have come, at where I am now, and at where I am going, with God's will. And wherever that will be, I shall remain ever your loving

Yehuda ben Shmuel Halevi

13

FIRST PORT
OF CALL: ORAN

Soon after the harbour pilot boarded at dawn off Cape Falcon, the *Sultan's Ship* rounded the final headland into the Bay of Aiguades. With a growing sense of excitement, most of the passengers flocked to the foredeck to catch the first sight of the port of Oran. Solomon ben Joseph pushed through the mass of passengers, asking those he recognised, 'Have you seen Master Yehuda?' A woman pointed to the prow, where the old man was holding on to a forestay and gazing at the sea ahead, his robe billowing in the wind.

'Master!' Solomon called as he made his way forward. Turning, Yehuda beckoned Solomon to join him.

'Come here, Solomon, we're getting close, I can smell the land! Can you see, there it is, I think, the port of Oran, just to left of that promontory? All these days without a sight of land, and now at last we can see the port.'

Peering at the bay ahead in the morning light, Solomon could just make out a darker patch on the horizon. 'Yes, Master, I think I see it.' As the ship lurched, he grabbed a stay to steady himself. 'Are we safe, here in the front of the ship? It feels a lot more stable on the main deck.'

'Safe, my boy?' Yehuda smiled. 'The sea is full of storms and pirates and disease. There's no safety here!'

They heard a splash in the sea and, to Solomon's alarm, Yehuda leaned yet further over the gunwale. He shouted back to Solomon, 'Look, the dolphins have come to welcome us ashore.' Edging closer to the gunwale, Solomon saw four or five dolphins swimming alongside and in front of the ship, cavorting playfully as if challenging the ship to a race. Other passengers soon saw them, and there was a delighted murmur as they moved towards the gunwale for a closer look.

'Ladies and gentlemen!' The purser – the *wakil* – was shouting to make himself heard over the rattle of the rigging and the babble of the crowd. 'I must ask you to move away from here. The crew will need to get to the for'ard anchor, so please move towards the main deck.' As the crowd reluctantly started to move aft, he added, 'Would those merchants who have goods to land at Oran please go below decks and stand by your bales, so that you can ensure that the correct goods are taken.'

Yehuda approached the *wakil*. 'Ismat,' he said, 'did you say anchor? Are we anchoring?'

Surprised by the question, the old purser said, 'Why yes, my lord, have you not been to Oran before? The *Sultan's Ship* has a very deep draught, so we can't risk running aground on the sandbanks off Hai Omaria, especially with the wind so fresh from the west.'

'Not go into port?' said Solomon. 'Really?'

Yehuda patted Solomon on the back. 'Oh, poor lad. I'm disappointed too. I'd hoped to make landfall. But it seems our ship is too big and must anchor in the roads.'

'You can go ashore if you wish, sir,' said Ismat. 'We'll be here a day or two, and there are many barges due to carry cargo and passengers to and from the ship, so you can hitch a ride on one of them.' He looked around to see that no one was in earshot and leaned towards Yehuda. 'Best not to leave your own goods alone too long though, sir, some of them coming on board from Oran are a rum lot, I hear.'

Yehuda matched the *wakil*'s conspiratorial tone. 'What do you mean, Ismat, a rum lot?'

'Well, sir, some of them are refugees from Tlemcen, fleeing from the Almohads, and not all of them so innocent either, I'm told. It's—'

Solomon interrupted, bursting with the news, 'Yes, so I've heard too. Eli told me – you know, Eli the son of Nathan, the scribe – well, he spoke to the pilot, who said that Abd al-Mumin's Almohads are on another campaign, this time in Tlemcen. They're killing hundreds of Jews.'

'Yes, Solomon,' said Yehuda gently, 'the ship is full of stories. But the *wakil* here probably knows more than we do, since he'll be making up the passenger manifest. Who are you expecting, Ismat?'

'Well, Rabbi, with respect, the Almohads are killing more than Jews – Christians too and any Muslims they think are heretics, which means anyone who sets a foot wrong or mutters a word against them. There's many have fled to Oran – Muslims, Christians and Jews. People in Oran are afeared – they think Al-Mumin is planning to lead his Almohads against them and bring down the whole Almoravid amirate.'

Looking up at the gulls quarrelling above the ship, Ismat muttered, 'Two gulls at the mast, not such a good omen.' He spat over the rail and turned back to Yehuda. 'I'm sorry, my lord, I must return to my duties. But if you and Master Solomon want to go ashore, you just make your way amidships when the barges come out. I'll make sure you get to see the officials first to clear your papers.'

'Thank you, Ismat, you're very kind,' Yehuda said as the *wakil* saluted and moved aft. 'So, Solomon, let's go and find Isaac and prepare ourselves to go ashore.'

*

At the quayside, Isaac ibn Abraham leapt off the barge first and held out his hand to Yehuda, who stepped up to the quay, followed by Solomon. 'Well, we were fed up with the movement of the *Sultan's Ship*,' Yehuda said, 'but it was positively stable compared to that little barge. I felt, as Shmuel the Nagid put it, like a little worm on a splinter! Thank you again for your hand, Isaac – I'm not as nimble as I used to be.'

He straightened up and took a deep breath, revelling in the sensation of standing on solid ground, and taking in the smells of the port – the spices, the smoke from the cooking fires and, he thought, even the scent of soil. Isaac and Solomon were gazing in wonder at the bustle on the waterfront. The sailors from the *Sultan's Ship* were already heaving bales off the barge. The stevedores dragged them to the loading compound for Ismat to check against his cargo manifest. In the compound, half a dozen merchants from the ship gossiped with their Oran agents. Several carts, already heavily laden, rumbled cautiously away along the crowded quay to the enormous warehouses that cut off the view of the city, apart from the mosque and citadel perched at the top of the Aljibal Algharbia hills to the west, glowing in the light of the morning sun.

'Can you feel the change, boys?' Yehuda said. 'After all that time at sea, standing on land feels as if it's the earth that is moving and we who are steady. *Blessed are you, our living God, whose presence journeys with Your people.*'

'Amen,' Solomon and Isaac responded.

Isaac smiled. 'I love to hear the buzz of business at a port. It's like coming back to life after the confinement of the ship!'

'Yes, yes indeed, Isaac, it is delightful,' Yehuda said.

'So, Master, where do we go now?' Solomon asked.

Yehuda looked around. 'Well, I'd like to begin with something to eat. In the excitement of landing I haven't yet broken my fast. Let's find the *suq* and see if we can find some decent food.' He grinned. 'Just think of it, my friends, fresh bread and fresh fruit!'

As the three of them began to stroll towards the town, they saw half a dozen men pushing through the bustle towards them. Like Yehuda, they were dressed in the fine linen robes and turbans of Jewish courtiers and scholars, sober browns and maroons brightened by flashes of colour at the cuffs. The old man in front was looking in their direction, shouting, 'Master Yehuda? Yehuda Halevi?' Reaching the three companions, he stopped, breathing heavily, as the other men caught up with him. 'Forgive me, sir, but are you Master Yehuda Halevi?'

'Yes, sir, I am. What do you want of me?' Yehuda replied warily.

'I'm sorry, Revered Master, we should have been here to greet you sooner. I am Nachum ben Shlomo HaCohen, Warden of the community here in Oran.' Yehuda bowed slightly, and Nachum returned the bow. 'It's an honour to have you visit our city, sir. We have come at the request of the nagid to invite you to do him the honour of meeting him and the members of the community.'

'I'm most appreciative of your gracious welcome, Rab Nachum,' Yehuda replied, bowing slightly again, 'but how did you know I was coming?'

'We had a letter two days ago, brought on Captain Akwal's fast *khiti*. My business partner in Almería wrote to say that you were planning to sail to Alexandria on the sultan's new ship. We're so glad to have found you!' Finally, suppressing his excitement, Nachum took a deep breath and straightened up, adopting a tone more suited to his office. 'Esteemed Master, the community of

Oran and our leader, Nagid Gideon ben Moses, invite you to come and spend a little time with us while you are here.'

Deborah had warned Yehuda that he would often be expected at ports of call, and that fame had its obligations. Again, he longed for her to be with him, this time not just for her company. She was so much better at this sort of gathering, making community events less of a strain for him when she was around. But Deborah was not here. He would have preferred to take some food in the *suq* with Solomon and Isaac and wander quietly around the town. Having no choice, however, he gracefully accepted the invitation, and the men conducted the three travellers to a large compound to the east of the port.

Once inside the compound, Yehuda was able to relax a little. The courtyard was crowded with people who had come to greet the great scholar and poet, but Nagid Gideon had provided a light meal for Yehuda, Solomon and Isaac in a side room, where they ate and rested before encountering the community.

Yehuda agreed to lead a study session on the week's portion of the Torah, insisting that the women be allowed to attend the session. Some of the elders frowned and exchanged glances, making it clear that they considered this rather perverse, but nobody openly objected, and some women did pluck up the courage to sit at the back of the room. The Torah portion dealt with the detailed instructions for the robes of Aaron the High Priest, from the golden diadem on the turban to the golden bells and pomegranates all around the hem of the robe of the ephod. The women in particular were captivated by Yehuda's account of the meaning of the materials, the colours and the stitching of the robes.

The familiar, quiet concentration of the *shiur* was a delight to Yehuda after the bustle and noise of the sea voyage, and he was in fine form. As always, his deep scholarship, light touch and genius for telling stories enthralled the audience. Responding to their enthusiasm, he soon forgot his desire for a quiet time in the town.

One of the women seemed particularly interested in Yehuda, staring at him throughout the session. She was old, probably as old as Yehuda, and not dressed like the women of Oran. He guessed that she might be one of the refugees from Tlemcen. She seemed tired and defeated – she never joined the laughter when a joke was made, nor the brief exchanges between the women when a difficult point was being discussed.

When the session ended, the old woman was among those who approached Yehuda to congratulate him on the session or to ask further questions on the Torah portion. Nervous and ill at ease, she held back at the edge of the group, but when it began to break up, she approached Yehuda and touched his sleeve.

'Rabbi Yehuda, I don't suppose you remember me?' she said quietly. She raised a hand to brush back a loose strand of hair from her eyes, which, though sad, were clear and alert, belying her age. The expression on the woman's face stirred a faint memory in Yehuda.

'Why yes, madam,' he replied. 'You do look familiar – I thought so when I saw you at the back of the *shiur*. But I'm sorry, I can't remember where we've met.'

She shrugged, a little crestfallen. 'No, Rabbi, I'm not surprised, it was a very long time ago and I was only a serving girl then.' She looked up at him. 'My name is Rebekah bat Nathan, but you would only have known me as Rebekah. When...'

'But of course!' Yehuda exclaimed, clapping his hands. 'Rebekah! Now I remember. Yes, of course it's you, I can see that now. You worked for Isaac ibn Ezra in Córdoba. There was you and – what was her name – Chaya?'

'Yes, that's right, sir, me and Chaya. So you do remember!' Rebekah's smile lasted only a moment. 'Chaya, poor Chaya, she died last year.'

'That is sad. You had stayed in touch with her, then?' Yehuda felt drawn to this woman, intrigued by the evident depth of her sadness. He could see that she needed to tell someone her story.

'Yes, sir, when things got bad in Córdoba and Master Ibn Ezra and his family left the city for Toledo, both my family and Chaya's moved, first to Algeciras and then to Sijilmasa and Tlemcen. Oh, God in Heaven, I wish we'd stayed in Córdoba. It was…'

She was interrupted by Nachum HaCohen, the warden, who was pushing officiously towards Yehuda and Solomon. 'Sir,' he called, 'the nagid would be grateful to see you now, if you would be so kind. He has a few disputed cases on which wants your opinion – and he'd like to hear about the state of affairs in Andalucía.' He called to Solomon and Isaac, who were talking to another group nearby, 'Rab Solomon, you and the Master are to go and see the nagid. And you also, Rab Isaac ibn Ezra.'

'Yes, Rab Nachum,' Yehuda said, 'please go ahead with Solomon and Isaac and I'll join you very shortly.' He raised his hand to silence the warden's protestation. Nachum wasn't used to people keeping the nagid waiting, but he wasn't about to start an argument with Yehuda Halevi, so he shook his head and led Yehuda's companions towards the nagid's study. Yehuda turned back to Rebekah. 'I'm very sorry, Rebekah, I need to go, but I'd like to have a chance to speak to you some more. Are you staying around here?'

'No, Rabbi, but we'll have plenty of time to speak – I'm travelling on the *Sultan's Ship* to Alexandria, so we'll be together on the ship.'

'Why, that's excellent, Rebekah, we can continue our conversation on board!'

'If that's what you want, sir,' Rebekah answered with a wry smile. Yehuda watched her as she left the compound, her shoulders hunched once again. When she had disappeared from sight, he turned towards the nagid's study.

14

AT SEA, OFF TRIPOLI

Sailing from Oran, the *Sultan's Ship* was joined by another large merchantman, the *Salim*, a *qunbar* carrying silk, spices and timber, as well as by three light galleys. After the noise and bustle of the departure, the sailors had secured the sheets and gone below for their midday meal. The convoy began to make good headway in a moderate westerly wind and the passengers settled on deck to enjoy the sunshine as the ship rode the gentle swell of the sea. Those who had boarded at Oran found berths for themselves and started to get acquainted with their new neighbours.

While Yehuda sat in his usual place on the foredeck with his writing board, Solomon leaned on the gunwale, enjoying the gentle breeze and watching the other ships in the convoy.

'Those galleys are slowing us down,' Solomon said, to no one in particular, 'the *ghurab* is designed as a rowing vessel. It's true that it's a light vessel, but it doesn't have enough sail. So it's even slower than the heavy merchantmen like us and the *Salim*.'

'What a sailor you've become, my boy,' said Yehuda, 'but speed isn't everything. The *ghurab* can strike sail and use its oars in a gale. If our ship founders in a really bad storm, we'll be glad we have the galleys to rescue us. I'd rather travel slowly and safely than fast and perilously.'

'But God will protect us, Master: whatever happens is God's will,' said Solomon. 'As King David said in his Psalm:

If I take wing with the dawn, if I dwell at the ends of the sea,
there too Your hand leads me, and Your right hand seizes me.'

A pair of gulls squawked loudly over the mainmast, startling the men. Standing up as if to better see the gulls, Yehuda moved closer to Solomon and lowering his voice said, 'I have told you before, Solomon, you need to pay more attention to the rabbis and less to Al-Ghazali and the Sufis, wise though they are. Yes, whatever happens is God's will, but that doesn't mean that we're not responsible for what we do – God gives us the power to act, to change our destiny and that of the world.'

'But we don't determine the outcome, God does.'

'Yes, of course, but it's always a dialogue, it's a covenant between us and God. Do you remember that verse I wrote?

I asked to be near You,
with all my heart I called to You
and going out to seek You
I found You seeking me.

'We are Children of Israel, and *Isra'El* means "the one who struggles with God". The name "Israel" was given to the Patriarch Jacob after he wrestled with the angel.' Yehuda looked down at his gnarled hands, stained with ink, his right hand still holding his quill. 'We wrestle with God.' He lowered his voice again. 'We don't pay as much attention to submission as the Muslims

– after all, *Islam* means submission, but Jacob did not submit to the angel!'

Solomon was about to respond, but the *wakil*, Ismat, approached and saluted Yehuda. 'Excuse me, Rabbi, but there's a woman on the lower deck who told Isaac ibn Ezra that she wants to speak to you. She says you know her – name of Rebekah.'

'Ah, yes, Ismat, I do indeed know Rebekah. I haven't had a chance to exchange more than a few words with her since we boarded at Oran. Would you be so kind as to show her up with Isaac?'

'With pleasure, sir.' Ismat bowed and returned to the companionway to fetch Rebekah and Isaac.

'Sorry, Solomon, where were we?'

'We were wrestling with God, Master, but maybe we can continue after you've spoken to Rebekah.' He pointed to starboard, where a high breakwater was just visible, with two domes and four or five minarets rising behind it, shimmering in the morning sun. 'Do you know what that is on the horizon?'

'Ah, that's Tunis, sir,' said Ismat, arriving with Rebekah and Isaac, who had been waiting for him at the foot of the companionway. 'You're lucky you can see Tunis – we don't normally sail this close but we're hugging the shore as we sail into the Gulf of Hammamet, on account of the pirates out of Tripoli.'

'Pirates! What else must we endure now?' Rebekah shaded her eyes with her hand and stared nervously out to sea as if expecting the arrival of a pirate fleet at any moment.

Solomon smiled at Rebekah's agitation, but Yehuda and Ismat exchanged glances: both of them knew what it felt like to escape one horror only to be confronted with a new danger.

'No need to worry, ma'am,' Ismat said gently. 'The Fatimid Governor here has put a lid on the Tripoli pirates. They've been quiet all this year, though I doubt it'll last much longer. We also have some Egyptian soldiers with us on their way home – they're on that green *qunbar* on our port side. The pirates wouldn't mess with them. It's not only storms that make it safer to sail in convoy!'

Seeing that Rebekah was calmer, Ismat nodded at Yehuda and left.

Yehuda sat down and put aside his quill, ink and writing board. 'Rebekah,' he said, 'come and sit with us. Solomon, would you mind bringing extra cushions from the locker?'

Rebekah took a final glance at the empty sea and sat with Yehuda, Isaac and Solomon on the cushions, plucking at a loose thread in her worn woollen shift. She had asked to see Yehuda, but she was obviously uncomfortable to be at last in the company of the great scholar and poet, though Yehuda was looking at her with a benign smile.

It was Isaac who broke the silence. 'So, you two knew each other in Córdoba?'

'Yes,' Yehuda replied, 'I met Rebekah the first time I visited Córdoba to stay with Deborah's father – it must be about fifty years ago. Rebekah was working for Isaac then, weren't you, Rebekah? I remember you as a rather feisty young woman!'

Rebekah sighed and looked up at Yehuda with a wry smile. 'Yes, Rabbi, I was feisty then – and as for you, you were rather a cheeky young man, I recall. You took all sorts of liberties, just like Deborah. But all the feistiness has been knocked out of me.'

'Tell me about it, my friend. But first, let's give thanks that we've been brought together again. I think a *bracha* is appropriate.' Rebekah, Isaac and Solomon bowed their heads as Yehuda recited in Hebrew, '*Blessed are you, our Eternal God, Sovereign of the universe, Who has kept us alive and supported us and brought us to this season.*'

Solomon and Isaac responded 'Amen', but Rebekah said, 'Well, yes, I suppose we should be grateful that we've been kept alive, but it's been a close call these last years. How to tell you about it? I don't know where to begin.'

'Well,' said Yehuda, 'the last I heard of you was when I married Deborah in Toledo. You couldn't come to the wedding because by then you'd married and moved to Sijilmasa in the Atlas Mountains – the City of Gold!'

Rebekah's eyes lit up at the memory. 'Yes, I was so excited. It was a bustling city and, being married to Joseph ben Japhet, one of old Master Isaac's business partners, I was right at the centre of Sijilmasa life. You should have seen what a beautiful city it was. All the gold that came from the Empires of Ghana and Mali through Timbuktu came to Sijilmasa. The people were rich and varied, all life passed through the city, and travellers often stopped at our home. Northern Berbers, Lamtuna, Jews, even Africans as black as ebony. The Almoravids had been there for many years, so by the time Yusuf ibn Tashfin left the Maghreb to cause chaos in Andalucía, Sijilmasa had become a settled place. Yes, it was a wonderful life.' Rebekah closed her eyes, savouring the memory of the good times.

'But then the Almohads came,' said Yehuda.

'Yes, then the Almohads came.' A gull swooped down from the top of the mast, flying close to the gunwale as it dived for fish in the bow wave of the ship, but it came up with an empty beak, settling on the water with a forlorn cry. 'We first heard about them twenty years ago, when Ibn Tumart went around Marrakesh overturning the wine vats and smashing the musical instruments.'

'What, he did that?' said Isaac. 'I hadn't heard of that. How ironic! I remember reading in the journal of Ibn Abi Zar that when the Almoravids first invaded Sijilmasa eighty-five years ago their imam also "chopped up the instruments of music and burned down the shops where wine was sold". So what the Almoravids had done before, the Almohads did to them!'

'Yes,' said Yehuda, 'but the Almoravids gradually became less fanatical. Now we all live together in peace under their rule. On this ship we have thirty-seven Jews and three hundred Muslims – Muslims of all kinds: Sunni and Shi'ite, Malikite and Zahirite. Maybe the Almohads will also mellow just as the Almoravids did.'

'No, my lord.' Rebekah was trembling now. 'The Almohads will not mellow. They're different. At that time, Ibn Tumart even assaulted the sister of the Almoravid amir Ali ibn Yusuf because she wasn't wearing a veil, even though no Lamtuna woman wore a veil in those days. When she refused his order to cover her face, Ibn Tumart slapped her horse and it threw her to the ground. But even then the amir didn't punish Ibn Tumart, he only banished him – he fled to his home town of Iglitz in the Atlas Mountains.'

'Was that when the Almoravids built their string of fortresses to guard against the Almohads?' Isaac asked.

'You're right, Isaac,' said Yehuda. 'I was back in Córdoba by then and we couldn't understand why Amir Ali didn't attack and kill Ibn Tumart. He could have done that – he was much stronger then. Instead, he just built up defences to keep the Almohads out.'

'We didn't really understand either,' said Rebekah, 'but we thought we were safe behind those defences – the mighty Jebel Mudawwar fortress was only ten miles from Sijilmasa. We thought no one could pass that. But the Almohads on the other side just grew stronger and more aggressive. Any Muslims they thought heretical, which meant anyone who criticised them or disagreed with them, were killed. Jews were forced to convert or killed if they refused. So were Christians. That's what happened to poor Chaya.'

Rebekah brushed away a tear with the back of her hand. Yehuda leaned forward to offer her a kerchief, but she waved it away awkwardly. 'Thank you, sir, but I don't need it, I'll be all right in a moment.'

'So that's how Chaya died?'

'Yes, she came to Sijilmasa at the same time as I did, but her husband moved to Taroudant just before the Almohads started their persecutions. She and her husband were murdered there because they refused to convert. Chaya seemed so shy and delicate, but she had the courage of a lioness. A lioness, she was.'

As Rebekah paused, covering her eyes, Yehuda waited in silence. The wind veered slightly southwards, rattling the rigging and causing the sails to shudder. Two sailors came onto the fore-deck to trim the jib staysail, talking quietly to each other while they worked. As they left, Rebekah looked up, watching them descend the companionway.

'A couple of years ago Amir Ali started to grow sick, and people began to get anxious. His son Tashfin is able enough, but the Almohads are getting stronger every day. They've broken through the defences in many places and destroyed some fortresses. Where they break through, they treat people on the other side even worse than those in their own towns. That's how my husband…' She sobbed, her face contorted with grief as she leaned forward, wringing her hands.

Yehuda, in silence, leaned over and took her hands in his. 'Go on,' he said after a while.

'That's how David died. Last year. He was on his way to Marrakesh to buy silk when the Almohads broke through at Ouarzazate and attacked the caravan. They killed almost everyone. One of the apprentices was wounded but lived, and he told me that David fought bravely, but was overwhelmed.

'After that, we decided to leave. My two boys went ahead to set up a new life in the East. Now they're in Alexandria and want to stay there. They've sent for me at last, so I can leave this whole nightmare behind. I don't think it'll be long before the Almohads take Sijilmasa, and they won't stop there. Nowhere is safe, not Oran or Marrakesh.'

The four of them sat in silence, listening to the creak of the ship's timbers and the gentle rattle of the rigging, while each of them reflected on Rebekah's story. After a while, Yehuda leaned back to reach for the wine tray. 'Here, Rebekah, take a little wine with me.' He poured the wine and passed beakers to Rebekah, Isaac and Solomon. 'Let's drink to our reunion and to a better life for both of us, for you in Alexandria and for me in Jerusalem.'

'And you, Solomon and Isaac, where will you be?' asked Rebekah.

'Where God wills,' said Solomon, 'but my wife, daughter and son are back in Andalucía, so I hope it will be there.' He and Yehuda exchanged glances.

'And I expect my business to keep me in Egypt for a while, Rebekah,' said Isaac, 'so we may get to know each other.'

Yehuda raised his beaker. 'So, wherever we are – to Life!'

'To Life!' Rebekah, Solomon and Isaac responded, and they all drained their beakers.

15

AT SEA, OFF LAMPEDUSA

Sailing from Tunis to Tripoli, the captain decided not to hug the shore as usual but to take advantage of the prevailing northwest wind by sailing across the Gulf of Hammamet towards the Pelagie Islands. This proved to be an unfortunate choice.

As the convoy approached the western end of Lampedusa, the green silhouette of the island could be seen across the calm sea, which was sparkling in the afternoon sun. Yehuda and Solomon were, as usual, sitting on the foredeck of the *Sultan's Ship*, enjoying the breeze and discussing philosophy, while Isaac ibn Ezra was below deck, talking to Rebekah and some of the refugees from Tlemcen. The mild following breeze was a mixed blessing, constantly threatening to blow away the texts they were studying, especially when Yehuda or Solomon raised a hand in a gesture. Since gesturing was indispensable to their style of argument, this happened often, but they hardly noticed the inconvenience, so focused were they on the intricacies of the dispute within Islam between philosophy and mysticism. Yehuda had long been an admirer of Al-Ghazali's *The Incoherence of the Philosophers*, a vehement rejection of Aristotle and Plato.

'How can you side with Al-Ghazali on this, Father-in-Law?' asked Solomon. 'As a physician you're a devoted follower of the Greeks – always quoting Hippocrates or Galen or Discorides or some other Greek! And we know them only because the Arabic philosophers preserved and translated their work.'

'You're absolutely right, Solomon. I am devoted to Greek medicine – because it works, because my experience is that when I treat a patient with a herb recommended by Discorides, the patient gets better. The Greeks, even Aristotle, based their medical and scientific work on years, on decades, of observation.'

'Exactly, and even Al-Ghazali follows Ibn Sina in stressing how important experience is, as you keep telling me. Since that recommendation is based on Aristotle, what do you have against Aristotle?'

Yehuda put his papers in his portfolio and got stiffly to his feet. He stretched, raising his face to the sun and closing his eyes. He looked as contented as Solomon had ever seen him. 'Ah, Solomon,' he said, 'is it not pleasant to feel the warmth of the sun, yet to have a gentle breeze to keep one cool?' He leaned against the gunwale and looked down at Solomon, still sitting cross-legged on the deck. 'I have nothing against Aristotle in general, Solomon, when he writes of the real world; but when it comes to metaphysics and the origins of the universe, he abandons his own principles and indulges in pure speculation. He ignores experience, especially our experience of the divine through revelation. So he and his fellow philosophers come to conclusions that conflict directly with the Torah – and for that matter, with the Quran. Do you remember my verses?

Don't let Greek philosophy seduce you:
it may have flowers, but it will never bear fruit...
Just hear the incoherence of their doctrines,

constructed out of chaos and pretension;
they only leave a hollow in your heart,
and nothing in your mouth but syllogisms.'

'I don't know,' said Solomon, also rising to his feet and gathering up his papers, 'many scholars disagree with you on this, and—'

He was interrupted by a shout from a sailor at the masthead, who was calling out and pointing ahead. Yehuda and Solomon looked where he was pointing and saw a war galley with two rows of oars emerging from behind the cliffs of Cape Ponente at the western end of Lampedusa. At the stern of the galley they saw its flag, a red Maltese cross on a white background. The sailor, who had scrambled down from the masthead, ran to the gunwale beside them and shaded his eyes as he stared at the galley.

'What's that, Ahmed?' asked Yehuda. 'Is it crusaders?'

'No, sir,' replied Ahmed, 'that's no crusader vessel. The crusaders haven't been using rowing galleys for thirty years or more – they all use sail now. Look, there's another galley rounding the Cape. They're flying crusader flags but for sure they're pirates, probably Italian pirates.'

By this time, many passengers had seen the galleys and were milling around the foredeck, some crying out in alarm.

'Ahmed, Ahmed,' the captain called from the bridge, 'get all the passengers below – right now!'

'Please keep calm, everybody,' Ahmed shouted, 'and get below deck as quickly as you can. We'll soon see these ruffians off.' He turned back to Yehuda. 'Don't you worry, sir, we have our own galleys, and good Fatimid soldiers on the *Salim*. We'll be safe enough, but best get below decks now – it's going to get rough up here.'

As the passengers came down from the deck to the ill-lit hold, now even more crowded than usual, Yehuda had the impression that he could smell the fear in the fetid air. There was a constant murmur as the passengers shared their fears or consoled each other.

'They're pirates, I heard the sailors say – they'll be after the cargo.'

'It's more than cargo they want, it's slaves. They'll be taking slaves.'

'Slaves? God help us!'

'I hear they take the young and kill the old.'

'Nonsense, they'll be after ransom as well as slaves. They'll take the old too.'

'What? D'you think that makes me feel better?'

'Who cares what they want? We have the soldiers to protect us.'

'Yes, the pirates couldn't see the galleys behind our ship – as soon as they see them, they'll turn and run.'

'And if they don't, we've also got the soldiers on the *Salim*.'

'But the pirates will get to us first!'

Yehuda was sitting on a bale of cloth, his eyes closed, half listening to these exchanges, when Isaac quietly interrupted his reverie. 'Master, Rebekah is coming over. I think she wants to speak to you.'

Yehuda kept his eyes closed a little longer, holding up his hand to prevent further interruption, but he looked up as Rebekah reached their alcove. She was trembling violently, unable to speak.

Yehuda stood up and put his hand on Rebekah's arm. 'We're all afraid, Rebekah. We have no choice but to put our faith in God's protection. Remember the Psalm:

The curs came all around me,
 A pack of the evil encircled me…
But you, Eternal God, be not far.
 My strength, to my aid O hasten!
Save from the sword my life,
 From the cur's power my person.'

Rebekah took a deep breath and her trembling slowed down. 'Rabbi, I barely escaped the Almohads, and now it's crusaders or Christian pirates. Will I ever see my sons again? I thought that we... my God! What was that!'

The sound of a scuffle at the companionway hatch was followed by a crash as Ahmed fell into the hold, landing hard on his back and dropping his scimitar and shield. The passengers cried out as a pirate in ragged clothing scrambled down the companionway and stood over Ahmed, raising a bloodied broadsword, with both hands on the hilt. Before he could strike, Solomon, who had been standing beside Isaac and Rebekah, grabbed Ahmed's fallen scimitar and slashed wildly at the pirate, cutting into his left shoulder. The pirate roared in pain and anger as blood began to flow from the wound. He turned on his assailant, his eyes widening in surprise as he saw who it was.

'So,' he shouted, 'first a feeble Mussulman and now a mewling Jew. Then it's you who'll die first, Jew-boy!' Hefting the sword in his right hand, he ran at Solomon, who tripped as he stepped back, falling onto a pile of grain sacks. The pirate roared again and raised his broadsword in both hands, but as he brought it down Solomon rolled aside and managed to deflect the sword with the scimitar. Solomon leapt to his feet as the pirate lifted his sword a second time. The pirate rushed at Solomon just as he was raising the scimitar. The point of the scimitar dug deep into the pirate's midriff.

Rebekah screamed as both men fell between her and Yehuda, knocking her off balance. Solomon, pinned under the dying pirate, pushed him off with Isaac's help, then plunged his scimitar into the pirate's chest, making sure of his death. Blood spurted from the pirate's wound and ran onto the deck, mingling with the grain spilt from the damaged sacks. The smell of blood and barley filled the dusty air.

'Well done, lad!' Ahmed said, by then having recovered his breath and got to his feet. Picking up his shield, he reached out his hand to Solomon. 'Best give me the scimitar, young man, so I can get back to the fight.' The sounds of battle were getting louder overhead. Above the din they heard new cries of *Allahu Akbar!*

Ahmed smiled. 'Aha, the soldiers from the galleys or the *Salim* must have reached us. I'd like to give them a hand against these rogues.' He kicked the blood-soaked body of the pirate and held out his hand again to Solomon.

Giving the scimitar to Ahmed, Solomon said quietly, 'I want to fight them too.'

Yehuda took hold of Solomon's arm to restrain him. 'Solomon, Solomon, please,' he said, his voice trembling with alarm, 'you're no soldier. Leave it to Ahmed and his companions.'

'Rabbi, we need all the hands we can get,' Ahmed said. He turned back to Solomon. 'If you really want to fight, pick up the pirate's broadsword and follow me, but don't do anything stupid. Just stick with the rest of us and protect our backs.'

With a defiant glance at Yehuda, Solomon took the pirate's sword and followed Ahmed up the companionway into the fray.

The passengers in the hold lapsed into fearful silence, listening to the noises from above – the scuffle of feet on the deck, the clash of swords, voices cursing or shouting orders – as if they could decode the sounds and work out how the fight was going. Martha, a freed Christian slave girl who had befriended Rebekah during the voyage, helped her to get to her feet and dabbed at the bloodstains on her shift.

'Come, Rebekah,' she said, 'let's get away from this stinking pirate – and I mean stinking. I could smell his rank clothes as he came down into the hold, and now he smells of blood too, thank God.' She smiled and Rebekah cautiously returned her smile. 'The fight has kicked up a cloud of dust from the grain sacks,' Martha continued. 'Let's go forward: I can see your rabbi has gone to talk to some of the other Jews from Tlemcen. Let me take you over there.'

Martha and Rebekah went across to where a group of refugees were gathered round Yehuda and Isaac, who quietly led them in prayers and the reciting of psalms. It seemed natural for Martha to join them and listen to their chanting, though she didn't understand the Hebrew. The rhythm of the psalms was frequently interrupted when a crash or a shout from above caused them to stumble over the familiar phrases.

A mother screamed when a trickle of blood from above fell on her sleeping infant's hand and tunic. The child woke at her mother's scream and started to cry. Some of the group pulled away from them in horror, but Yehuda took off his prayer shawl and used it to wipe away the blood, speaking softly to the mother and the child. 'Don't fear, my child, God will protect you, here on the *Sultan's Ship*, like the eagle it resembles.

With His pinions He shelters you;
and beneath His wings you take refuge;
a shield and buckler, His truth.'

As Yehuda began to fold away the blood-stained prayer shawl, they heard a loud cheer from the deck above, and repeated shouts of '*Allahu Akbar*'. Ismat, the old *wakil*, climbed down the companionway, his clothes torn and stained with blood. The women at the foot of the companionway gasped and started to get to their feet. The infant's mother cried out and her child must have felt her terror: it shrieked loudly, spreading waves of anxiety through those huddled in fear in the dark pit. As Ismat turned, those near him gasped to see the blood on his torn clothing.

'Don't worry, folks,' he said with a smile, realising the terrifying vision he presented. 'that's not my blood – it's the blood of those accursed pirates. Accursed and cowardly, it turns out. We've beaten them off – those who still live have fled on their galleys.'

There was a cheer from the passengers, and cries of 'Thank God' in many languages.

'Does Solomon live?' Yehuda asked Ismat quietly.

'Yes, Rabbi, he certainly does, and a brave lad he was too.' Ismat raised his voice again. 'The captain has asked me to apologise for the inconvenience,' he continued, raising a laugh from most of the passengers, 'and to ask you to remain here while we clear up the decks. After that, our companions will be prepared for burial. As for the pirates…'

Everyone knew that the bodies of the pirates would be dumped unceremoniously overboard, and some fancied that they could hear the sound of that happening already, though no one could be sure because the ship was once again under sail and the splashes and creaks of normal progress had resumed.

A sailor's head appeared in the companionway hatch. 'Ismat,' he said, 'the decks are more or less clear now. The captain says that passengers can come back on deck if they want to.'

'Thank you, Hamid,' Ismat said. Raising his voice again he called out, 'Ladies and gentlemen, God has been merciful and we have overcome the pirates. The ship is more or less back to normal and you can go up on deck if you wish. I'm going to go to my quarters and get a good wash and change my clothes.' The passengers cheered and shouted, 'Thank you, Ismat' and 'God be praised'.

As Ismat led the way up the companionway, Martha knelt and spoke quietly to Rebekah, who was sitting in the corner of an alcove, crying. 'No need to weep, Rebekah,' she said, 'it's all over now. We're safe.'

'Yes,' said Rebekah, with a gentle smile, 'that's why I'm crying! These are tears of relief, not grief!'

'Let's go on deck, then, and get some air – I'm suffocating in all this dust.' Martha took Rebekah's hand and they joined the line of passengers waiting to climb the companionway.

When Yehuda and Isaac emerged on deck, Ahmed approached them to say that the captain wanted a word with Yehuda. As they reached the bridge, the captain was discussing the burials with Qadi Abdul al-Rafi, a senior judge who was travelling on the ship to Tripoli. 'I agree, Qadi,' the captain was saying, 'we all want to give our men a decent burial on land, but those pirates could have been from Genoa or Venice or Sicily. Whichever they were, it would be too dangerous to land the bodies in Lampedusa. The pirates may be there, and the Sicilian authorities would turn a blind eye if the pirates attacked us – assuming the authorities don't attack us themselves! Unfortunately, there's nowhere safe to land within a two-day journey even if we turn back, not with the wind from the northwest.'

'I see,' said the qadi, closing his eyes and stroking his beard. As he looked up, he caught sight of Yehuda. 'Good day, Rabbi. What to do? We Muslims have the same law as you Jews – we both require burial to be as soon as possible after death.' Yehuda nodded and Al-Rafi turned back to the captain and said, 'Many Sharia authorities say that if someone dies on a ship and it's impossible to bury him on land, then it's permissible for the body to be lowered into the sea, with due rites. I'll go to the foredeck and help your crew to prepare the bodies.'

After the qadi left the bridge, the captain said, 'So, Master Yehuda, your son-in-law turns out to be a real soldier!' He pointed to the rear of the bridge, where Solomon was sitting, exhausted, nursing the pirate's broadsword. His clothes were torn and bloodstained and his hair and face filthy, but he was smiling broadly, his eyes glittering.

'Thank you, Captain, yes, he's a brave lad indeed,' Yehuda said. He and Isaac approached Solomon, and Yehuda crouched beside him. 'Are you all right my, son?' he asked quietly.

'I've never felt better, Master. It was wonderful. I was very frightened but I felt alive, truly alive. As the psalmist says:

God is my strength and my shield.
In Him my heart trusts.
I was helped and my heart rejoiced,
and with my song I acclaim Him.

'I could see, see clearly, that *Allahu Akbar.*'

Yehuda looked round nervously and sat beside Solomon. 'We've all been citing the Psalms a lot, not surprisingly,' he said quietly, 'but maybe we should be careful about using the *Takbir* – it's a Muslim phrase and your use of it might be misunderstood.'

'Why should it be misunderstood?' Solomon replied, keeping his voice low despite his agitation. '*Allahu Akbar*, God is great. Arabic is our language, and Allah is a name of God in Arabic and God is indeed great, as Jews and Christians also keep saying. In any case, the Muslims behave as if they actually *believe* that God is great. They fight, they fight the *jihad*, while we cower behind the protection of amirs or allow ourselves to be massacred. I want to fight. I want to crush our enemies, not to capitulate like sheep in the slaughterhouse.'

Yehuda and Isaac exchanged a worried glance. Isaac knew only too well where this line of thought led: he had himself been through the same process and only the intervention of his father, Abraham, had prevented his conversion to Islam. Yehuda tried to hide his apprehension at Solomon's state of mind as he said, 'Yes, Solomon, I understand how you feel. We can discuss this later, but for now, let's get you cleaned up and let's deposit that sword in the ship's armoury.'

16

ALEXANDRIA

I have taken a city of which I can only say that it contains 4,000 palaces, 400 theatres, 1,200 greengrocers and 40,000 Jews.

'Amr ibn al-'As, Muslim conqueror of Egypt, writing to the caliph in Baghdad, 640

The weather started to deteriorate after the *Sultan's Ship* left Barqa, culminating in a storm that hit the ship the night before she reached Alexandria. The storm abated just before dawn and Yehuda rose from a much-disturbed sleep and gathered his cloak about him. I'm too old, he thought, to sleep on a bale of hides in a crowded, stinking hellhole of a cabin, and to eat the muck that they've been feeding us on this ship.

He climbed up to the deck and took a deep breath. The sea air and the cool breeze revived him as he joined some of the other passengers at the rail. The harbour pilot had already been brought out from the Om Zegheo headland and boarded the *Sultan's Ship* to guide it into port – they could see his tender returning to shore. Yehuda's attention was caught by a light, low on the horizon, far out across the starboard bow against the pink-ish glow of the dawn sky.

When the captain crossed the deck to where he stood, Yehuda asked, 'Captain, what's that star on the eastern horizon? There shouldn't be a star there, certainly not that low. It's like a new Morning Star, shining as the sun rises.'

'That's no star, sir,' the captain said. 'We're nearly at Alexandria – what you're seeing is the Pharos lighthouse on the other side of the promontory.'

'The Pharos!' One of the Seven Wonders of the World – Yehuda had never seen it but his merchant friends back in Córdoba spoke in awe of the Pharos. 'We can really see it from here?'

'Just wait till we round the headland into the Bay of Alexandria and you'll see the whole Pharos in full daylight. It's a magnificent sight. The pilot tells me that great crowds of people are heading toward Pharos Island today. He says he's never known anything like it, the size of the gathering. Hundreds of people are coming to see the Wonder of the World.'

'What do you mean, Captain?' Yehuda asked. 'They can see the Pharos any time they like. Why are they gathering now?'

The captain smiled. 'No, you don't understand, Rabbi. It's not the Pharos they're coming for, it's you, sir. You, Yehuda Halevi, are the Wonder of the World that they are coming to see!'

As Isaac joined Yehuda on the deck the captain told them that he thought the storm the previous night must be a precursor to the storms that marked the end of the favourable summer trade winds. No ship would now risk setting out on the voyage from Alexandria to Ascalon. Yehuda was going to have to overwinter in Alexandria. Sensing Yehuda's disappointment, Isaac pointed out that they would be spending time in Egypt, which was also a land that figured in the Bible story, but Yehuda did not find this a great consolation.

The ship sailed in calm waters towards the Eastern Harbour, approaching the Pharos lighthouse on the starboard side. Anticipating the curiosity and wonder of the passengers, the captain had stationed the *wakil* and other members of the crew on deck to warn them that the ship would list dangerously if they all crowded along the starboard rail. The Pharos was big enough to see from any point on the deck, they said. That proved to be true: the base alone, towering over the harbour entrance, was 350 cubits high. From the base a further three stages rose to a chapel, on top of which was a massive mirror that reflected the sun by day and a huge burning brazier at night.

As Yehuda, Solomon and Isaac stood gazing at the lighthouse, Isaac said to Solomon, 'There you are, the chapel at the top is attributed to your namesake, King Solomon.'

'I think that must be false,' Solomon said. 'The Pharos is older than the Kingdom of Israel – the name Pharos means Pharoah's Island, doesn't it?'

'Maybe it does, but that probably refers to the island rather than to the lighthouse built on it.'

'My friends,' Yehuda said, 'maybe you can continue this learned disputation later. For now, let's just look on this wonder and appreciate the works of which humankind is capable. I don't think there's a specific blessing prescribed for a building like this, but there is one for the learning and skills of human beings: *Blessed are You, Eternal God, Sovereign of the Universe, who has given of Your wisdom to flesh and blood.*'

'Amen,' Solomon and Isaac responded, and then fell silent.

As the ship rounded the Pharos into the harbour, the passengers saw crowds of people around the foot of the structure and on top of the base.

'There you are, sir,' the *wakil* said to Yehuda, 'it's just like the pilot told us, all those people have come to see you arrive. But they're going to be disappointed.'

'Why disappointed, Ismat?' asked Isaac.

'Because you won't be disembarking today, nor probably tomorrow. We're anchoring here in the Eastern Harbour
because of all the merchants on board with goods to tranship to
Nile vessels. There are lots more customs officials here than in
the Western Harbour, but it'll still be a long time before we can
disembark. It's not just about the cargo – there's also all those
refugees out of Oran.

'You'll still see some of your friends soon, though. The Alexandria agents will be allowed to come aboard at the same time as
the customs men. Yes,' he said, looking towards the shore, 'there
are the tenders coming out now.' He pointed to two *ghurab* boats
coming out from the al-Tahrir quay.

As the ship dropped anchor and the tenders came alongside,
the crowds around the Pharos began to disperse. The word was
getting around that they would not be seeing the great Yehuda
Halevi for a while yet.

Soon after the agents had scrambled aboard the ship a tall
man, elegantly dressed, was brought over by the *wakil*. He was
introduced to Yehuda, Solomon and Isaac as Amram ben Isaac,
who had come to greet the visitors on behalf of Yehuda's friend
Halfon ben Nataniel. Once the formal introductions were made
the *wakil* bowed and left.

'It's a great honour to meet you, Master,' Amram said to
Yehuda, 'but for your part you must be disappointed that Rab
Halfon isn't here to greet you in person.'

Yehuda was indeed disappointed – Halfon had become a dear
friend and but had not been to Andalucía for a year or so. Yehuda
had been looking forward keenly to their reunion – but he didn't
want to appear ungrateful to Amram, so he said, 'Yes, I am sorry
not to see him yet but I quite understand. It's only five days until

the New Year and I realise that Halfon needs to be with his family in Cairo to prepare for Rosh Hashana and Yom Kippur. And his absence means that I can get to know you better – Halfon has spoken warmly of your courtesy and your efficiency.'

Amram smiled. 'Halfon is a flatterer! If I'm as efficient as he claims, however, you'll have much need of it. The customs men are overwhelmed at present. They're not only inspecting the cargoes but also checking that all the *dhimmis* – all Christians and Jews – have paid the appropriate *jizyah* taxes in their regions of origin.'

'Well, we're safe on that point,' said Solomon, 'our cargoes are legitimate and all three of us have certificates of payment of our *jizyah*.'

'Of course you have – I'd expected nothing less. But the whole process may need to be completed for everyone before any passengers are allowed to disembark. Most of the refugees from Tlemcen won't have *jizyah* certificates.'

Isaac pulled a long face. 'That's frustrating. I'd been hoping to see Alexandria again soon and to show Solomon around. You've not been here before, have you, Solomon?'

'No, I haven't. And in any case, I've had quite enough of the *Sultan's Ship*, well-appointed though she is.'

'There will be plenty of time to see Alexandria, boys,' Yehuda said, 'since we will have to overwinter here in Egypt. I had thought to make Alexandria a place of transit, but it seems that it is not to be.' Yehuda's voice was trembling. He had not yet come to terms with the news that it would be months before he could fulfil his dream of reaching Jerusalem.

Amram, seeing the disappointment on Yehuda's face, started to bring the papers out of his portfolio. 'My duty is clear. I must do my best to get you off this ship as soon as possible. Let's go below, check your cargo and gather all your papers together so that I can start work with the customs men.'

As they turned towards the entrance to the hold, Isaac pointed to a small group by the gunwale. 'Look, Master, there's Rebekah with two men – they must be her sons.'

'Yes, Isaac, you're right. Amram, would you mind going ahead with Solomon and Isaac to check the cargo and I'll join you shortly – Rebekah is an old friend in distress and I'd like to reassure myself that she's safe now.'

'Of course, Rabbi, we can review the cargo first and deal with the other formalities when you come down.' He gestured to Solomon and Isaac to go down the companionway ahead of him.

As Yehuda approached Rebekah, she greeted him warmly and introduced her two sons, both well-dressed and handsome, around the same age as Solomon. They told him that they had settled in Alexandria and already started to make a good life for themselves. The older, Kiram ben David, was a wax-maker and the younger, Benjamin ben David, was a scholar and scribe. They had found that Egypt under the Fatimids was an even better place for Jews and Christians than Andalucía, free of disruptions and the tensions between Arabs and Berbers there.

'Yes, I've heard this and I pray that it continues,' Yehuda replied. 'There's always been constant change in these matters. But, Rebekah, that's beside the point. What matters today is that you are here, safe with your sons and able at last to settle in some security.'

'Yes, Rabbi, thanks be to God,' Rebekah said. 'And it was also a blessing to see you again after such a long time. I hope that you'll come and visit us while you are in Alexandria. You were so kind to me on the ship.'

'Of course you must come and see us, sir,' Kiram said. 'We share a house at the end of Wax Makers Street, next to the bath house.'

'I'd be delighted to do that, Kiram. It's not going to be easy, though, even if we get off this vessel before Rosh Hashana. I'm told that etiquette demands that I visit or receive all the notables among the Jews here, and that they are all pushing to be the first. But I promise that I'll come and visit your house as soon as I can.'

*

The passengers were allowed to disembark on Wednesday morning, three days after the *Sultan's Ship* had reached Alexandria. After a tumultuous welcome by crowds of admirers on al-Tahrir quay, Yehuda and his two companions were led by Amram to the estate of Aaron ibn al-'Ammani, the dayan, the chief justice of the Alexandria Jewish community, who lodged them in one of his houses. The dayan and his household did their best to give Yehuda some privacy but, as Amram had warned, the notables of Alexandria, or those who thought themselves notables, all sought the honour of visiting or being visited by the great man.

On Friday afternoon Yehuda was able to escape and make his way to Wax Makers Street to keep his promise and call on Rebekah and her sons. Isaac, who knew Alexandria well, agreed to show him the way. Progress was slow in the busy streets. It was not only the Muslim day of prayer and the eve of the Jewish Sabbath but also the eve of Rosh Hashana. Crowds of Muslims were leaving the mosques after the *Zuhr* prayers while equal numbers of Jews were converging on the *suqs* and merchant houses in a last-minute rush to buy provisions for the High Holy Days – wine and bread for the *Kiddush* prayer, honey to bring in a sweet year, meat for the Sabbath meal, spices, candles and gifts. Yehuda didn't mind the slow progress, enchanted as he was by the bustling world into which he had been released after days enclosed in the dayan's house.

He was a city dweller, well used to the crowds of Granada, Córdoba and Seville, but he had never seen anything like Alexandria. The most cosmopolitan city in the world, it was teeming with people and goods from all around the Mediterranean, East Africa and India.

The market district was even livelier than in Seville, and more varied. The bustling spice market was pervaded by the seductive odours of cloves, cardamom and coriander, laid out in neat, colourful mounds on each stall alongside a profusion of other spices in all the colours of the rainbow. In the spice market and in Clothmakers Street, Yehuda was bombarded with the noise of stallholders shouting out their wares. Bakers Street was quieter and the smell of bread from the ovens less varied than in the spice market, but no less seductive. Potters Row was also quiet, apart from the subdued sounds of kneading and hammering from the workshops behind the stalls. The stallholders there were not shouting for attention, preferring to let their goods speak for themselves.

Yehuda kept stopping, begging Isaac to wait while he admired the varied faces and costumes of the people passing by, or examined exotic ceramics, glass and textiles, as well as beautiful Fatimid artefacts. He bought a delicate cut-glass dish from Mesopotamia as a gift for Dayan Aaron and a set of Persian glass beakers for Rebekah, after which Isaac was finally able to persuade him to move on.

The entrance to Wax Makers Street was almost impassable. Candles were in high demand at all times but particularly during the High Holy Days, when synagogues sought to provide a blaze of light during evening prayers, and hosts lit their homes as well as they could afford. As they approached the street, Yehuda heard someone calling his name. Turning, he saw Kiram coming out of the building next to a bath house, holding a large basket of candles in each hand.

'Good afternoon, Rabbi Yehuda,' Kiram said, 'are you coming to visit us?'

'Yes, Kiram, but I see you're busy' – he gestured at the teeming street – 'as is everyone here. We don't want to interrupt your business.'

'Nonsense,' said Kiram. 'We're very busy – I can hardly keep up with the demand for candles – but I'm never too busy to see you, Master, after what my mother has said about you. It's a privilege and a pleasure to meet you again. Please do come up.'

'We'll come up with you but then you must leave us and finish your work – we can spend time with Rebekah and Benjamin until you return.'

They walked past a bakery on the ground floor of the building and Kiram's workshop on the first floor to a small apartment above. Benjamin was sent out to buy wine and cakes for their guests. Kiram also left, promising to return as soon as he had delivered his candles.

Yehuda and Isaac sat with Rebekah on the *martaba* and she talked of her joy at being free of the terrors of Tlemcen and the perils of the voyage. Fortunately, the caliph had sent a decree from Cairo that *dhimmi* refugees without *jizyah* certificates were to be allowed into Alexandria, so Rebekah had disembarked on the same day as Yehuda. Now she was reunited with her sons and looking forward to settling in with them, putting the apartment in order and above all getting them married off as soon as possible.

Yehuda smiled. 'I can see that the Rebekah I knew in Córdoba is beginning to come to life again. To help you enjoy your new home, Rebekah, we hope that you will accept this small gift from us.'

He unwrapped the set of cut-glass Persian beakers and put them in front of Rebekah. Head bowed, Rebekah took a deep breath as she looked at the glasses. Yehuda sensed that she was still scarcely able to believe that she was now safe and among friends, and each reminder almost brought her to tears. He and Isaac sat in silence as she reached out and delicately touched the rims of the glasses, as if afraid of breaking them. After a while she looked up and said, 'Thank you very much, Master Yehuda, Master Isaac, I am deeply moved by your kindness.' Picking up one of the glasses and examining it, she smiled at last. 'These are exquisite. Here we are on the eve of the Days of Awe and you're tempting me with luxury. I'll feel almost guilty using them!'

Yehuda patted Rebekah on the hand. 'You certainly don't need to feel guilty, Rebekah. We're allowed to enjoy the gifts of God, and those of our friends. Indeed, we're obliged to do so. We're not meant to live as ascetics.'

Benjamin, returning at that moment with the cakes and wine, concurred. 'Yes, Mother, as it is written, "The divine law does not require us to serve through asceticism. Rather, we should do so through moderation, giving each faculty of the soul and the body its just share, provided we are not excessive."'

'Benjamin, I'm amazed!' Yehuda exclaimed. 'You're quoting from *The Kuzari*! Have you read it?'

Benjamin was pleased with the impact of his intervention. 'Yes, Rabbi,' he said modestly. 'You sent a copy to Rab Halfon ben Nataniel in Cairo and he had it copied and sent to Dayan Aaron. The dayan was so delighted with it that he asked me to copy it for his friends. And of course, a scribe is allowed to read the book he is copying!'

'Indeed you are, Benjamin, but the dayan hasn't mentioned it to me. He…'

'The dayan has hardly had a chance to speak to you since you got here, Master,' Isaac interrupted. 'You've been too busy engaging with all the people who've been flocking to see you. Much to your credit, given how tedious some of them are!' Yehuda shook his head, frowning, but Isaac went on, 'Dayan Aaron himself told me how much he loves the book. And he hopes that you'll have some time to discuss it during your stay.'

'Meanwhile, gentlemen,' Rebekah said, 'it's time to enjoy the good things that Benjamin has brought. Let's drink our wine from these wonderful beakers.'

When Kiram came back the conversation returned to the subject of *The Kuzari*. Kiram told Yehuda that Benjamin was entranced by the book and kept quoting passages from it until Kiram himself almost knew it by heart. Yehuda, flattered, asked Benjamin if that was true.

'Yes, Rabbi, I was so taken with it that I'm making an extra copy for myself.'

'Which we can scarce afford,' Rebekah added. 'While you're making a copy for yourself, you're not earning a fee by making a copy for someone else! Nevertheless, it's a joy to see you so loving your work.'

'Yes, Mother, and I'll work that much harder to make up for the time! But, Rabbi, if I may, I have a question for you about the book.' When Yehuda nodded, Benjamin went on, 'I understand your emphasis on action – as the Chaver says at the end of Book Five, neither intention without action nor action without intention will suffice. But why, as his ultimate action, does the Chaver decide to go to Jerusalem? As the King of Khazars points out to him, with the Temple destroyed the Divine Presence is gone from that place. Closeness to God can be achieved anywhere.'

'That, Benjamin, is a crucial question, but one that's hard to answer. I'm not the Chaver, and what he says in the book may not always be exactly my own opinion. But, of course, my present pilgrimage means that in this case I agree with the Chaver. So why must I go to Jerusalem? Give me a moment.' Yehuda took a sip of wine. He stared into the beaker, running his finger around the rim. From the street, the noises from the market grew louder as more people hurried to buy their candles and provisions before the Sabbath and Rosh Hashana came in. The smell of the last loaves being taken out of the ovens in the bakery below drifted into the apartment, along with the aroma of beeswax from Kiram's workshop.

Yehuda began to speak of his own spiritual development. From his very first discussions with Moses ibn Ezra, he had come to understand the importance of experience, of direct experience. God did not choose to be revealed to the Jews through philosophical discourse, but through revelation, physical revelation, culminating in the revelation on Mount Sinai. Yehuda had learned from the Sufis that this is a two-way process, that human beings need to recognise and respond to what they experience, to manifestations of *amr ilahi*, of divinity. That is why the Chaver had said in *The Kuzari* that it was entirely legitimate to focus on objects and places, and to recognise the divinity inherent in them.

While Rebekah and Kiram listened politely and seemed to be taking in something of what Yehuda was saying, Benjamin responded with restless excitement.

'I see, I see,' he said, 'so that's why, as the Chaver says, God gave us so many physical manifestations to focus on in the Wilderness – the pillar of cloud by day and the pillar of fire by night, the two tablets of stone, the Ark. And the Chaver talks of the divinity that people attribute to a place also, especially Jerusalem.'

Isaac, who had been listening with his head bowed, straightened up and looked at Yehuda. 'Yes, I can understand what Benjamin is saying, and it appeals to me a lot. But what about the golden calf? Worshipping the golden calf was the gravest sin the Children of Israel committed. Wasn't that also attributing divinity to an object? Doesn't the Torah endlessly warn us against idolatry?'

The sound of the muezzins began to drift through the city, one after another, calling the *Asr* prayers. Yehuda leaned across and put his hand on Isaac's shoulder. 'You are completely right, Isaac, but so is Benjamin. The Chaver answers your question, but I'm afraid that will have to wait. It's getting late and we need to leave now – Rebekah and her sons must prepare for the Sabbath and the dayan's household will be wondering where we are. So, we'll resume the discussion later. Don't be offended, Isaac, but you haven't read the book yet, unlike Benjamin. I haven't had a spare copy to give you.'

Isaac did indeed look a little put out, but he responded gently, 'You're right, Master. But we have a solution right here.' He gestured towards Benjamin. 'I'll commission a copy from our scribe, if he has time. We're going to be in Egypt until at least the spring.' Benjamin nodded, smiling.

Yehuda and Isaac took their leave of Rebekah and her sons, promising to come and see them again soon. As they walked through the crowded streets, Isaac asked Yehuda to give him a brief answer to his question. Yehuda told him about the Chaver's argument that the intention of the Jews in making the golden calf was not in itself sinful. They felt abandoned by Moses, waiting for him to come down from the mountain. Their intention was not to deny God, but to have something in front of them when recounting God's wonders, something on which they could focus, just as all the other nations did. Their sin was not the making of an object in itself, but making an object, an idol, that was forbidden to them – and then attributing divinity to that object that they themselves had constructed without the sanction of God, projecting their image of a god onto the golden calf. They were making God in their own image.

'So, how do you know, Master, when you talk about the holiness of Jerusalem, or of anything else for that matter, that you're not doing the same thing – attributing divinity because of your own desires, not because God wills it?'

'You don't ask easy questions, do you, Isaac? But the short answer is that we rely on God's revealed will where it is absolutely clear, and on our tradition on the frequent occasions when it is not clear.'

'In the case of Jerusalem, I suppose, it's not only our tradition. The Muslims and the Christians also revere Jerusalem.'

'Exactly. Though…'

'I'm sorry to interrupt you, Master,' Isaac said, 'but we'll soon reach the dayan's house and be plunged into the business of the High Holy Days and there's an important matter that has just now occurred to me. Can I make a suggestion?'

Isaac told Yehuda that he was worried about Solomon, who seemed to be increasingly attracted to Islam. He understood the symptoms well, having himself nearly converted. He was prevented only just in time by his father's visit to Alexandria, when his father had persuaded him that what he was seeking could be found in Judaism.

'But Solomon is rather different,' Isaac went on. 'The attraction of Islam to him is an attraction to the active life. The fight against the pirates was a turning point. He's disillusioned with scholarship and he wants action – he sees the Muslims as fighters and we Jews as passive, as feeble.'

'I know, Isaac, but that's the problem.' Yehuda paused while he and Isaac stood aside to let a laden mule pass them in the narrow alley. 'I can't argue him out of that position precisely because he sees all my arguments as scholarly obfuscation.'

'Exactly, Master, and that's why it may be a mistake for Solomon to accompany you to Jerusalem. He'll see how some of the crusaders treat Jews and Muslims and hear stories of the constant struggles of the Muslims to keep the Frankish Christians at bay. He may then find Islam and its jihad irresistible. He'd be responding to experience, as the Chaver might say he should!'

'Yes, Isaac, I can see that. So…?'

'So in the spring he does not go with you to Jerusalem. He goes back to Miriam and his children and Deborah in

Córdoba. I know how much he misses them, so he might be willing to do so.'

'Isaac, my young friend, you have your father's wisdom. The situation is increasingly unsettled back at home. That means not only that Solomon will be back with his family, but also that he'll feel called upon to keep them safe and defend them against the Almohad jihadists.'

'Which he may indeed need to do.'

'Yes, yes.' Yehuda's face broke into a smile. 'And the other advantage is that my arguments may not prevail, but if he goes home he won't be able to withstand the combined opposition of Miriam and Deborah to his conversion.'

'Nobody could withstand that! So, it's worth trying this solution.'

'If Solomon does return to Córdoba, I'll have to find someone else to accompany me to Jerusalem. Which, alas, you can't do.'

'No, I can't. My business will keep me here for at least six months. But I was watching Benjamin as we were talking just now about Jerusalem. I have a feeling that he might love to join you on your pilgrimage.'

Yehuda stopped and turned to Isaac, a broad smile on his face. 'Yes, yes, you're right, I saw the shine in his eyes as we talked about it. And he'd make a good companion. I liked him. Scholarly but lively and interested in the world. Let's talk about this with Benjamin when the time seems right.' He smoothed down his robe. 'Meanwhile, we must get to the dayan's house before Sabbath.' Yehuda and Isaac walked on together towards the dayan's estate.

17

CAIRO

How can we sing of the Eternal God
   on foreign soil?
Should I forget you, Jerusalem,
   may my right hand wither.
May my tongue cleave to my palate
   if I do not recall you,
if I do not set Jerusalem
   above my chief joy.

Psalm 137:4–6

A few years before Yehuda arrived in Egypt, a dispute arose over which of Caliph Al-Hafiz Il-Din Allah's two sons, Ismail or Joseph, should succeed to the caliphate. Fearing that this would result in civil war, the caliph asked two physicians at his court, Ibn Kirfa, a Christian, and Samuel ben Hanania, a Jew, to poison Joseph. Samuel declined to cooperate but Ibn Kirfa did as he was asked. The caliph soon came to repent the killing of his son. He never forgave Ibn Kirfa, who was imprisoned and eventually executed. He rewarded Samuel by appointing him as chief physician at the court and by giving him all Ibn Kirfa's property. Samuel soon became the *nagid*, the head of the Jewish community in Egypt. By the time Yehuda reached Alexandria, therefore, Samuel was the most powerful Jew, and one of the most powerful men, in the whole of Egypt. So when Samuel ben Hanania let it be known through Halfon ben Nataniel that he wanted to meet Yehuda, it was not so much an invitation as a command to come to Cairo.

Nevertheless, Yehuda resisted the nagid's summons, reluctant to abandon the pleasures of Alexandria. His host, the dayan, was, like himself, a scholar and poet. He and his five sons did all they could to make Yehuda's stay as happy as possible. Yehuda wrote to a friend back in Andalucía,

> *I'm being cared for in a palace here in Alexandria,*
> *a golden palace, a mine of precious ore –*
> *Aaron's house, a place of holiness and song,*
> *of gardens, wells and pools,*
> *the dwelling of a scholar and a sage,*
> *a rabbi and a judge, a righteous, pious man.*

He wrote of twelve wells and a spring of water, of almond blossoms and the lovely fragrances of nard and henna, of seventy palm trees.

Faced with this reluctance, Halfon called in reinforcements. The *chaver* Nathan ben Samuel, a renowned scholar, was court scribe to the nagid and also secretary of the Fustat yeshiva. He exchanged letters with Yehuda, in which he took a polite but increasingly forceful line. Eventually, Yehuda surrendered. At the end of November, just before the festival of Chanukah, Halfon came to Alexandria to accompany Yehuda, Solomon and Isaac up the Nile to Cairo.

When they got to Cairo, Halfon insisted on hosting the three travellers in his house in Fustat, the old part of the city, near the Ben Ezra Synagogue. It was in this crowded district of narrow alleys that most of the Jews of greater Cairo lived. Behind a blank wall facing one of the alleys, Halfon's house, like many others in Fustat, was large and spacious, arranged around a pleasant courtyard of trees and flower beds.

Yehuda was as feted there as he had been in Alexandria, in demand as a famous scholar, poet and physician. As a physician, Yehuda was also called upon to occasionally support Samuel ben Hanania in his medical work at court in the new part of the city – al-Qahira, Cairo proper, the fortress and royal city built by the Fatimids. When Yehuda saw the elegant buildings and spacious squares of al-Qahira he was reminded of the Amir's Palace in Granada, though al-Qahira was on an even larger scale. The great parade ground of the Bayn al-Qasran was three times the size of the Royal Courtyard in Granada. The elaborate ceremonies held there put those of Granada into the shade.

Solomon, who often accompanied Yehuda to al-Qahira to assist him, was overawed by the spectacle. Even more wonderful for them was the Dar al Ilm, the House of Knowledge – the university established by the previous caliph – where controversies about the problems of government and religion were freely discussed.

Yehuda and Solomon were sometimes able to spend an afternoon in the Dar al Ilm with a group of Muslim scholars, discussing the glories and the limitations of Greek philosophy. They were often in agreement, though Benjamin and the Muslim scholars were less critical of the Greek philosophers than Yehuda was. On one such afternoon the discussion was interrupted by Isaac, sent by Halfon to ask Yehuda and Solomon to return to the house early. Halfon had asked Chaver Nathan ben Samuel over for a study session and for dinner and wanted his visitors to join them.

Nathan was about the same age as Yehuda, but he looked a lot older – his back bent from years of Talmud study and his face deeply lined. His mind, however, remained lively and he was a perceptive and sympathetic colleague to both teachers and students at the yeshiva. These qualities were evident during the *shiur* that he led in Halfon's house that afternoon. It was February and the weekly Torah reading that they discussed, from the Book of Exodus, covered the story of Jethro, the Priest of Midian, who was Moses's father-in-law. Jethro saw Moses exhausted by the constant work of judging cases and answering questions brought to him by the people. He told Moses, 'The thing that you are doing is not good. You will surely wear yourself out – both you and this people that are with you.' Jethro persuaded Moses to delegate some of his work to leaders who would take on the burden of judging cases, enabling Moses to concentrate on his primary tasks of strategy and leadership.

In the *majlis* after dinner, the conversation turned again to the wisdom of Jethro.

'Sometimes I know how Moses felt,' Yehuda said. 'I also find the constant demands of public work exhausting.'

'So,' Nathan said with a smile, 'you compare yourself to Moses?'

Yehuda returned the smile. 'No, Chaver, not at all. But here in Fustat, as in Alexandria, I'm always at the beck and call of the community. It's pleasing and flattering to be sought after, but it's also exhausting.'

'Yes,' said Halfon, 'you wrote the same thing to me from Alexandria. Let's see, I was looking at your letters only this morning.' He turned to a pile of papers on the corner of the *martaba* and shuffled though them. 'Ah, here it is:

*The community showed me so much kindness and acceptance,
acclaim, thoughtfulness, courtesy, and honour that I was
embarrassed. I participated outwardly. Inwardly, it was very
burdensome for me. Because I did not come for any of this,
and all I want is the opposite – isolation and solitude – as
appropriate for me who is near to expecting death any minute.'*

'That's very strongly put, Father-in-Law,' Solomon said. 'I didn't
detect that feeling in Alexandria at the time. You hid it well. Was
it really so bad for you?'

'No, Solomon, you're right, it wasn't that bad, and I wasn't
actually ill, as the text implies. I was thinking, in my depressed
state, of the Talmudic instruction to live each day as though it is
one's last.' He looked over at Halfon. 'But it was clumsily put and
it's rather unkind of Halfon to quote that letter now!'

'I'm sorry, Yehuda, I meant no harm. Let me make amends by
offering you some more wine.'

Yehuda smiled. 'No offence was taken, my friend, but I'll
happily accept your offer of wine!'

The wine was passed around and the conversation turned to
other matters, but Nathan sat silent for a while, watching Yehuda.
At the end of the evening, he asked if he could call on Yehuda the
following morning.

*

Arriving at Yehuda's apartment the next day, Nathan was clearly
troubled. After the usual exchange of formalities, he took a breath
and said, 'Yehuda, I would like to give you some advice, but it
means that I'll have to be rather blunt with you. Do I have your
permission to speak, even though my words may offend you?'

After a moment's hesitation, Yehuda said, 'Of course, Nathan,
you must say what you've come to say. I saw yesterday that you

were concerned. I'm grateful for your concern and your friendship. In that spirit I'll listen to what you have to tell me, however hard it may be to hear.'

'Yes, it's in the spirit of friendship that I'm here. Both as your friend and as secretary to the nagid, I'm delighted that you're spending time with us in Egypt, even though it's the result of unfortunate necessity. But as your friend, and as someone who has gained some insight in my many years as a teacher in the yeshiva, I'm also troubled by how you're using your time here.'

He paused. Yehuda gestured for him to continue.

'In the letter that Halfon read out last night, you wrote of "being near to death any minute". This struck me as only an oblique reference to what really concerns you. Am I right?'

'Yes, Nathan, the nearness of death doesn't trouble me at all. Rabbi Eliezer taught, "Repent one day before your death". He meant that a person should be in a process of reflection and repentance every day, since we never know which will be the day we'll die. I'm not afraid of death.'

Nathan nodded but remained silent. After a pause, Yehuda continued, 'What really troubles me are the distractions from my true purpose, my pilgrimage. I don't want to offend people by seeming distant, and in any case, to be honest, the attention and praise are flattering. But I do feel a duty to seek what I called in the letter isolation and solitude, to pray and to study. That's my task as a pilgrim; it's essential as preparation for the final stage of the journey to Jerusalem. It's also what I truly desire. As I wrote to Halfon, even from Córdoba, "My heart is urging me to go up to my Temple, see my city." That's where my focus should be. Can Cairo contain me when my soul is rushing towards Zion?'

This was what Nathan had suspected was troubling Yehuda, and he was encouraged that Yehuda was willing to be honest about it. Getting him to recognise the solution, however, was not going to be easy, even though the solution was obvious to Nathan. He would have to tread carefully. 'I understand exactly what you mean, Yehuda,' he said. 'You're both drawn to and resentful of the distractions of Egypt. And it's not just the attention and praise that distracts you, is it? You're also seduced by Egypt itself…'

'Seduced is rather strong, Nathan!'

'It is, but I stand by the word. In the first place, you're rejoicing at being in a place that figures in the biblical narrative – the Nile and Goshen and Pithon and Ramses. Secondly, you're enchanted by the beauty of the country and its people.'

'Yes, I am. That's another part of the problem, I admit.'

'But I think you may be mistaking what the solution to "the problem" is, Yehuda.' Nathan paused. He closed his eyes and rubbed his forehead. Yehuda waited, unable to imagine where Nathan was taking the conversation. Eventually Nathan sat up and reached for his outer robe. 'Come, let's go for a walk – it'll be easier for me to explain what I mean if we go out.'

Yehuda was even more perplexed by this, but he assented and they left his apartment and walked towards the Nile. They passed between the communal dwellings that lined the streets to the west of Fustat, each of them five, six or seven stories high, where rich and poor lived in close proximity. The noise was overwhelming, as was the smell from the waste tips between some of the buildings. It was a relief to escape through the fragrant Market of the Fruit Sellers to the Qasr al Sham fortress. Yehuda relaxed a little as he took in the panoramic view from the fortress walls – the busy port to the north, the riverside walk below him and to the south, and the green island of Jazira just opposite. He took a deep breath, savouring the fresh smells from the gardens along the riverside.

As they stood in the morning sun, Nathan asked, 'Do you remember, Yehuda, that poem you sent to me from Alexandria, the one about the Nile? *Has Time thrown off its robes of trembling and clothed itself with treasure?'*

'Yes, you showed it to your colleague, Dayan Hiyya ben Yitzhak, and he wants to add it to his *diwan* of my poems. Another flattering temptation!'

'The Nile here in Cairo isn't so different from the Nile in Alexandria.' He pointed to some young women strolling on the riverside walk. 'Look at those women down there. They remind me of lines from that poem; I think they go thus:

Beside the Nile are girls, and not just one or two;
gazelles, yet different from gazelles, for not as fleet –
their arms weighed down with heavy bracelets,
golden anklets heavy on their legs.
They steal your heart, they make you forget your age;
your mind goes back to youths and girls
from other times and places.'

'You have a good memory, Nathan.'

'I remember it because you write memorable poetry, Yehuda!'

'Maybe, but that's part of what troubles me. Why am I writing such poetry when I'm on a pilgrimage, a holy journey?'

Nathan abruptly turned from the view of the river to face Yehuda. 'That's exactly what I wanted to discuss, my friend. Your question is... misguided. You think of all this – the beauty, your fame, the public demands on your time – as a distraction. They're not a distraction. They are an opportunity.'

'What do you mean, Nathan? An opportunity for what?'

'An opportunity to learn.' Nathan took a deep breath. 'Look, a pilgrimage, this pilgrimage that you're on, it isn't a withdrawal from normal life. It's an intensification of normal life. You yourself wrote in *The Kuzari* that the divine law doesn't require us to serve through asceticism. A pilgrimage is not a retreat into an ascetic denial of the world – quite the opposite: it's a microcosm of life's journey through the world. Far from regretting the experiences you're having, what you're required to do is to fully engage in them, to pay attention to them and to learn from them. That's the true purpose of a pilgrimage.'

'But surely the point of the pilgrimage is the destination, is reaching Jerusalem?'

'Yes, reaching Jerusalem is important, but so is how you get there. Remember Sedra Masei in the Book of Numbers. In that Sedra, every single one of the forty-two stops that the Children of Israel made between Egypt and the Promised Land is named, and some of them are described. There's a *midrash* that God said to Moses, "Write down all the places through which Israel travelled, so that they may remember the miracles that I wrought for them." The Torah is telling us that freedom from the slavery of the world is important, but so is the journey from slavery to freedom. If you're to be worthy of Jerusalem, you need to learn from the journey. As I said, a pilgrimage is a microcosm of life's journey.'

Staring at Nathan, Yehuda opened his mouth to speak, then closed it again. After a long pause, he reached out to Nathan and grasped his hand. 'Nathan, my friend, my teacher, I can't thank you enough. You've rebuked me and liberated me at the same time. I envy your students at the yeshiva!'

Nathan laughed. 'So now it's your turn to tempt me with flattery? All I have is the experience that enables me to see the truth, which does indeed have a habit of both rebuking and liberating us. But it's time to go and find Solomon and Isaac – we're due to call on the nagid this afternoon.'

*

The Nagid Samuel ben Hanania, as chief physician to the caliph, was required to visit the palace in al-Qahira almost daily. He therefore had a house north of the Ben Ezra Synagogue and the Mosque of Amr, closer to the Mosque of Abu Su'ud. Even so, it was an hour's walk from his house to the palace. When Nathan, Yehuda, Solomon and Isaac arrived, he had not yet returned from a morning summons to tend to one of the caliph's wives. They were shown into the private quarters to wait for him.

The buildings occupied by the nagid were large and elegant, with an official reception hall on the northern side of the central courtyard, the religious law courts to the east, Samuel's medical consulting rooms on the west and the rooms occupied by his extensive staff in the south. The private quarters, reached through the consulting rooms, were modest, in contrast to the grandeur of the rest of the house. The family *majlis* was quiet and comfortable and its brass lamps, carpets and cushions were old and worn. In his private space, Samuel liked to surround himself with familiar and well-loved furnishings.

The visitors did not have to wait long. As they were being served with mint tea by an elderly maid, the nagid appeared and joined them on the *martaba*. Taking a cup of the infusion himself, he held it to his nose and breathed in deeply.

'Dina,' he said to the maid, 'what magic have you performed on this mint? It has the most invigorating aroma; it fills the room.'

The maid smiled. 'Thank you, my lord. I only use mint picked just before flowering, and I've added a small pinch of cardamom to the infusion.'

'I thought so,' Yehuda said. 'I thought I detected a hint of cardamom. Dina, you're a physician as well as a cook! Pedanius Discorides says that mint and cardamom work together to aid digestion, and they both help to cleanse the breath.'

'Yes, they do, sir, but I didn't learn that from the gentleman you mentioned. I learned it from my mother.'

Samuel laughed. 'There you are, Yehuda, more proof that experience is as good a teacher as the Greeks are. Dina's been with my family for years. She looked after my sons and daughters when they were younger, and she was always telling me which herbs were the best medicines, which explains why they're all so healthy!'

'Thank you, my lord.' Dina curtseyed, smiling at the compliment. 'Will that be all?'

'Yes, thank you, Dina.' When Dina had left the *majlis*, the nagid turned to his guests. 'Thank you for waiting so patiently for me, gentlemen. I know you're all very busy, so let's get down to our business.'

He explained that he wanted to discuss Yehuda's plans for the next few weeks. The weather would not be favourable for the journey from Alexandria to Palestine until sometime around Shevuot, in April or May, so Yehuda would have to stay in Egypt until then. Samuel hoped that Yehuda might stay in Cairo until after Passover rather than going back to Alexandria early: he was going to be very busy with his community duties in the run up to Passover, and would welcome Yehuda's help with the medical work, at the palace and in the community. He would also welcome Yehuda's support with some of the religious cases he would have to deal with. Yehuda willingly agreed. He said that Halfon ben Nataniel had also been urging him to stay in Cairo and had offered to extend his hospitality for a few more weeks.

'What about you, my friends?' Samuel asked, turning to Isaac and Solomon. 'Will you also stay on here?'

'I'll have to stay in Cairo for some time, even after Passover, as Rabbi Yehuda knows,' Isaac said, 'so I won't be going with him to Alexandria. My father has written to tell us that he plans to go and meet a group of scholars in Paris, and then possibly in Oxford. They want him to help them with the Greek texts preserved in Arabic. That means that I'll have to secure our business affairs in Cairo and then return to Córdoba to continue the work.' He turned to Yehuda. 'I'm sorry to have to part from you, Master, but to be honest, I'll be glad to go back to Córdoba.' Yehuda nodded.

The nagid turned to Solomon. 'And what about you, Solomon ben Joseph? Will you travel with your father-in-law?'

'I'll return with my father-in-law to Alexandria, whenever he goes. After that, I'm not so sure. I think I might like to stay in Egypt.'

'To stay in Egypt? For what purpose, Solomon?'

Solomon hesitated, but then looked up at Samuel and said, 'I think I have a lot to learn here in Egypt.'

'But nothing is decided yet, is it, Solomon?' Yehuda said.

'Not yet, sir,' Solomon replied, looking down at his hands.

The nagid steered the conversation on to other matters. As the meeting drew to a close, he asked Solomon and Yehuda to stay behind for a while.

'Solomon, my son,' he said after the others had left, 'you said earlier that you have much to learn in Egypt.'

'Yes, my lord.'

'I understand that you are not only focused on the Greek philosophers at the Dar al Ilm. My sources tell me that one of the subjects you're particularly interested in is Islam. Is that right?'

Solomon shifted uncomfortably on his cushions. 'Yes, it is right, my lord. I am interested in Islam.'

'In converting to Islam?'

Solomon calmly held the nagid's gaze. 'That's something I have not yet decided.'

Yehuda started to speak, but the nagid raised a hand to silence him. 'So tell me, my son, what is it that can stop you from such taking such a foolish step?'

Solomon straightened his shoulders and looked defiantly at the nagid, his face flushed. 'I don't see it as foolish, my lord. It's we Jews who are the subject people, the *dhimmi* ruled by Muslims. They're the successful ones, they're the strong ones who fight for what they believe. Muslims are strong, as their faith is strong, but they are also enlightened. They respect learning and art. Are they foolish? I think not.'

'No, I agree with you, my son, the Muslims are not foolish at all, or at least no more foolish than anyone else. What I say would be foolish is for you to become a Muslim.'

'Why? Why would it be foolish?'

'For many, many reasons, Solomon. First of all, you say that you want to fight, but what do you want to fight for? You have a wife and two children in Córdoba, a city whose peace is threatened by the weakness of its rulers and the rise of the Almohads. Don't you have a duty to protect them? Wouldn't fighting for them be more important, and more honourable, than fighting some religious *jihad*? Secondly, honour apart, do you really value enlightenment above Miriam and your children, even if the enlightenment of Islam were greater than that of Torah, which it is not? Do you want to put yourself in a position where you'll never see them again? And that's the third reason – conversion would be irreversible. If you convert to Islam you will never, ever be able to return to your people. It's a capital offence for a convert to abandon Islam. Do I need to go on? There are other reasons.'

Looking down at his hands, Solomon shook his head. After a long silence Yehuda put his arm round Solomon's shoulder and said gently, 'Solomon, I know how difficult this is for you. There will be time to consider it further and I beg you not to rush into a decision. Of course you don't need to come with me to Jerusalem – we can find another companion, such as Benjamin the Scribe. Samuel's advice is wise. It may be God's will that you should return to Miriam and the children in Córdoba. But you don't need to decide just yet. We should let the matter rest for now.'

He helped Solomon to his feet and silently they took their leave of the nagid.

18

RETURN TO ALEXANDRIA

Save me from my enemies, my God,
 over those who rise against me make me safe.
Save me from the wrongdoers,
 and from men of bloodshed rescue me.
For look, they lie in wait for my life,
 the powerful scheme against me—
  not for my wrong or my offence, Eternal God.

Psalm 59:2–4

'Yehuda, my good friend, I have a confession to make.'

'That's intriguing, Aaron. Your normal task as a judge is to hear confessions, not to make them.'

Yehuda was sitting with Dayan Aaron ibn al-'Ammani in the *majlis* of the dayan's guest house. Yehuda and Solomon had left Cairo for Alexandria shortly after Passover. Now, a week later, they were lodged once again in the house that the dayan had first allocated to them when they arrived in Egypt. The morning sun shone through the lattice of the *mashrabiyya*, dappling the red Armenian rug with bright patches of yellow. The murmurs of the nearby *suq* could be heard through the lattice windows, punctuated by the occasional cries of the stallholders and water carriers, 'Fresh fruit, ripe pomegranates!', 'Henna and dyes, the finest colours!', 'Hoi! All who are thirsty, come and drink!'

The dayan shifted on his cushions. 'We all do things we regret and I'm no exception, Yehuda. The thing is, while you were in Cairo, I collected some of the occasional poems you wrote to me and to our friends and assembled them in a new *diwan*. I had several copies made, without your permission. They were widely circulated…'

'… but they were not well received.'

'No, they… I mean, it's true, but how did you know?'

'I also have a confession to make, Aaron. I had a letter before Passover from our friend Abu'l Ala, telling me all about it, but I decided that it was best to let the matter pass. So I didn't mention it to you.'

'Ah yes, Abu'l Ala, he did berate me for publishing the *diwan*. What did he say in his letter?'

'He said quite a lot. That the publication was impolitic and indiscreet. That feelings were hurt – there was jealousy on the part of people to whom I wrote poems that weren't included in the *diwan*, and resentment by notables who hadn't succeeded in meeting me and had therefore got no poems. Others were shocked by my frivolity. How could a man on a holy pilgrimage spend his time writing a poem in praise of a gift of chickens? The *diwan* even included the poem I addressed to a razor blade. Not to mention the more sensuous poems. According to Abu'l Ala, the *diwan* has caused quite a stir here in Alexandria.'

'Yes, it did and I'm truly sorry, Yehuda. I thought people would see the poems as you intended them, as innocent amusement. They're brilliant and witty and I wanted to share them, that's all.'

Yehuda waved his hand, brushing the problem aside. 'Don't blame yourself, Aaron. You meant no harm, and no real harm has been done.'

'But I should have known, I do know, how prone this community is to squabbling and slander. I've been a judge here for so many years.'

'Yes, that's the point. The squabbling of squabblers is just *hevel*, just a breath of empty wind. I know, and you know, that those poems were harmless. And I know that being a pilgrim doesn't require me to lose my sense of humour! So, I'll forgive you for publishing the poems if you'll just pass me some more of those delicious dates.'

As Aaron reached across for the bowl, Yehuda said, 'There is one piece of business that I need to mention. We have some money, a bill of exchange, for someone here. His brother in Alexandria asked us to deliver it to him. His name is Abraham ibn al-Basri: do you know where I can find him?'

Aaron, startled, dropped the bowl of dates on the rug. 'Al-Basri? There's only one Ibn al-Basri here in Alexandria. Al-Basri – the Jew who converted to Islam.'

'Yes, that's him. His brother was, of course, very distressed that he had converted, but he still wanted to send the money.'

Aaron picked up the bowl and started gathering the dates. 'Yehuda, he's a dangerous man. Having converted, he's become hostile to our community. He's not to be trusted.' He put the bowl of dates aside. 'Shall I send for some clean dates?'

Yehuda shook his head. 'No, no, that's fine, thank you, Aaron. I'll manage without. Yes, I understand the risks, but all I have to do is keep my promise to deliver the bill of exchange to him.'

'I'm not sure when you'll be able to do that, in any case. I heard that he's gone to Damietta on business and may not be back for some time. In a few weeks the trade winds will be returning and you'll be sailing to Ascalon.'

'If God wills, yes. But I don't want to send the bill by courier to Damietta. It's thirty dinars.'

'Thirty dinars! That's a lot. It's enough for him to live comfortably for a year or so!'

'Exactly, so if he's not back by the time I sail, then maybe I'll have to entrust the money to you to give to him.'

As Aaron hesitated, considering his reply, they heard voices in the courtyard and turned to the door as Solomon entered.

'Solomon,' Yehuda said, 'welcome back. You're just in time. Could you please let me have that bill of exchange and letter from Al-Basri's brother?'

Solomon looked puzzled. 'But I don't have them, Father-in-Law. You asked me to look after them for you during the journey from Cairo, but I gave them back yesterday. Don't you remember?'

'I'm sorry, Solomon, yes, I remember now. They are in the coffer in my room. I'm afraid I'm becoming a forgetful old man.' He gestured to the cushions on the *martaba*. 'So, tell me, how did you get on with Benjamin the scribe?'

As Solomon sat down, Aaron got to his feet and picked up the bowl of dates. 'I'm sorry to interrupt you, Solomon, but I need to get ready for court, so I'll have to leave you now. Can I send in some mint tea? And some fresh dates?'

'Yes please, Dayan, that would be welcome.'

After Aaron had left the room, Solomon told Yehuda that he had found Rebekah and her sons at home. The good news was that Benjamin was more than willing to be considered as a companion for Yehuda on the trip to Jerusalem, now that Solomon had decided to return to Córdoba. It was agreed that they should all meet the next day to discuss the possibility and make a final decision.

*

Three weeks later, Ibn al-Basri concluded his business in Damietta and returned to Alexandria. Yehuda and Solomon had not yet been able to leave the city, so they arranged to call on him. After he had converted to Islam, Al-Basri had left the western quarter of the city, where most Jews lived, and moved south of the harbour to Al Attarin. Once a prosperous area of spice merchants, this was now a rather run-down quarter, though Al-Basri's apartment was in one of the more salubrious buildings.

The manservant showed the visitors into a small but well-appointed *majlis*, furnished with blue and black damask cushions and a rich Moroccan carpet. Al-Basri rose from the cushions, his body tense, his expression inscrutable. He was a young man, squat and ugly. Solomon thought he looked rather like a frog, one of the plague of frogs described at the recent Passover Seder meal. Dismissing the image from his mind, he bowed to Al-Basri.

'Sir, may I present my master and father-in-law, *Al-Muhadhab* Yehuda ben Shmuel Halevi. I am your humble servant, Abu l-Rabi Solomon ben Joseph ibn Gabbai.'

Al-Basri bowed in response. 'You are both welcome. How tactful of you, sir, to give your master a physician's title, rather than that of rabbi or *chaver*. To what do I owe the honour of this visit?' His tone, though not hostile, was rather sour, and he did not invite the visitors to sit.

Overlooking the slight, Yehuda said, 'We've come to deliver to you a letter and a bill of exchange from your brother Naphtali in Cairo.'

He reached out his hand to Solomon, but before Solomon could give him the documents, Al-Basri shouted, 'How dare you!' Yehuda and Solomon both took a step back in surprise as Al-Basri lowered his voice and went on in a tone of suppressed anger, 'Don't you know that it's a capital crime for me to return to Judaism? And, what's more, it's a capital crime for you to try to persuade me to do so!'

'I have no idea what you mean, sir,' Yehuda replied. 'All we're doing is delivering a letter and money from your brother.' He pointed to the letter in Solomon's hand. 'We said nothing about conversion.'

'You didn't have to say it. I've already had word from Naphtali to tell me that you'd be bringing the money and that, as a condition of accepting the money, I must accompany you to Jerusalem. The crusaders rule there, not the caliph, Naphtali wrote, so I can return to Judaism in Jerusalem without risking my life. I'm sure he says the same in that letter that your son-in-law is holding.'

'We know nothing about this, Al-Basri,' Solomon said. 'My master simply undertook to deliver the money and letter safely. We haven't read the letter, obviously.'

Al-Basri's face grew red and his tone menacing. 'Nevertheless, the letter is an attempt to suborn my return to Judaism. That's a criminal offence, and you are parties to that crime.'

'But…'

'Silence!' Al-Basri took a deep breath and said, more quietly still, 'I must ask you to leave my house at once. I will have to report this to the police, if only for my own protection.'

Yehuda again began to speak but Al-Basri held up his hand and left the room with a final, 'Go now.'

Solomon made a move to follow him, holding out the letter, but Yehuda put his hand on his arm. 'No, Solomon, there's nothing we can do. We must leave now. We'll ask the dayan for his advice on what to do if Al-Basri carries out his threat.'

Solomon put the letter back in his bag and they left together.

*

The following day, Yehuda and Solomon were summoned by the nuzzar Ali bin Ahmed, head of the Alexandria secret police. They were apprehensive – the secret police had a reputation for strict interpretation of Sharia law. Dayan Aaron reassured them that the nuzzar was strict, but not a fanatic. He offered to accompany them to the interview, an offer that they gratefully accepted.

When the nuzzar expressed his intention to question Yehuda in the presence of Ibn al-Basri, the dayan quietly intervened. He explained who Yehuda was and how important this distinguished scholar was to the nagid and to the Jewish community. After a moment's thought, the nuzzar had Al-Basri brought in. He declared that this matter was one for the Sharia court, not for the police. If Al-Basri wished to lay an accusation, he must go to the court. That ended the meeting, but Al-Basri then appealed to the amir as the caliph's representative. He got the same response: this was a matter for the Sharia court.

The dayan tried to reassure Yehuda, pointing out that the response of both the nuzzar and the amir were evidence of the respect for the rule of law that characterised the Fatimid caliphate. But his reassurances did little to lessen the impact of the court summons when it came a few days later. Yehuda was a Jew facing capital charges before a Sharia court, in a city that had been, and still remained, less tolerant of Jews than Córdoba or Cairo. Such a court had, not long before, condemned a Jew to death for exactly the same offence – attempting to suborn the return to Judaism of a Jewish convert to Islam.

On the appointed day, Yehuda appeared at the main court-house next to the Sheikh Al-Qabari mosque, accompanied by Dayan Aaron, Solomon ben Joseph and Benjamin the Scribe, Rebekah's son. The main courtroom, built only twenty years before, exemplified the elegant Fatimid style. Rows of fine columns were topped with arches of coloured stones. The walls were covered in friezes decorated with elaborate bas-reliefs. But it was not the elegance of the hall that impressed the defendants as they entered; it was the host of people who had come to witness the trial. The murmur of the crowd could be heard from the outer courtyard, but a silence fell as Yehuda and his companions entered the hall. All kinds of people, Jews and Muslims, rich and poor, were crammed together, sitting in every available space. The only open areas were the empty dais on which the qadi and the *fuqaha*, the judges, were to sit, the space to their right where Ibn al-Basri was already standing, and the space to their left allocated to Yehuda and his friends. Al-Basri was standing alone, dressed a blue linen *thawb*. He glared at Yehuda's party as they took their places in front of the dais.

The spectators soon resumed their conversations but fell silent again as the qadi and his two fellow judges appeared from behind the dais and took their seats. Qadi Mahmud Abu Sadiq, though the senior *faqi*, was noticeably younger than his junior colleagues, his black beard trimmed in the square style fashionable among young men in Alexandria, and his robes lined with fine green damask. Seeing that his colleagues were settled and ready, the qadi raised both his hands, palm upwards.

'In the name of God, the Compassionate, the Merciful, we declare these proceedings open. Let it be recorded that this court has convened at the Sheikh Al-Qabari mosque on this, the tenth day of Shawwal in the year 535, Mahmud Abu Sadiq presiding. May God lead us to the right path, the path that God has favoured. Ameen.'

As the responding Ameen arose from those present, the qadi turned to Al-Basri. 'The court recognises Abraham ibn al-Basri, who has petitioned this court to assemble and hear his accusation against this person. Tell us whom you are accusing and what is the charge. You may speak.'

Al-Basri bowed. As he straightened up he took a deep breath and pointed at Yehuda, his hand visibly shaking. 'This, my Lords, is Yehuda ben Shmuel Halevi of Córdoba. I accuse him of attempting, against the law of the holy Quran, to tempt me to abandon the true faith and return to Judaism.'

Not a sound could be heard in the courtroom as Al-Basri lowered his arm and turned back to the qadi. Everyone knew what the charge was going to be, and what the penalty was.

The qadi asked Al-Basri to specify what he was alleging that the accused had done.

'My lord Qadi, he came to me with money and a letter from my brother. He came with his son-in-law Solomon ben Joseph, who is standing with him in this court. The money was thirty dinars.' The revelation of the amount started a ripple of comment in the crowd, but the qadi held up his hand for silence and nodded to Al-Basri to continue. 'In return for the money I was to accompany Yehuda Halevi to Palestine and there return to Judaism, out of the jurisdiction of the caliph, peace be upon him.'

'Is this what they told you?'

'No, my lord, my brother had sent me word previously about the conditions, which were repeated in the letter that they carried.'

'Yehuda ben Shmuel, how do you respond to this charge.'

'I reject it, my lord, I deny it completely.'

'So, Ibn al-Basri, do you have the letter?'

'No, my lord, I refused it and they took it away with them.' Again, the qadi had to silence a murmur from the spectators as Al-Basri continued, 'But they must surrender the letter and the bill of exchange to the court, and in any case, I will swear on oath that this was their mission.'

'Do you have the letter and the bill of exchange, Yehuda ben Shmuel?'

'No, my lord, I do not. I have no letter and no bill of exchange.'

'Liar!' Al-Basri said.

'Enough, sir, be silent and wait.' The qadi turned to his colleagues and after a whispered consultation with them he announced, 'The court will be adjourned and resume tomorrow morning after the *Zuhr* prayers. The accused will bring the letter and bill of exchange, if he has them. If not, then testimony will be taken on oath.' He paused, looking at Yehuda's party. 'Do I see the Dayan Aaron ibn al-'Ammani in the court?' The dayan bowed. 'Dayan, I'd be grateful if you would come to my chambers when we adjourn. I want to seek your advice on the protocols for a Jew to take an oath, since the accused is a Jew...'

Yehuda thought he heard the judge nearest him mutter '...if not the accuser', as the qadi adjourned the court.

*

'Qadi,' Dayan Aaron said, standing at the entrance to the judge's chambers, 'would it be permissible for me to be accompanied by Benjamin ben David? He's a scribe and notary and is familiar with the Jewish protocols for oaths.'

'By all means, Dayan, bring him in.'

Aaron gestured to Benjamin and they came into the room. The qadi wore fine clothes for public appearances, but his room was modest and sparsely furnished, its main feature being the numerous books and scrolls scattered over the carpets. The son of a distinguished *alim*, Qadi Mahmud was a scholar by temperament. His room was at the back of the court building overlooking the spice market, and the aroma of cinnamon and cardamom mingled with that of parchment and ink.

'Do sit down, Dayan, and you – Benjamin, is it?'

'Yes, my Lord Qadi, I am Benjamin ben David the Scribe, at your service.'

As the two visitors sat, Mahmud said, 'Let's not stand on ceremony and titles here, Aaron, we know each other well enough to speak frankly. But first, would you like something to drink? I have sherbet here, or I could send for a hot infusion if you'd prefer.'

'Thank you, Mahmud, sherbet would be fine for me' – he looked over at Benjamin, who nodded – 'and for Benjamin.'

Settling back on his cushions after administering the drinks, the qadi sighed. 'My friend and colleague, I need your help. The court's in an impossible position. We can't spare Yehuda if he's found guilty, yet it would be a travesty to condemn this great man to death. He's a scholar and physician highly respected in the Muslim community as well as among the Jews. I know the amir wants him to go free – preferably to leave for Palestine as soon as possible.'

Not sure where this was leading, Aaron responded, 'As the Arab proverb says, Mahmud, the mouth should have three gate-keepers: Is it true? Is it kind? Is it necessary? Even if you think Al-Basri's accusation is true, it's neither kind nor necessary to condemn Yehuda to death.'

'Come, Aaron, you know as well as I do that this won't work. I like the proverb, but it doesn't apply to the law. The law is clear. If he's found guilty, then he must die.'

'Then there's only one solution. He must not be found guilty.'

'Exactly, Aaron. And that's where we need your help.'

Exchanging glances with Benjamin, the dayan asked, 'Help? How can we help?'

'This is the position,' the qadi responded. 'I'm assuming that the accused will not bring a letter and bill of exchange tomorrow, in which case the court will have to rely on testimony taken on oath.'

Benjamin burst out, 'They can't bring the letter because…'

The qadi held up his hand and gently interrupted, 'Yes, my son, because they don't have it, or at least that's what they say. My point is that if we don't have the documents then we have to rely on sworn testimony.'

'Yes, my lord, I'm sorry.'

'That's all right, Benjamin, I understand your anxiety.' The qadi took a deep breath and exhaled slowly. 'So, sworn testimony. Now, as you know, in a Sharia court, if someone makes a deposition on oath in front of the court, then that oath is regarded as probative. The court must take as fact whatever is stated in the deposition. That applies of course to a Muslim taking an oath on the holy Quran, but it also applies equally to an oath taken by a Jew on the Torah. Or a Christian on the Christian Bible, for that matter. As I think you know, Benjamin.'

'Yes, sir, indeed it does.' Benjamin was becoming animated. 'I have myself been summoned before Sharia courts to testify that the scroll on which a Jew was swearing was a true Torah scroll. If it was, then their testimony was accepted as fact.'

'Good, you clearly see my point, young man. Do you, Dayan?'

'Yes I do, Mahmud. Al-Basri can testify only that he believes his accusation to be true. He hasn't even read the alleged letter or the bill of exchange. If Yehuda testifies that he doesn't have them, then you and your colleagues must conclude that he doesn't have them. So…'

The qadi put his finger to his lips. 'Enough,' he said quietly, 'that's as far as we can go. I am not here to coach you on how to conduct Yehuda's defence; I only wanted to clarify the law, which' – he smiled – 'is my sole concern.'

Returning the smile, Aaron said, 'Of course it is, Mahmud, of course it is.'

'Unless you have any other questions, or advice on Jewish law, then I think that concludes our business.' Aaron and Benjamin shook their heads. 'Good, then my colleagues and I will see you tomorrow after the *Zuhr* prayers.'

*

The dayan and Benjamin returned to the dayan's house to make the necessary arrangements with Yehuda and Solomon. They agreed that the trial was likely to result in Yehuda's acquittal, but everyone knew that this was not a certainty.

The next day, Benjamin, carrying a small Torah scroll, waited at the edge of the spice market to meet Yehuda, the dayan and Solomon.

'What's that noise, Benjamin?' Solomon asked as they met. 'Is there a crowd outside the court? It sounds rather ugly.'

'Yes, there is a crowd and they're not happy.' Seeing the concern on the faces of his companions, he added, 'No, don't be worried. They're angry with Al-Basri, not with us. The Jews don't like him because he's a convert. The Muslims don't like him because he's a Jew, especially since he's testifying against one of his own, and especially against someone they respect! I know that's a contradiction – they don't like Jews, but they respect a particular Jew – but when was anyone ever consistent in their likes and dislikes?'

'Wise words, Benjamin,' Yehuda said, 'and comforting – or at least I think so. But let's go into court. It's time.'

As they entered the courtyard, they saw Al-Basri being escorted by the muhtasib and his officials through the hostile crowd, who were shouting insults – 'Lying Jew!' 'Who do you think you are?' and even 'Kill the liar!' But the presence of the officials restrained the crowd from physically attacking Al-Basri. As he disappeared into the courthouse, people in the crowd saw Yehuda and his colleagues arriving, and they parted silently to let them pass and go inside. The courtroom itself also fell silent as they entered.

At first the trial proceeded as expected. Ibn al-Basri swore on the Quran that Yehuda had tried to bring him back to Judaism. Yehuda swore on the Torah that he did not have the letter or the bill of exchange. But before the qadi could announce that they must find Yehuda not guilty, Al-Basri intervened.

'If Yehuda Halevi doesn't have them, Solomon ben Joseph must have them. He was holding them when they came to me. I accuse him too, so he must swear.'

The qadi, sighing, glanced at his colleagues, who nodded. 'Very well. Abu l-Rabi Solomon ben Joseph ibn Gabbai, do you possess the letter and bill of exchange as alleged by Abraham ibn al-Basri?'

'No, my Lord Qadi.' He gestured to Benjamin, who brought the Torah scroll to him. Putting his hand on the scroll, Solomon intoned, 'I swear by Almighty God on this sacred Torah, that I have no letter or money for Abraham ibn al-Basri from his brother nor from anyone else.'

As he took his hand from the scroll and Benjamin moved back towards his place, Al-Basri pointed to Benjamin and shouted, 'Then Benjamin ben David, he must have them.'

The qadi jumped to his feet. 'Silence!' He looked sternly at Al-Basri. 'How dare you? Are we to get every Jew in Alexandria to swear that they have no letter to you?' The crowd laughed and some of them jeered at Al-Basri, until the qadi called again for silence. 'That's enough. The court will now consider its verdict.'

The qadi sat, and after a very short exchange with his colleagues, he raised his voice and declared, 'In the name of God, the Compassionate, the Merciful, this court finds the accused, Yehuda ben Shmuel Halevi not guilty of attempting to suborn the return of Abraham ibn al-Basri to Judaism.' The crowd started to shout abuse at Al-Basri but the qadi raised his hand to silence them yet again. 'Let it also be known, however, that no fault whatsoever attaches to the said Ibn al-Basri, who made the accusation in good faith, wrongly believing it to be true.' There was a growl from the crowd, but it subsided as the qadi added, 'I summon Ibn al-Basri, Yehuda Halevi and his companions to my chambers to complete the formalities of this case.' Nobody, including his fellow judges, knew quite what to make of this last declaration, but the qadi, unconcerned, left the courtroom.

The judge's chambers were a little crowded, but the visitors all managed to find somewhere to sit: Yehuda, Solomon, the dayan, Benjamin and Al-Basri. The qadi explained that his fellow judges had agreed that there were possible anomalies in the testimony. Not wanting to risk the trial descending into a farcical succession of impromptu oaths, the judges had agreed that the qadi should establish if there was still a case to answer.

'Let's get straight to the point,' he concluded. 'Abraham ibn al-Basri, you said that you saw the letter and the bill of exchange in Solomon's hand. Is that so?'

'Yes, my lord, I did see them.' Al-Basri was subdued now, nervous about his position, even though the qadi had exonerated him in the courtroom.

'What you saw were some sealed documents,' the qadi said. 'We need to establish whether the documents were what you allege they were.' He turned to Solomon. 'In court, Solomon ben Joseph, you swore that have no letter nor money for Abraham ibn al-Basri. You said that you 'have' no letter or money, which means that they are not in your possession now. Benjamin the Scribe has a Torah scroll on his lap. Are you prepared to swear in court on that Torah scroll that they have never been in your possession? Will you swear that you have never had, held or carried any documents sent by Naphtali ibn al-Basri to his brother?'

Solomon hesitated. He looked at the dayan, who shrugged slightly and shook his head.

'Take your time, Solomon,' the qadi said gently.

Solomon's eyes moved first to the Torah scroll and then to the qadi. When he spoke, his voice was almost a whisper, 'No, my lord, I am not prepared to swear to that.'

In the silence that followed this admission, Al-Basri visibly struggled to restrain himself from speaking. Eventually, the qadi turned to Yehuda.

'Am I right to assume that you would also refuse to take such an oath?' Yehuda nodded in affirmation. 'So, now we have reason to believe that Yehuda Halevi and Solomon ben Joseph may at some time have had documents from Al-Basri's brother. On the other hand, we have no evidence that indicates that they knew what was in those documents, even if they did have them. No one could be condemned to death under Sharia law on this basis.

'However,' he added, before Yehuda and his companions could react to this good news, 'there are grounds for concluding that Abraham ibn al-Basri had reason to believe that something amiss may have happened here, and he was right to bring the accusation. I therefore suggest that, as a gesture of goodwill, Yehuda volunteers to pay Abraham the sum of ten dinars. This will signal to the Jewish and the Muslim communities that Yehuda and Solomon bear no ill will towards Abraham ibn al-Basri, and that will draw the case to a satisfactory conclusion for all concerned.'

The arrangement was agreed, and Yehuda promised to send the ten dinars to Al-Basri that very day. As the visitors were leaving, the qadi asked the dayan to stay behind.

'So, Aaron, as I said, a satisfactory conclusion for all concerned. Even for Al-Basri, who would have been obliged to refuse the thirty dinars, but now receives ten.'

The dayan smiled. 'Assuming, of course, that there ever was thirty dinars on offer in the first place, Mahmud, which we do not accept.'

'Yes, my friend, and that's what I wanted to talk about. If, in the course of time, young Benjamin happens to come across a bill of exchange for, say, thirty dinars to which he is not entitled, I suggest that he gives ten dinars to Yehuda to compensate for Yehuda's payment to Al-Basri. He might give the other twenty dinars to charity. In the circumstances, I would suggest that it should be a Muslim charity.'

The Dayan returned the qadi's smile. 'I can't, of course, say whether or not Benjamin will find such money, Qadi, but your point is taken. I'll advise them accordingly. Thank you a thousand times for your help.'

'My help? I was only serving the law and my amir. Who, by the way, thinks that it would be prudent if Yehuda and Solomon were to leave Alexandria as soon as possible. The trade winds are about to return.'

'That is, and has always been, their intention, Mahmud.'

*

The trade winds did indeed resume within a few days. Solomon took his leave of Yehuda and their friends in Alexandria and sailed west on the *Sultan's Ship* for Córdoba. A few days later, on 5 May 1141, five days before the festival of Shevuot, Yehuda and Benjamin boarded the ship of the Amir of al-Mahdiyya bound for Ascalon. They were less fortunate than Solomon, however. No west wind came, so the passengers had to stay on board until the eve of Shevuot, when the wind finally arrived and the ship set sail for Ascalon.

19

YEHUDA'S LAST LETTER TO DEBORAH

Alexandria, on board The Mahdiyya,
5 Sivan 4901 [9 May 1141]

To my darling Deborah, beloved of my soul, greetings.

It has been a long wait – I have been on board for four days
– but at last we have a westerly wind and we are now due to sail
tomorrow, God willing.

> *This wind of yours is a perfumed wind, O West,*
> *with saffron in its wings and apple scent,*
> *as if it came from the perfumer's chest,*
> *not from the chest of the winds.*
> *The wings of swallows flutter to your breath.*
> *You set them free,*
> *like myrrh tears, from a bundle poured.*
> *And how we long for you,*
> *we who ride a board on the back of the sea!*

So, Benjamin and I will ride a board on the back of the sea towards Ascalon and Jerusalem. I think I told you that when Benjamin and I first met in Alexandria, he asked me about the end of *The Kuzari*, when the Chaver decides to go to Jerusalem and the King of the Khazars challenges his decision. He and I returned to this discussion yesterday and I was reminded that when I wrote the king's challenge in the book, I used the very words that you had used when you challenged my decision to go on this pilgrimage.

> *What do you seek today in Jerusalem and the land of Canaan? The Divine Presence is gone from those places! Closeness to God can be achieved in any place, with a good heart and strong desire. Why, then, should you place yourself in danger from deserts, oceans and various hostile peoples?*

In *The Kuzari*, the Chaver answers with certainty that only the Divine Presence that was seen face-to-face by the prophets is gone, but the hidden, intangible Divine Presence remains. The land is still especially reserved for God, and one's deeds cannot be entirely complete in any place except there. My answer to you in Córdoba, and to Benjamin here in Alexandria, was less certain than that. I am not the Chaver and I understand your reservations about my argument.

Nevertheless, I have become even more convinced during these last weeks that Jerusalem may be a place in which divinity is inherent as it is nowhere else in the world and that I must visit it. That conviction has been reinforced while I have been in Egypt, experiencing the places where we Jews were slaves for so long, and from which we were freed to receive the Torah – on Shavuot – and to make ourselves worthy of the Promised Land, which I long with all my heart to see. As I wrote in Córdoba:

My goal is set to the Fragrant Hill –
to Zion, if it be God's will.
If I had dove's wings,
to fly and alight –
I would go to the Mount of Myrrh, the hill of Frankincense.

I lift my eyes to the lofty heights –
Whence will the shining spheres be revealed to me?
I long and yearn
to go to my king.
When will I go and see the face of God?

At last, at last, that longing is to be fulfilled, if God wills it. Our voyage is expected to be about ten days to Ascalon, where the Fatimids still rule securely, and I understand that the road from there to Jerusalem remains open, so that I shall be able to proceed to Zion soon after we land. The current friendly negotiations between the Amir Mu'in al-Din Unar of Damascus and King Fulk and Queen Melisende of Jerusalem also mean that the city should be at peace.

My pilgrimage therefore nears its goal, but it is hard to keep focused on it. I miss you, I miss you terribly. You are constantly in my dreams.

As your image passes through my dream,
    So I beg you to let me pass through yours…
I cannot hear your voice, but in the secret places
    Of my heart, I hear your footsteps.

I am resolved to return to you once the pilgrimage is complete. That is my ultimate goal.

I am giving this letter today to my friend Amram ben Isaac before we sail – he will despatch it to you by the *fayj tayyar* express courier, so I hope you will receive it very soon after you and Miriam are reunited with our son-in-law Solomon, who sailed westward on Thursday last. I pray to God that I will before very long be able to join all of you and complete our family once again.

Until that time, I pray for you and the family and remain your devoted and faithful,

Yehuda ben Shmuel Halevi

AFTERWORD

It is not known when, how or exactly where Yehuda Halevi died. He certainly left Alexandria in early May 1141 and reached the Holy Land, where he died sometime in June or July that year. He therefore had plenty of time to visit Jerusalem and stay there for a while.

The Jerusalem that Yehuda Halevi would have entered in 1141 was very different from the Jerusalem of the early years of the Christian conquest. The story of the brutal massacre of Muslims and Jews in 1099, when the crusaders first took Jerusalem is now well known. Less well known, perhaps, is the gradual assimilation of the crusaders into the more open world of the Levant as they settled and made their homes in the region. Fulcher of Chartres, who chose to stay on after the First Crusade, famously wrote around twenty years later, 'We who were once Occidentals have now become Orientals.'

Twenty years after that, when Yehuda reached Ascalon and Jerusalem in 1141, the process had gone even further. The new culture was exemplified in an incident observed around that time by Usama ibn Munquidh, a famous Arab aristocrat, diplomat and poet, when he was an emissary to Jerusalem for Amir Mu'in al-Din Unar of Damascus. The amir went hunting in Acre with King Fulk of Jerusalem. He admired the goshawk with which the king was hunting. The king immediately gave the hawk to him, along with a retriever dog. Usama ibn Munquidh noted that 'Anyone who is recently arrived from the Frankish lands is rougher in character than those who have become acclimatised and have frequented the company of Muslims.'

By that time King Fulk had resolved his dispute with Queen Melisende, his wife and co-ruler in Jerusalem. She was the daughter of King Baldwin II of Jerusalem and his Armenian queen. Fulk, formerly Count Fulk V of Anjou, had left Anjou to marry Melisende. The dispute, and its resolution, reflected the tension between the 'old Franks' and the 'new Franks', but that is another story.

So, the Jerusalem that Yehuda and Benjamin entered in 1141 was at peace, though a rather fragile peace. Hardly any Jews lived in Jerusalem, but Jews were allowed to visit the holy places as pilgrims.

Yehuda and Benjamin would have visited Mount Zion and the Mount of Olives and wandered around the Old City. The city was still in the process of transformation by the Christians, who had already converted many mosques into churches and were building new churches and markets. On Mount Moriah, the Temple Mount, the pilgrims would have seen the cross that had been put on top of the Dome of the Rock (renamed the Temple of the Lord), and the Templar's Palace in and around the Al-Aqsa Mosque. They may then have descended to the Western Wall, the square in front of which was at that time a cattle market.

I like to think that Yehuda had an opportunity to pray at the Western Wall, and that afterwards he and Benjamin might have shared a cardamom tea at the market in Temple Street (now Aqbat e Saraya Street) with Usama ibn Munquidh and perhaps a knight of the Knights Templar, whom Usama called 'my friends'.

The exact date of Yehuda Halevi's death is unknown, though a letter from an acquaintance to Yehuda's friend Halfon ben

Nathaniel indicates that Yehuda died in June or July 1141 (Av 4901). In his wonderful account of Yehuda's pilgrimage, *The Song of the Distant Dove*, Raymond Scheindlin speculates, 'Perhaps he held out until the Ninth of Av [11 July], the summer fast day commemorating the destruction of Jerusalem, when, in post-destruction times, Jews had customarily made pilgrimage to the Mount of Olives.'

זיכרונו לברכה – *May his memory be a blessing.*

WHO'S WHO
IN THE STORY

The list below covers characters who appear repeatedly in the novel (people who appear only once in the story, where their role is clear in the text, are not listed here). The list also includes the names of certain writers frequently referred to in the story, even though they do not appear in the story in person.

Real people are named in plain text and fictional ones in italics.

Abd Allah ibn Buluggin Amir of Granada, reigned 1073–1090

Abd al-Mumin (1194–1163) Leader of the Almohads, succeeded Ibn Tumart in 1130

Abigail Servant to Yehuda's family in Toledo

Abraham ibn Daud Physician in Granada to whom Yehuda was apprenticed

Abraham ibn al-Basri See Al-Basri

Abraham ibn Ezra (1089–1167) A distinguished biblical scholar and author of a widely read commentary on the Torah. A friend of Yehuda (born, like him, in Tudela)

Ahmad bin Ali Abu Umar Ahmad bin Ali bin Hazm, friend of Yehuda in Córdoba, great-grandson of Ibn Hazm

Alfonso VI of León-Castile King of León-Castile, reigned 1077–1109

Alfonso I, 'The Battler' King of Aragon and Navarre, reigned 1104–1134, married Queen Urraca of Léon-Castile in 1109 and became king of the combined kingdom

Al-Basri Ibn al-Basri, the Jewish convert to Islam who was Yehuda's accuser in Alexandria (His first name is not known, so we have given him the name *Abraham*)

Al-Ghazali Abū Ḥāmid Muḥammad ibn Muḥammad al-Ghazālī (1058–1111), one of the greatest Muslim scholars, jurists and mystics

Al-Hafiz Il-Din Allah Fatimid caliph of Egypt, reigned 1130–1149

Ali ibn Yusuf Ali ibn Yusuf ibn Tashfin, Amir of the Faithful (1084–1143) son of Yusuf ibn Tashfin

Ameira Name used here for the queen mother of Amir Abd Allah of Granada (whose name is uncertain, but who is referred to in Abd Allah's memoir, *The Tibyān*)

Asim ibn Muhammad *Muhtasib* (supervisor of markets and trade) in Córdoba

Benjamin ben David A scribe in Alexandria, son of Rebekah bat Nathan

Bahya ibn Paquda Theologian and philosopher, author of *Duties of the Heart* (late eleventh, early twelfth century, dates uncertain)

Bertha Queen of León-Castile, third wife of Alfonso VI, from about 1095; died late 1099 or early 1100

Chaya Servant of Isaac ibn Ezra in Córdoba

Claudia Lady of the Bedchamber, first to Queen Bertha then to Queen Isabel

Constance of Burgundy Queen of León-Castile, second wife of Alfonso VI, 1079–1093. Mother of Urraca of León

David bin Avram Secretary to Rabbi Yitzchak al-Fasi, head of the yeshiva at Lucena

Deborah bat Isaac Yehuda Halevi's wife. We know of course that he had a wife, but we know virtually nothing about her, except that he loved her very much

Discorides Pedanius Discorides (*c.*40–*c.*90 CE), Greek physician and pharmacologist

Faruddin the Scribe Amanuensis to Amir Abd Allah of Granada

Fuad ibn Said Merchant in Granada, executed by order of Yusuf ibn Tashfin

Guy de Clamency Physician to Queen Constance and Queen Urraca of Burgundy

Halfon ben Nataniel Halevi Abu Said Halfon ben Nataniel Halevi, Egyptian merchant, close friend of Yehuda (dates uncertain)

Hannah Wife of Solomon ibn Ferruziel

Hannah bat Solomon Granddaughter of Yehuda Halevi (apart from young Yehuda, the identity of *Miriam*'s children is uncertain)

Ibn Hamdin Abu Abd Allah Mohammed ibn Ali ibn Hamdin, Qadi of Córdoba under Ali ibn Yusuf

Ibn Hazm Abū Muḥammad ʿAlī ibn Aḥmad ibn Saʿīd ibn Ḥazm (994–1064), Andalucían poet, philosopher and jurist

Ibn Paquda See Bahya ibn Paquda

Ibn Sina Abu 'Ali al-Husayn ibn Sina, also known as Avicenna (980–1037), physician, astronomer and philosopher

Ibn Tumart Abu Abd Allah Muhammad ibn Tumart (1080–1130), Berber religious scholar and teacher, first founder and leader of the Almohad movement

Isaac ibn Abraham Son of Abraham ibn Ezra

Isaac ibn Ezra One of four brothers of Moses ibn Ezra

Isabel Fourth wife of Alfonso VI (probably formerly Zaida of Seville, probably mother of Sancho), c.1100–1107

Ismat Wakil (purser) of the *Sultan's Ship*

Jamal bin Qasum Captain of the guard at the palace of the Amir of Granada

Joseph ben Samuel ibn al-Ukhtush Friend of Yehuda and of Halfon ibn Nataniel. A merchant, probably based in Granada

Joseph ibn Ferruziel (c.1055–1145) Physician and adviser to King Alfonso VI of León-Castile – father of Solomon ibn Ferruziel

Joseph ibn Migash (1077–c.1141) Student under Yitzchak al-Fasi at the Lucena yeshiva (when he was twenty-six, in 1103, Al-Fasi ordained him as a rabbi and nominated him as his successor as head of the yeshiva)

Mahmud Soldier in the Almoravid army that conquered Granada in 1090

Mahmud Abu Sadiq A qadi in Alexandria

Meir ibn Kamniel Physician to the Amir of Seville, allowed to continue as an administrator and physician after the Almoravids conquered the city in 1091

Miriam bat Yehuda Daughter of Yehuda Halevi. (It is known that he had a daughter, probably the only child to survive beyond infancy, but her name is unknown)

Moses ibn Ezra (1058–1138) Great poet, linguist and philosopher

Nathan ben Samuel Court scribe to Samuel ben Hanania, nagid of the Jewish community in Egypt in 1140, and also secretary of the Fustat yeshiva (active 1128–53)

Rachel bat Shlomo (1070–1105) Also known as Bella: daughter of Rashi

Rashi (1040–1105) Rabbi Shlomo Yitzhaki, Torah scholar and commentator in Troyes, France, father of Rachel bat Shlomo

Rebekah bat Nathan Servant of Isaac ibn Ezra in Córdoba; later met Yehuda on his voyage to Egypt

Samuel ben Hanania Nagid of the Jewish community in Egypt, 1140–1159, and physician to the caliph

Sancho Son and heir of Alfonso VI, born *c.*1094, died at the battle of Uclés, 1108

Shalom ibn Japhrut Poet in Córdoba

Shulamit Servant of the Halevi family in Córdoba

Solomon ben Joseph Accompanied Yehuda on his voyage to Egypt. (It is not certain that he married Yehuda's daughter Miriam, but it is possible.) Full name Abu l-Rabi Solomon ben Joseph ibn Gabbai

Solomon ibn Ferruziel (*c.*1050–1108) Son of Joseph ibn Ferruziel. Counsellor to King Alfonso VI of León-Castile, murdered in Toledo, 1108

Yehuda ben Shmuel Halevi (*c.*1075–1141) The protagonist of our story

Yehuda *ben Solomon* Grandson of Yehuda, son of his daughter *Miriam* and Solomon ben Joseph (It is by no means certain that Solomon was his father, but it is possible)

Yitzchak al-Fasi Yitzchak ben Yaakov al-Fasi Hacohen (1013–1103), great Talmudic scholar and Jurist, moved from Fez to become head of the yeshiva at Lucena

Yusuf ibn Tashfin Ruler of the Almoravid empire (reigned *c.*1061–1106) and founder of Marrakesh

Urraca of León (1079–1126) Daughter of King Alfonso VI and Queen Constance of León-Castile; Queen of León-Castile after Alfonso VI's death, reigned 1109–1126, and Queen of Aragon and Navarre when she married King Alfonso I in 1109

Urraca of Zamora (1033–1101) Wife of King Alfonso VI of León-Castile

Wallada bint al-Mustakfi (d. 1091) Daughter of the Umayyad caliph Al-Mustakfi (976–1025) loved by the poet Ibn Zaidun (1004–1071)

Zaida (b. 1063) Daughter-in-law of Amir Al-Mutamid of Seville, (probably) converted to Christianity and became Isabel, fourth wife of King Alfonso VI and mother of Sancho

Zipporah Wife of Moses ibn Ezra

GLOSSARY

Arabic words are in plain text, Hebrew words are in italics, words in other languages underlined.

alim A scholar, a learned person, a religious teacher. Plural, *ulama*

Almohads A puritanical Islamic reform movement founded in the twelfth century, originally among the Berbers of southern Morocco, which eventually conquered the Maghreb and Andalucía, replacing the Almoravids

Almoravids An Islamic reform movement of the eleventh and twelfth centuries, originating among the Sanhaja Berbers of western Morocco, which came to rule the Maghreb and Andalucía, but was overthrown by the Almohads

Al-Muhadhab Literally 'The Accomplished' a courtesy title for a physician

'aqid A drink of milk curds dissolved in water

Ashkenazi Jews of France and Germany (supposedly descended from Ashkenaz, a great-grandson of Noah)

bet midrash A Jewish study hall

bracha A blessing

book The word 'book' is used here for what would more properly be called a 'codex', a manuscript in book form: printing had not yet been invented in Europe so all 'books' were handwritten

chaver A study companion in a *yeshiva*. Also used as a title of respect for a *yeshiva* official or a rabbi: the Chaver is the representative of the Jews in Halevi's book, *The Kuzari* (in modern Hebrew it means 'friend')

cubit Ancient measure of length, the length of a forearm – typically about 18 inches or 44 cm. So the Pharos, at 450 cubits, would have been about 675 feet or 200 metres high

dayan A judge in a Jewish religious court

dhimmi Literally 'a protected person'. Dhimmi were non-Muslims given protected status under Sharia in Muslim states in return for payment of a *jizya* tax. Principally the 'people of the Book', i.e., Jews and Christians

diwan A collection of poems, usually by one author

faqi An Islamic jurist or judge, expert in Islamic law, *fiqh*. Plural, *fuqaha*

Fatimid caliphate An Isma'ili Shi'ite caliphate first established in Sijilmasa and the Maghreb. The Fatimids conquered Egypt in 969 CE and established their capital in Fustat. The caliphs claimed descent from Fatima, daughter of the Prophet Mohammed

funduq An inn or caravanserai

fuqaha Plural of *faqi*

ghurab A light galley, principally propelled by oars, but sometimes with supplementary sails

hypereikon Greek for St John's wort

ijtihad Literally 'striving' – in theological terms, striving to understand and interpret the meaning of the Quran, the Hadith and Sharia

jizyah The tax paid by *dhimmi* as protected persons under Sharia

khadim A servant

khiti A ship built for speed

majlis The living room or reception room of a private house, where guests were entertained; also, a place used for study of religious law

martaba A raised platform or set of sofas covered in cushions

mashrabiyya A wooden latticework screen over a window or a balcony

Mozarabs Iberian Christians who spoke mainly Arabic, most of whom followed the ancient Visigothic rite of St Isidore

muhtasib An official under the *qadi*, whose principal function was the supervision of markets and trade

mulukhiya A thick soup made of garden mallow

nagid The leader of a Jewish community in the Middle Ages. In Fatimid Egypt the *nagid* had the power of a ruler over the Jewish community. (From the biblical Hebrew for prince or leader)

nuzzar Inspector of police, or of the secret police

qadi Principal or senior judge of the Sharia court

qunbar A very large ship designed to carry heavy cargo and passengers

Rosh Hashana The Jewish New Year, beginning of the Days of Awe leading to Yom Kippur

ruach The spirit, part of the soul

Sharia Islamic law

Shevuot The Jewish Festival of Weeks (Pentecost), which commemorates the giving of the Ten Commandments on Mount Sinai

Shir ha'Shirim *The Song of Songs*, a book of the Hebrew Bible

shiur A religious seminar or study session

taifa states The warring Islamic states that arose out of the civil strife following the fall of the Umayyad caliphate of Córdoba

thawb An ankle-length robe with long sleeves

wakil A commercial agent, including the purser of a ship

yeshiva Jewish seminary and centre of learning

Yom Kippur The Jewish Day of Atonement

FURTHER READING

For those who want to know more about Yehuda Halevi, his life, his poetry and his pilgrimage, I strongly recommend Raymond P. Scheindlin's, *The Song of the Distant Dove: Judah Halevi's Pilgrimage* (Oxford University Press, 2008). Anvil Press has published a volume of outstanding translations of Halevi's poetry by Gabriel Levin, *Yehuda Halevi, Poems from The Diwan* (Anvil Press Poetry, 2002). Yehuda's pilgrimage is covered in more detail in Joseph Yahalom's *Yehuda Halevi, Poetry and Pilgrimage* (Hebrew University Manes Press, 2009), and his full life in *Yehuda Halevi* by Hillel Halkin (Schocken Books, 2010).

If you want to know more about the lives and poetry of Halevi and other Jewish 'courtier-poets' of medieval Andalucía, I recommend two more books by Raymond Scheindlin (whose titles are self-explanatory): *Wine, Women and Death: Medieval Hebrew Poems on the Good Life* (Oxford University Press, 1986/1991) and *The Gazelle: Medieval Hebrew Poems on God, Israel and the Soul* (Jewish Publication Society, Philadelphia & New York, 1991). Another excellent collection is by Peter Cole, *The Dream of the Poem: Hebrew Poetry from Muslim and Christian Spain, 950–1492* (Princeton University Press, 2007).

As for Yehuda Halevi's philosophy and in particular its debt to Sufi philosophy, Diana Lobel has published an authoritative and readable account in *Between Mysticism and Philosophy: Sufi*

Language of Religious Experience in Judah Halevi's Kuzari (State University of New York Press, 2000). The most accessible translation of Halevi's book, *The Kuzari*, is *The Kuzari: In Defense of the Despised Faith*, translated and annotated by N. Daniel Korobkin (Jason Aronson Inc., 1998).*

There are a number of excellent studies of the wider story of relations between Muslims, Jews and Christians in the medieval Muslim world. Three studies I would recommend as a starting point are Jacob Lassner, *Jews, Christians and the Abode of Islam: Modern Scholarship, Medieval Realities* (University of Chicago Press, 2012); María Roda Menocal, *The Ornament of the World: How Muslims, Jews and Christians Created a Culture of Tolerance in Medieval Spain* (Little, Brown & Co, 2002); and Ross Brann, *Power in the Portrayal: Representations of Jews and Muslims in Eleventh- and Twelfth-Century Islamic Spain* (Princeton University Press, 2002). A fascinating account of the Crusades from the Arab perspective is given in Amin Maalouf, *The Crusades Through Arab Eyes*, translated by Jon Rothschild (Saqi, 2004).

---

* It should be noted, however, that this is translated from Ibn Tarfon's later translation of the book into Hebrew, not from Halevi's original, which was written in Arabic.

ACKNOWLEDGEMENTS

I am grateful to the numerous people and organisations who have helped me to get to the point of publishing this novel. Among the organisations, I am particularly grateful to the Arvon Foundation, having attended many of their superb residential creative writing courses. Every one of the tutors on those courses has been outstanding, but I owe a special thanks to Carol Ann Duffy for her encouragement of my translations of Halevi's poems, and to Lindsay Clarke, who followed up his fiction course with a monthly writing workshop. Lindsay and the participants on the workshop helped me to shape the work over many months.

As an alumnus of Cambridge University I am fortunate to have lifetime access to the University Library, a warm and welcoming treasure house of scholarship and literature.

In terms of getting the book completed, I thank my first structural editor, Laura McFarlane, and also the beta readers whom I found through The History Quill, who made invaluable suggestions for polishing the work.

The book would certainly not have got this far without the support of the whitefox team who have managed the publication process, including Silvia Crompton, my editor, and Emma Ewbank, the brilliant cover designer.

Last but not least, I thank my family and friends for their patience and support, listening to me talking endlessly about the work and giving me helpful advice, and also organisations like Limmud and Finchley Reform Synagogue, my community, for giving me the opportunity to test some of my ideas by delivering workshops on the history and culture of this fascinating period.

COPYRIGHTS

Most of the dialogue in this novel is fictional, but in some cases I quote actual writings by or about the character or period. In such cases I have often used translations or quotations from other works. I am grateful for permission to use the material from the copyright holders as follows:

© Robert Alter, *The Hebrew Bible: A Translation with Commentary* (W. W. Norton & Co., 2019)
© Yehuda Amichai, *Selected Poetry of Yehuda Amichai*, edited and translated by Chana Block and Stephen Mitchell (University of California Press, 2013 edition)
© Peter Cole, *The Dream of the Poem: Hebrew Poetry from Muslim and Christian Spain, 950–1492* (Princeton University Press, 2007)
© Laurence Durrell, Introduction to E. M. Forster, *Alexandria: A History and Guide* by E. M. Forster (1922, paperback 2014, I. B. Tauris, an imprint of Bloomsbury Publishing Plc.)
© Fulcher of Chartres, *A History of the Expedition to Jerusalem, 1095–1127*, translated by Frances Rita Ryan; edited with an introduction by Harold S. Fink (University of Tennessee Press, 1969)
© S. G. Goitein, *A Mediterranean Society: The Jewish Communities of the World as Portrayed in the Documents of the Cairo Geniza*

(University of California Press, paperback edition, six volumes, 1993)

© Abraham Joshua Heschel, *Heavenly Torah: As Refracted through the Generations*, edited and translated by Gordon Tucker with Leonard Levy (2007, Continuum Publishing US, an imprint of Bloomsbury Publishing Inc.)

© N. Daniel Korobkin, translator, Yehuda Halevi, *The Kuzari: In Defense of the Despised Faith* (Jason Aronson Inc., 1998)

© André Raymond, *Cairo*, translated by Willard Wood (Harvard University Press, 2000)

© Ronald A Messier, *The Almoravids and the Meanings of Jihad* (2010, Praeger, an imprint of SAC-CLIO, LLC)

© Christopher Middleton and Leticia Garza-Falcon (eds), *Andalusian Poems* (David R. Godine, 1993)

© Gabriel Levin, *Yehuda Halevi, Poems from The Diwan* (Anvil Press Poetry, 2002)

© Janina M. Safran, 'The politics of book burning in al-Andalus', *Journal of Medieval Iberian Studies*, Vol. 6, Issue 2, 2014

© Raymond P. Scheindlin, 'Rabbi Moshe Ibn Ezra on the Legitimacy of Poetry' in Maurice Clogan (ed.), *Medieval Poetics* (*Medievalia et Humanistica*, N.S., 7 (1976)), pp 101–115)

© Raymond P. Scheindlin, *Wine, Women and Death: Medieval Hebrew Poems on the Good Life* (Oxford University Press, 1986/1991)

© Raymond P. Scheindlin, *The Gazelle: Medieval Hebrew Poems on God, Israel and the Soul* (Jewish Publication Society, Philadelphia & New York, 1991)

© Raymond P. Scheindlin, *The Song of the Distant Dove: Judah Halevi's Pilgrimage* (Oxford University Press, 2008)

© Amin T. Tibi, translator, Abd Allah ibn Bullugin, *The Tibyān: memoirs of ʿAbd Allāh b. Buluggīn, Last Zīrid Amīr of Granada*, translated from the emended Arabic text and provided with an introduction, notes and comments by Amin T. Tibi (Leiden, E. J. Brill, 1986)

© J. Spencer Trimingham, *The Sufi Orders in Islam* (Oxford University Press, 1971/1998)

© David J. Wasserstein, 'Ibn Hazm and al-Andalus' in Camilla Adang, Maribel Fierro and Sabine Schmidtke, *Ibn Hazm of Cordoba: The Life and Works of a Controversial Thinker* (Brill, 2013)

ABOUT THE AUTHOR

Having gained a PhD in history and political anthropology from Cambridge University, Robert L. Stone has worked for many years advising governments on strategies to fight poverty, particularly in the wake of conflicts. He has a lifelong interest in how different cultures and ethnicities relate to each other – this, combined with his love of literature, is the inspiration for *The Golden Bell*.